THE UKRAINE

THE UKRAINE

ARTEM CHAPEYE

Translated by ZENIA TOMPKINS

SEVEN STORIES PRESS

new york • oakland

Seven Stories Press
140 Watts Street
New York, NY 10013
www.sevenstories.com

College professors and high school and middle school teachers may order free examination copies of Seven Stories Press titles. Visit https://www.sevenstories.com/pg/resources-academics or email academic@sevenstories.com.

[Library of Congress Cataloging-in-Publication Data

Names: Chapeye, Artem, author. | Tompkins, Zenia, translator.
Title: The Ukraine / Artem Chapeye ; translated by Zenia H. Tompkins.
Other titles: Ukraine. English
Description: New York : Seven Stories Press, 2024.
Identifiers: LCCN 2023041059 | ISBN 9781644212950 (trade paperback) | ISBN
   9781644212967 (ebook)
Subjects: LCSH: Chapeye, Artem--Translations into English. | LCGFT: Short
   stories.
Classification: LCC PG3948.C46 U5713 2024 | DDC 891.7934--dc23/eng/20231014
LC record available at https://lccn.loc.gov/2023041059

This collection was originally published in Ukrainian as *The Ukraine* by Books XXI (Chernivtsi, Ukraine) in 2018. The following stories were previously published in English:

"Sonny, Please . . ." in a different translation in the anthology *Best European Fiction* 2016 (Dalkey Archive Press); "My Daughter Still Doesn't Understand" in a different translation in the collection *Refugees Worldwide*; "Feel Unique" in the Spring 2021 issue of *Apofenie Magazine*; "The Ukraine" in the April 4, 2022 issue of *The New Yorker*.

The following stories were published in Ukrainian prior to inclusion in this collection:

"Pan Ivan and the Three Bears" in the collection *I Like Ukraine!* (Nora-Drunk Publisher, Kyiv, Ukraine, 2016); "The First" in the collection *About Us*; "The Bazaar Never Sleeps" in *Insider UA*; "Did You Fall Off the Moon, or What?" by *Insider UA*; "Rymma Hryhorivna Is Craving Human Contact" by *Insider UA*; "Marmelade" by *Insider UA*; "Feel Unique" in the magazine *ShO*; "This is *My* Home!" in the magazine *ShO*; select texts in Artem Chapeye's travelogue *Travels with Mamayota in Search of Ukraine* (Nora-Druk Publishers, Kyiv, Ukraine, 2011).

TRANSLATOR'S NOTE

The following stories are possibly based on real events. They were written as standalone texts over the course of eight years. Faithful to the linguistic realities of pre-invasion Ukraine, they have been translated from standard Ukrainian, Russian, Surzhyk (the Russified vernacular form of Ukrainian used widely in the east prior to 2022), and an array of Ukrainian dialects and regiolects. This is the Ukraine Russia invaded on February 24, 2022.

Contents

A Million Stories

Preface to the English Edition

As I begin to write this, my wife, my two sons aged seven and nine, and our Jack Russell Terrier are staying in a tent city for displaced persons outside Przemyśl on the Polish–Ukrainian border. Relatively speaking, they've been lucky.

The child of one of my close friends is in intensive care in Dnipro after the entire family was trapped in the basement of a building in Mariupol ten days earlier, which had collapsed from a Russian bomb strike. This friend wrote me to share that the boy had undergone an operation right there in Mariupol, then another one after his evacuation to Dnipro, and now the "worst is behind them" and the teenager's condition is "critical but stable." I'm too scared to ask what exactly that means.

Another friend of mine just tried fleeing to Kyiv from Irpin, a suburb of Ukraine's capital, after her house was hit by Russian shelling. Her car got stuck in a forest because the road was blocked by a fallen pine tree. Google Maps doesn't show all the forest trails that are drivable, and she doesn't know what to do. She wrote a post about this on Facebook. Some friends recommend that she walk through the woods to Kyiv on foot because it's just ten or fifteen kilometers. Others caution against this because of mines left behind by the Russians and instead recommend that she head back home on the same road that she took from Irpin and hope for an organized evacuation later. Since that post, there's been no word from her, even now as I write this.

Meanwhile, my mother's brother, who had moved from Ukraine to Russia back when all this was still the USSR, initially responded to our messages to him after the start of Putin's full-scale invasion of Ukraine with, "These are all fakes." After his own sister told him that I—her son and his nephew—was in a bomb shelter, my uncle mustered the maximal compromise he was capable of: "You've got your own truth, and we've got ours." I'm still unable to fathom how it's possible to believe government propaganda over the eyewitness accounts of your own relatives. But it evokes bleak thoughts about humanity.

I'm typing a draft of this text on my phone, in my downtime after a day's service in Ukraine's Armed Forces, in which I voluntarily enlisted a few weeks ago. One of my duties as part of my army service is to relay information about missile threats up and down the chain of command as it's released by the air defense. Yesterday, we had multiple explosions. Today, all the threats have so far passed "quietly," that is, without exploding rockets: over the last month, we've already grown used to the constant air-raid alert sirens themselves.

Over the days that I add to this text—paragraph by paragraph, in brief chunks between army duties, and before and after shifts—increasingly terrible things are being added that are happening to people increasingly close to me. Right now, with the wounds still fresh, it feels brazen to reconstruct this suffering simply for the purposes of a text. Yet experience has taught me in recent weeks that the human capacity for empathy is rather limited: You describe the horror and tortures you've experienced and watch as the person you're talking to, out of an instinct for psychological self-preservation, refuses to absorb your story to its fullest extent. Over a century ago, Mykhailo Kotsiubynskyi, likely the strongest prose writer in the history of Ukrainian literature, wrote a short story in which the narrator is reading a newspaper story about peasants being killed during a strike in 1905, all while munching on a sweet, juicy plum. The narrator proceeds to lick his fingers with relish.

On February 24, 2022, my wife and I woke up from the first explosions in the predawn darkness with the words, "*Tse vono*"— "This is it" or "It's here." We were ready to leave within fifteen minutes because we already had a go bag packed, even though we hadn't believed what we had been warned about. Come on, it's impossible for something like this to actually be happening in twenty-first-century Europe!

A year ago, we finally finished paying off our apartment. Now we don't know if we'll ever come back—though our building, as I write this, hasn't yet been damaged by Russian bombs. But that has turned out to not be the most important thing. We only took one backpack for the four of us because we don't own a car and were getting a ride out of Kyiv from friends (who, quite possibly, saved our lives). Legal documents, cash, bank cards, and three days' worth of all kinds of energy bars: everything else we owned we lost. The only thing that I regret not having taken is the science fiction novel that my nine-year-old son was writing by hand in a notebook. We couldn't pack this literal *manu scriptus* in advance, since my son added a few pages to the story every day. I was remembering this notebook, I was remembering it—but in the panic of the moment, I forgot. It's the only thing I cried over. All other material objects ceased to matter. Now, I sometimes cry over more serious, nonmaterial "things"—such as the stories relayed here.

All of these stories have been reproduced in millions of copies. Each of them is unique, and all of them are similar. At the moment of my writing this, half of Ukraine's children have left their homes. Four million people have fled abroad. Hundreds of thousands of men and women have joined the Armed Forces of Ukraine or Ukraine's semi-amateur Territorial Defense Forces.

On the day that I was leaving my parents' house in western Ukraine, where we had initially evacuated to from Kyiv, to join the army, my children gave me a cheap Rubik's Connector Snake. Naturally, the vein that kept the pieces together broke before I even boarded the train. But now these little plastic triangle pieces are a metaphor for our shattered life. And these little toy fragments have suddenly become the most valuable things that I have with me. My wife Oksana told me that, for the sake of the children, she's trying to not feel, to become numb. I, conversely, want to feel everything, and I'm so happy that Oksana, our children, our parents, and my brother simply exist. It's a love that's more acute than ever.

During the first days of the war, I felt a lot of love toward everyone around me and sensed that it was mutual. In the bank where you've been sent to be issued an army ID card, chairs are pushed up for you and you're offered delicious, freshly brewed coffee. At the neighboring tables, queues of people line up, making financial donations to the army. In the barracks, there are pails of fresh home-cooked foods from neighborhood grannies. "Eat, or it'll go to waste," they say. The attitude of the officers to the rank-and-file troops isn't the same as when I served as a young man in peacetime: this time, there's no bullshit with regulations, there's gentleness, there's humanity. "While you have the time, rest, here's a blanket for you," they say.

It is a strange and surreal war in the sense that it's taking place not just in reality, but simultaneously in the virtual world. It's possible that smartphones, despite the government's instructions to not share information that could benefit the enemy, lead to safety issues now and then—but I'm convinced that the cumulative effect of the constant support of loved ones outweighs this by orders of magnitude. I even have a psychotherapist for the first time in my life, albeit a virtual one.

Through this constant contact, I saw how feelings were reproduced, seemingly in millions of copies as well. The first all-encompassing love of everyone toward everyone else was, before long, replaced by a multilayered feeling of survivor's guilt—as if each person felt that he or she had been unjustly lucky in comparison to someone else, and that he or she was doing too little.

After this, there seemed to come a mass sense of "Hey-hey-hey! Russia's chipped its teeth, Putin's blitzkrieg spluttered! Why, we're becoming a legendary nation, we're creating an epos, we're Leonidas's three hundred Spartans! Instead of 'This is Sparta!' we're shouting, 'This is Bucha!'" In this suburb of Kyiv, entire streets were filled with burned tanks of the Russian–Fascist invaders. That's how we began to refer to them en masse, by analogy to the phrase "German–Fascist invaders," since World War II had in large measure trundled precisely through Ukraine. I was born two generations after that, but in preschool I was forever drawing downed Nazi bombers in flames. I think that Putin's invasion of Ukraine will be hardwired into our children's children the same way.

The emergency release of hormones couldn't last long. On the heels of the euphoric feelings of "We're still standing!," the emotional rollercoasters—and the impression that everyone you knew was experiencing them at the same time—began. Now, "a little more, and we'll kick out the occupier" changes to "this is going to be like Donbas, it'll drag on for years" ten times a day, every day. What's true, any thought of defeat isn't permitted. But, "Putinism will fall any day now" alternates with "What if he destroys the planet?" I'm aware that by the time this text is translated and published, many people will in retrospect think that I wrote nonsense here. Oh well. I'm describing the moment at the bifurcation point—when no one knows in which direction change will take us.

Here are some other thoughts that are coming now, at this moment of bifurcation. Maybe this is from lack of sleep after the night watch, but it seems that in the spring of 2022, we Ukrainians have ended up in a time and place when the planet's future literally depends on us. We're the sentinels of the fucking galaxy. We can't want others to risk or suffer in our stead—because then things might spin out of control, maybe leading to the death of the planet itself. As a child, I wondered what it must have been like to live in the 1950s in the menacing shadow of nuclear war. Well, now, at age forty, I know. Thank you, Putin, may you burn in hell.

We Ukrainians can't give up. We must wear out the dictatorship ourselves because otherwise life will be worse on this planet. Otherwise, there will be less freedom.

And, naturally, as soon as everything is over, those in the "nucleus of the world system" will again begin to forget about this semi-periphery, and they themselves will once more become paramount in their own histories, Biden's declarations, and *Saving Private Ryan*. Oh well.

As of right now, without the unprecedented solidarity and assistance that we're seeing, we wouldn't still be hanging on. Thank you, world.

I'm surrounded in my army unit by people seemingly out of unwritten stories from the book you've opened. A seminarian who voluntarily enlisted worries whether he'll be ordained a priest if he ends up having to kill someone. A bodybuilder who teared up while describing how, on the day that Russia attacked us, he and his wife were planning on making homemade dumplings together. A former head of a village council—a zoologist by education and the village philosopher by calling—who constantly impresses me, a professional philosopher by training, with his critical thinking: this head of a village council is much less susceptible than I am to our war propaganda. (Yes, we too have it, and even my wife, a Marxist sociologist, acknowledges that it's an indispensable moral support.) A hipster who vehemently battles with our commander to keep his beard.

All of them are, of course, imperfect. When we take a closer look at each other and at ourselves, we turn out not to be how we would like to present ourselves. That's true of me. And you, too. And of the entire countries and societies in which we live.

And perhaps that's exactly what *The Ukraine* is about.

These stories were written between 2010 and 2018. I hope they'll shed at least some light on why millions of Ukrainians—in many instances surprising even themselves—realized how much they love this imperfect country.

ARTEM CHAPEYE
March 2022, Ukraine

Pan Ivan and the Three Bears

He stood on the summit of the white mountain and gazed in our direction. The sun and the snow blinded us. Against the background of the jarringly blue sky, his dark figure, motionless, stood out starkly.

"He's like an Indian," Volodia said, turning to me, the snow beneath him crunching.

We had dropped our backpacks in the snow next to the trail and sat down on them to rest. We had no choice but to walk over trampled snow, following the existing tracks. It was tiring. But sinking knee-deep into snow was even more tiring.

"Yeah, his gaze is so intent . . ." I said, squinting at the figure on the mountaintop.

". . . and then he shoots to kill," Taras laughed, walking up to us.

Volodia and I chuckled too.

The figure tore away from the blue sky and began to swiftly approach us down the white slope of the mountain. No Indian in the prairies could have come down on horseback as fast as this man did on skis. With a quiet rustle, without kicking up a single flake of snow, Pan Ivan—Mr. Ivan, as we would end up calling him—came to a smooth stop in front of us.

"Good morning!" Volodia called out while the man was still braking.

"*Slava Issu,*" I said enthusiastically, mimicking the local Hutsuls. "Glory to Jesu—."

"Where you heading to, boys?" Pan Ivan asked.

His eyes and voice turned out to be gentle. His face was tanned and covered in wrinkles. His teeth were bad, but his body was strong.

"Wherever we get to," Taras answered. "Maybe up Sheshul Mountain. Maybe up Mount Petros."

"You won't make it up Petros today," Pan Ivan warned.

"Is it going to be cold at night?" Volodia asked.

"How should I know?" Pan Ivan responded with an honest shrug.

"But you're local," I said.

"And so, what—that makes me a weatherman?"

"Do you work at the bio-station?" asked Volodia.

"Well, yes."

"What station?" Taras asked.

"Students come from Lviv in the summer. There's a nature preserve here. They study plants, butterflies," Pan Ivan explained, smiling.

"And you look after it in the winter?"

"Well, yes. So that no one burns it down—or ransacks it. Both the bio-station and the mountain pasture."

"You yourself are from Kvasy, the village just west of here?"

"Well, yes."

Crunching snow, the rest of our group was approaching up the existing tracks. One after another, they dropped their backpacks, which sank into the snow with a scrunch, and plopped down on top of them. All of us were exuding steam. The afternoon had grown warmer than the forecast had predicted, and we had broken into a sweat.

"Oh, wow!" Maksym exclaimed, pointing at the man's skis. "Did you make the bindings yourself?"

"Well, yes," Pan Ivan replied with a quiet pride. "I fitted them to the skis. Because I don't own special shoes."

"And when you fall, do they unfasten?" Maksym asked. And then he reconsidered: "Or do you not . . . ?"

"I don't fall," Pan Ivan confirmed calmly. "I'm almost fifty-six already," he explained.

"Whoa!"

"Well, yes. At my age, no one in the village skis anymore. But I like it. I've been working here since the nineties. As if I'd be working here if I didn't love the mountains? I have a lot of work in the village too."

Our group spent a long time arguing whether to continue on or spend the night in the shepherds' huts in the meadow next to the bio-station. We asked Pan Ivan for advice. He proposed that we sleep in the warmth of his house. What, all twelve of us? We felt awkward at his proposal. Though for many, it was also tempting.

"Let's continue on," Taras said, a little irritated by now. "It's only midday. Why dawdle here?"

Pan Ivan listened for a long time. We looked to him for affirmation. He didn't try to win anyone over; he didn't take anyone's side. Suddenly, he had had enough: with a single sentence he bid us goodbye and, seconds later, was far away, descending on his skis to the wooden building of the bio-station.

We ended up continuing on. At night, it was minus twenty. The following morning, a wind picked up and five from our group descended down the mountain to the village. The remaining seven of us climbed up to the ridge. The wind was blowing up chunks of compacted frozen snow and tossing them in our faces. The exposed centimeters of skin felt like they were being cut by knives. At one moment, I was sure that my eye was on the verge of leaking out down my cheek.

I was among the four that eventually gave up and descended from the ridge. Only three from our group ended up climbing Sheshul. We agreed to meet up with them next to Pan Ivan's bio-station.

The four of us headed back down the mountain, submerged up to our balls in fluffy snow. We tried to slide down the incline on our asses but kept sinking in. Finally, we made it back by crawling to the path we had stomped out the day before. Heading back over our tracks at almost a run, we broke a sweat.

Pan Ivan saw us descending and started climbing to meet us halfway.

"We're coming to you!" I hollered immediately, unceremoniously.

"Have you frozen?" Pan Ivan asked, happy to see us. "I told you, you should have spent the night at my place, like normal people."

"But we wanted mountains," Volodia protested.

"And got more than our fill of them," I added.

"Let's go into the house," Pan Ivan said, turning around and waving for us to follow.

"This next part is my favorite part of traveling," I whispered to Volodia as we followed our host.

Taras and the final two of our group came down from Sheshul Mountain just in time for the epic about the bear, a story in three parts. Pan Ivan made hot sweetened tea for everyone and insisted, as he offered us *borshch*, "I'm going to throw it out tomorrow either way if you don't eat it."

Our shoulders warmed from the stove and our stomachs from

the *borshch*. We laughed lightheartedly: there was no need to freeze anymore. We asked Pan Ivan about life in the meadow during the winter.

"There are no bears here, are there?" Taras asked, his eyes exaggeratedly wide.

"Why wouldn't there be?" Mr. Ivan voiced his surprise at the question. "Of course there are."

"But they sleep all winter, right?"

"Well, yes. Though they do wake up on occasion." And that's how the first story began: one time, a bear woke up.

"One time, a bear woke up and was hungry. It came to the village. It tore apart a sheep. Then it tore apart another one. And it starts walking around. It kills a cow here, even a dog there. The people deliberated and decided to kill it."

"Is that allowed?"

"Killing a rampaging bear is allowed. The village men gathered and went off to look for it. One of them was this little old man who was cunning. He thinks to himself, I'll go off on my own. He stumbles onto the bear's trail and sees: the bear has gone uphill. So, the old man thinks to himself, Aha, there you are! So, I'm going to go around and climb up the other side faster than you."

"Now that's an old man!" Volodia exclaimed enthusiastically.

We laughed. But the old man succeeded in his plan:

"He walked around the mountain. And here they both are, climbing to the top—the bear on one side, the old man on the other. The old man makes it up there first, looks down, and sees the bear lumbering toward him. The old man reaches for his rifle and right in the bear's chest—pow! The bear is wounded but is running at the old man. And the old man doesn't have time to reload—nothing."

Pan Ivan demonstrated with his hand how the old man frantically tried to cock the rifle with his thumb.

"The bear reaches the old man and drags its claw over his face! The old man managed to spring back, but the bear ripped apart his cheek with a single swipe. Like this, from top to bottom."

Pan Ivan demonstrated on himself how the bear ripped apart the old man's face with its long claw, from the temple all the way down to the chin. We sat breathless.

"The old man's hat had fallen off and tumbled down the trail, and the bear thought that it was something scurrying away. It lets go of the old man and hurtles off down the mountain after the hat."

"Man, that old man was lucky!" Taras chuckled.

"While the bear is chasing after the hat, the old man reaches for his rifle. He reloads, but his legs are wobbling. Meanwhile, the bear sees that it's a hat, nothing living, and again heads for the old man. But the old man, now out of both barrels, right in the bear's chest—pow-pow! The bear is wounded but is still crawling toward the old man."

Pan Ivan demonstrated how the bear clutched its own chest with one paw and reached forward with the other.

"And the old man . . . well, he faints. He falls over. And he's lying—right there. He can't run away. And the bear is moving toward him."

Pan Ivan fell silent.

"Then what?!"

"The bear died two meters away from the old man. And that's how the village men found both of them."

Taras and I both exhaled noisily; we had been holding our breaths for a while by then.

"Epic," Taras murmured.

"Oof, Hollywood," I agreed.

Then Pan Ivan finished:

"The old man was taken to the district hospital in Rakhiv right away. There, he had an operation, got a blood transfusion.

They worked on him, worked on him . . . The old man died. From sepsis."

"Fuck, so it turns out that the bear chasing after the hat didn't help the old man?" Taras had started to laugh, then restrained himself.

We sat in silence, sipping the sweetened tea.

"Do bears wake up often in the winter?" Taras asked. "Because we'll have to head down to the village later."

"Not often. But it does happen. Right now—no. Right now, there's too much snow and it's too cold. But there was this one other time, when there was a thaw . . ." And that's how Pan Ivan began the second story.

"A bear was sleeping. But the weather warmed up, and the snow melted and flowed into its den. You could say the weather woke it up. It got up and went off roaming. And it killed a boar for itself."

"A domesticated one?"

"No, a wild one. Well, it ate what it ate, and the rest it covered with snow. The snow that hadn't melted yet. And here a forest ranger comes along, looks, and sees: a mound of snow, and all around it blood."

"Oh, wow!"

"Well, yes."

"The bear was clever in how it hid the food . . ."

"Well, yes. So, the ranger pokes open the mound with a stick, and sees: a boar's intestines, stomach, liver. He walks over to the second mound. He pokes it open, and finds a boar's head, hooves . . ."

"And flesh?"

"Well, yes, flesh too. The bear had eaten its fill and hidden the rest."

"For later?"

"Well, yes. The ranger has now climbed into those mounds and is examining them. And then he raises his head and sees: ten meters away, up the mountain, a bear is sitting and looking at him from above."

Taras burst into a loud laugh. I imagined the bear, not making a sound and its head tilted to the side, carefully watching a person rummaging around in its food.

"The forest ranger immediately reaches for his walkie-talkie—because there were other rangers not far away. And he says to them, 'There's a bear here.' And the head ranger replies, 'Don't kill it, let it go!' They knew that it was a she—because they had seen her peeing."

"So, what did she do?"

"She went off."

"She didn't bother them?"

"Bears don't bother people. If you don't attack them directly."

"But that was her food!" I said, then countered, "But the ranger hadn't eaten it."

Taras added with a laugh: "Imagine if he had shoved his head into the mound and started devouring!"

I imagined the man getting down on all fours and sinking his teeth into the bear's food.

"So, bears are smart!" I concluded, surprised.

"Ekh," Pan Ivan waved his hand. "Bears are like men. Only they can't talk."

And that's how he began the third story.

"Two people from our village were walking down a forest road. They come around a bend, and there's a bear sitting in the road. They freeze because they're close already, and the bear is coming toward them. One of the villagers runs off a ways, but the other is paralyzed with fear. And the bear is lumbering toward him. It approaches—and extends its paw to the man."

Pan Ivan demonstrated how the bear stretched his left paw all the way forward.

Taras let out a loud laugh.

"The man looks, and there's a large splinter in the paw. He pulls out his knife, unfolds it, then lifts the end of the splinter, and—y-y-yank! And he pulls it out! The bear roared—because it hurts, of course—and shoves its paw in his mouth. It's sucking at the blood."

Pan Ivan demonstrated how the bear jerked back its left paw and started to suck at its palm.

"The man's standing there, standing there: he can't budge from his spot. He was paralyzed with fear. He stood there and stood there—and then he fell. His heart couldn't take it."

"Really?" No one had expected such a turn of events.

"Well, yes."

"And the man died?"

"Well, yes, he died." Pan Ivan nodded calmly. "And the bear immediately heads over to him. It shakes him, then turns him this way, then that way. Like a doctor. It presses the man to its chest, embraces him. And when it realized that it was over, it sat down and started to cry. Like a man. What does that mean? It means the bear knew that the man had done something good for it. And then, for four days, they couldn't take the man away. The bear sat over him, guarding him, and chased everyone off. And then it dug a hole and buried the man himself."

And Pan Ivan demonstrated how the bear raked the ground apart with its paws, placed the man in there, and raked it back.

Sonny, Please . . .

Since her husband had died, things had gotten harder.

Her grandson Kolka had been scared of the old man, but these days he was completely out of control. He'd come by nearly every day: "Give me a bottle, Grandma. I know you've got one."

And when she ran out—because, for the love of God, she only had a dozen bottles for treating the neighbors should she have to ask for some help—Kolka started demanding money for booze. And she gave it to him, from what she had put aside for her own funeral. Grandma Nadia was a small and timid woman.

And Kolka would take it and would go drink with his friends. There was no work to be had in the village.

"Grandma Nadia, don't give it to him," her neighbor, a mustached and potbellied man of about fifty, would say. "Or, do you want me to sit him down for a man-to-man talk?"

Grandma Nadia would smooth out the folds of her skirt in silence.

"He's gotten way out of line," the female neighbors would say, shaking their heads. "But who else is there to look after him if his dad went off to earn some money and hasn't visited in a whole year?"

Kolko's mother had died long ago, and he lived in a dirty house alone. He'd bring friends over. The saleswoman in the shop tried not to sell Kolko alcohol, feeling sorry for his grandmother, so Kolko would go to the last house at the edge of the village to see Mykhailo, who sold booze even at night. But since his father sent money from Russia infrequently, Kolko never had enough. And Grandma Nadia would hand over some from what she had put aside for her funeral.

She needed to come up with some money from somewhere else.

Her sister in Baryshivka had it good: she took the commuter train from the suburbs to Kyiv and worked as a cleaning lady. Whatever the circumstances, she was guaranteed fifty-seven hryvnias every three days. But her sister was younger, only sixty-five, and had worked in an industrial plant before. Nadia, an uneducated old village woman, no one would hire.

So, Grandma Nadia got her hand cart out of the shed, the one that her husband had made for her in the early days of independence. She wiped the dust off the frame with her dry palm. The hand cart was big, almost as big as the old woman herself. Its wheels, taken from two wheelbarrows, were of solid rubber. The platform for a sack was made out of a piece of dark-brown plexiglass. Her husband had made this for her.

The old man, when he was still alive, was always constructing and tinkering. Their kids would make fun of him: he constructed a little plow based on sketches in the magazine *Home, Orchard, and Garden*, and then dragging that little plow proved harder than digging up the garden with a shovel; next, a wheelbarrow on two wheels that didn't fit through the narrow gate; and then a special apparatus for digging holes for potatoes, and while the old man was carrying it over to the potatoes and making a single hole, his old wife made ten with a hoe.

But he did make a cart for hauling a sack back when half the village was traveling to Kyiv to sell stuff, and everyone would tell Grandma Nadia that her hand cart was the best. The old woman would take quiet pride in it and silently forgive her old man for beating her on occasion. In his final few years, it's true, he grew calmer. After the heart attack. Not long before his death, the old man oiled that hand cart again. He liked order.

Back then, when everyone was traveling to Kyiv to sell stuff, Grandma Nadia even enjoyed it. But they were young at the time. Some of them had just retired, while others would have still had jobs if the collective farm hadn't been divvied up. They traveled a handful of women at a time. There were old men among them sometimes, but they were few. The first commuter train was at 3:47 am; the ride was free for senior citizens.

They worked as a group, one woman helping another load the sacks onto the train quickly. One, two—some with cucumbers, others with milk, sour cream, or cheese—they grabbed them and heaved them into the train's vestibule. And before they made it to Kyiv, they could even catch up on sleep, curl up on a bench for an hour and a half, legs tucked under. Or, whoever didn't want to, played cards. Or they just chatted—a good pastime too.

In Kyiv, they stuck together, so as to help one another. Plump Liudka, may she rest in peace, knew all the policemen: "This one's nice, he's got pity. If you tell him that you haven't sold anything, you can give him his cut next time. Or he might even let it slide. But that one, it depends on his mood. Now this one—look, you can't get around him—he's a scary man, it's better to have money on you to pay him off in advance. And even then, he might take it and still chase you off."

Back then, they would give the policemen two hryvnias each. Then it became five each. Nowadays, the mustached and potbellied neighbor told Grandma Nadia, it was twenty. And sometimes, they don't let you pay them. They just chase you off.

You need to really know where you're going and what you're getting into.

"Twenty hryvnias?" Grandma Nadia asked quietly. "What if you don't sell that much?"

The neighbor shrugged. "They'll chase you off, probably."

The neighbor was breathing heavily from excess weight and was sweating profusely in the sun.

These days, barely anyone sold stuff from hand carts the way she used to with the women from her village. Most everyone—like this neighbor of hers—would get into their little Zhiguli four-door and drive into the city with a trailer cart full of potatoes. But you needed a lot of money from the get-go to sell stuff like that.

Grandma Nadia sighed and went out to her garden. She opened the gate to the yard and shut it behind herself. They had put up the gate to keep the chickens out, though the old woman hadn't kept chickens since her husband's death: she didn't have the energy for that.

She plucked some scallions from their bed, then knocked the dirt off the roots against her dust-covered, dark green rubber boot. She found a few cucumbers hiding under some leaves. Had she known, she could've planted more. Maybe next year. For now, she'll have to bring potatoes, which are heavy. Her back's been aching constantly, her feet have been cramping, and both her big toes are completely crooked already.

Grandma Nadia held her back with her right hand as she walked over to the shed, pulling the hand cart with a blue-and-white checkered sack on it. The shed still bore the dry smell of chickens. The old woman bent over the crate where she kept the potatoes she had brought up from the root cellar and started picking out the prettier ones. She coughed a few times from the dust she had kicked up.

She'll have to ask the neighbor how much potatoes go for

these days in Kyiv and offer them a little cheaper; then they'll sell. If only some kind soul helps her lift the sack onto the commuter train. The train stops for three minutes.

"Grandma Nadia, are you here?" It was the neighbor, the mustached and potbellied one. He was peering into the shed from outside, squinting to make out the old woman in the semi-darkness. "My wife's telling me that you're planning on taking the train with sacks in tow? I'm heading to Kyiv tomorrow too, I can give you a ride."

The old lady felt awkward, but the neighbor insisted.

Where she ended up was all the same to her. It had been a long time since she knew where in Kyiv people sold stuff. She decided to go wherever the neighbor was going and would find a spot for herself somewhere there.

They were leaving late, at half past six. Grandma Nadia put on her newest headscarf, the yellow one with large green and red flowers. She was heading to the city, after all. She sat in the back seat, on the right side, her hands folded in her lap. She was wearing a dark blue blouse and a long, straight, dark brown skirt made out of a stiff fabric.

The neighbor was silent. The old woman gazed out the window, and, just like the trees and the fenceposts and the bushes and the fields, her thoughts floated by unnoticed: about her old husband and how, in the final years, he had grown quiet; about her son who was working at an oil field in Nizhnevartovsk in Western Siberia; about her daughter, who was living in the district center and had long been an alcoholic; about the good-for-nothing Kolka, who should find a job, but who would hire him; about the money for her funeral. Now and then, she adjusted her headscarf, then again placed her hands in her lap.

"Look, there are people selling stuff over there," the neighbor said, pointing at the sidewalk at an intersection, where a few women stood beneath chestnut trees, with cheese and sour cream, vegetables and flowers. "And when I finish up, I'll come get you."

The neighbor drove off to the closest residential neighborhood. He had a megaphone, and he walked through the courtyards of the apartment buildings hollering, "Potatoes! Potatoes for sale! Potatoes from Vinnytsia!"

He sold them by the sack and carried them up into people's apartments. He was still a strong man. He wore old clothes so as not to have to worry about the dirt. He and Grandma Nadia weren't from the Vinnytsia region, of course, but Vinnytsia potatoes were thought to sell better. In reality, he bought them in nearby villages.

Grandma Nadia's scallions and cucumbers sold right away, but the potatoes were barely moving, even though she was practically giving them away for two hryvnias each. The husband of the woman selling sour cream had already returned from the used car bazaar in his mustard-colored Lada Niva. They left for home. Even the Roma woman who had been selling flowers had gathered up the unsold ones and left.

"There might still be people coming back from work later. Maybe someone will buy some," a saleswoman working at a candy kiosk close by said to Grandma Nadia.

It started to get very hot, and Grandma Nadia rolled her hand cart over into the kiosk's shade. The saleswoman helped her move the sack onto the ground because Grandma Nadia was thinking of sitting down on the hand cart's platform. Her feet were hurting more and more, but she was worried that if she sat down, she'd have a hard time getting back up.

At four o'clock in the afternoon, the neighbor arrived.

"Ready to go, Grandma Nadia?"

"I'll probably stay a bit longer," she said quietly.

"Then you'll have to take the commuter train home. It's better that you come with me."

She looked over at the bag, which was still more than half full of potatoes. She thought about how the train was free for senior citizens, then she thought about her funeral and her grandson Kolko.

"Thank you, sonny. Maybe I'll sell the rest in the evening."

"OK, see for yourself," the neighbor replied with a shrug.

His cheeks were wet with sweat, and he was panting, his belly rising and falling. He wiped his forehead with a sleeve and glanced up at the sky.

"It's really hot today. Dragging sacks around is hard."

He climbed into his Zhiguli and drove off to the village.

After 6 p.m., a lot of people did pass by, and they bought another seven kilos of potatoes from Grandma Nadia. The old woman was happy that she hadn't stayed in vain. Maybe they'd buy them all, and then she could leave. There were three hours left till the last commuter train.

The stream of people was dwindling as she stood and timidly mumbled in the direction of the passers-by, "Who forgot to buy potatoes? Who hasn't bought potatoes yet?"

Barely anyone heard her soft voice. And that's when they appeared.

The senior sergeant had been drinking the night before in the police station's sleeping quarters because yet again that little bitch had not put out. She stood him up, just like the last time. The hangover had already passed, the alcohol flowing out together with his sweat into the armpits of his snug uniform (the senior sergeant had been putting on weight lately), but the sun shone right in his eyes no matter which way he turned all day long. And in the evening, tiny gnats appeared that also tried to get in his eyes. The whole day, the policeman had been scrutinizing from every angle the idea that maybe that little bitch was having a fling with that shaggy-haired dude he sometimes saw near her workplace. Because otherwise, what could it be?

His partner, still a young private who had just been accepted into the ranks of the Ministry of Internal Affairs, was walking a little behind him and watching the flock of pigeons feeding on a nearby public lawn. Should he rush at them for kicks or not?

"I'm going to buy some cigarettes," the private said.

"Go on."

The senior sergeant noticed an old woman in a yellow head-scarf in the shade of the aluminum candy kiosk on the public lawn. In front of her, on the sidewalk, stood a hand cart bigger than the old woman herself, a big, blue-and-white plastic bag next to it. The old woman was uneasily running her hands over her dark brown skirt. The senior sergeant walked over to her. The sun shone right in his eyes yet again.

"What, can't you read?" the senior sergeant snarled in lieu of a greeting.

Grandma Nadia had already noticed him approaching, but she couldn't leave quickly because her sack wasn't on the plexiglass platform of the hand cart. Her feet were hurting, but the old woman hadn't found the courage to sit down. Now the sack needed to be lifted.

A few meters from Grandma Nadia, twisted onto the trunk of a chestnut tree with wire at a height of about two meters, hung a dirty-white metal sign:

In case of unauthorized street vending,
please call the Patrol Service Regiment of the Dnipro
District Administration of the Headquarters of the
Ministry of Internal Affairs in Kyiv.
Tel: 559-63-62

Naturally, Grandma Nadia hadn't seen the sign. This was where everyone sold their stuff. The sign had rusted a little around the edges.

The old woman debated whether or not she should hand over a twenty. That was half of what she had earned that day.

"Go on, collect your things," the senior sergeant said.

The old woman began to bustle.

The old sergeant was standing over her. The old woman was bending down and approaching the sack from different sides, but she didn't look to be actually leaving. She just walked and walked, this way and that way, right in front of him. This way and that, this way and that. Worse yet, it was toward the sun, which yet again shone right in his eyes. And the senior sergeant snapped. The anger that had been sweltering in the sun the entire day finally found a way out of his body.

"Or should I help you?" the senior sergeant asked, taking a step toward the old woman.

"Sonny, please . . ."

She said it so quietly that he barely heard it. He ended up having to turn his ear toward her, and that exasperated him even more.

"Come on! Come on!"

Grandma Nadia was wrestling with the heavy sack, trying to stand it up on the platform, but she was having no success. The saleswoman who had helped her earlier in the day had now walked off somewhere. The old woman had no choice but to struggle on her own. The thin handles of the sack cut painfully into her dry palms.

"I'm sick of you people," the senior sergeant hissed and came even closer. The sun glared right in his eyes.

Maybe he had wanted to hold the hand cart steady, or to hoist up the sack to speed up the process. Or maybe he was just trying to walk past and his foot got caught. Regardless, the sack, the edge of which was already resting on the platform, proved heavier than the hand cart and, together with it, tipped over.

As he was getting his pack of cigarettes at another kiosk, the private heard the clang of metal against asphalt, turned his head, and saw potatoes bouncing along the sidewalk. A few potatoes skipped over the curb and rolled under a parked Jeep.

There were no passers-by in the vicinity.

The old woman was standing, her hands lowered along the sides of her skirt, and was repeating, "Sonny, please . . . Sonny, please . . ."

"A-a-a-agh!" The senior sergeant raised his hand and ran it over his cheek with force. He took a step back from the old woman, turned, and hissed over his shoulder, "You'd better be gone in five minutes." Then he hurried away, stepping over a potato.

"What was that?" the private called out after him. He started gathering up the potatoes but then decided that it wasn't befitting his position, straightened his uniform, and, with a quick gait, went off to catch up with his partner.

Later in the evening, Kolka, already drunk, came for money for his next bottle.

Rymma Hryhorivna Is Craving Human Contact

Every human being views themselves as a good person overall.

The police had slipped up yet again. Here in Ukraine, as everyone knows, the preceding government administration is always revealed to be if not a criminal gang then, at best, corrupt, and the police had once again defended the outgoing administration by dispersing a peaceful protest. It's understandable that, after yet another change of an "old bad" regime for a "new democratic" one, the police are more willing to communicate in order to vindicate themselves in the eyes of the public. They even want to unload a bit. And so, after a few hesitant comments on the part of the police, voiced almost as a warmup, something along these lines always slips out:

"Look, there's a certain government order in effect, and we're obligated to enforce it."

"Yes, I think that, in general, the police have been tasked with somewhat unusual assignments."

"They're talking about criminal orders? Do you remember the video about the protestors' combat weapons? What did the policeman hear? Articles 15 and 15a of the Law on the National

Police? What will that do?" an officer asks and pulls down his visor.

"I'll tell you about a criminal order!" another one chimes in. "It's when the Volyn riot police were first bussed into Kyiv in response to peaceful protests, then told, 'You're on your own. Figure out how to get back home yourselves.' Hang on, you brought us here!"

"And who came to power in the end? The same ones from a year and a half ago! Did someone new come? Huh?"

"And they want to put *me* through lustration, as if I've collaborated with the secret police? Well, if they lustrate me, my family will just say, 'Great, finally.'"

"During a protest, as you're standing there, you'll hear your fill of crap about both yourself and your mother . . . But what can you do in a uniform? So, you blink your eyes," a warrant officer says, standing at attention and bowing, "and say, 'Thank you, thank you.'"

"How do people view us?" a sergeant repeats with a snort. "Maybe you should spend a week on duty yourself. And better yet, in uniform."

The entire week that I spent on duty with the police, a line from The Who's "Behind Blue Eyes" kept whirling in my head:

No one knows what it's like to be hated.

I'm walking through a Kyiv metro station at night, together with my squad—true, not in uniform, because that isn't allowed. It's a wonderful job: twelve hours on foot, walking round and round in circles. It grows quieter and quieter. Our feet rustle over the scuffed granite of the station floors. After the metro closes for the day, the only ones left at the station are those who will spend the night there. They're getting ready to sleep sitting up on hard wooden chairs. Besides the people who are waiting for early-morning trains and the old women heading to bazaars in sheepskin coats that smell of hay and manure, there are the inevitable alcoholics and homeless.

It's obvious from the outset that I'm going to witness exemplary service that shift. That's why, with an eye on provocation, I tell each of my partners in turn about an incident that I had witnessed not long before. Right there, in a station of that same Kyiv metro. In the cold semi-darkness, beneath a set of stairs, a warrant officer, without uttering a word, quietly and methodically punched a homeless man in the stomach again and again. The man—unshaven, unbathed, wrapped in several layers of clothing, and with a face swollen purple—accepted his flogging equally quietly. "Enough!" I yelled, grabbing the policeman by the shoulder. "You're so smart, aren't you?" he asked, turning around, huffing and puffing. "Then take him home with you!" So, I left. The cop and the homeless man remained there, in the damp darkness beneath the stairs.

"I don't want to make excuses for anyone . . ." the supervisor, a young major, begins awkwardly, taken aback by the story. "I personally fired twenty corrupt cops prone to violence when I was transferred here."

"They're citizens of Ukraine too," the sergeant chisels a correct answer, as if on a school exam.

"Ohhhh! And they now know their rights!" the chief drawls sarcastically.

"No one does that sort of thing anymore," the deputy supervisor, a lieutenant, assures me.

But at one o'clock in the morning, a roundup does, in fact, take place. Indeed, the police don't do anything. Private security guards hired by the state-owned railway show up. Men in black walk up and down the rows of wooden chairs in the above-ground concourse. On each of them, someone is either sleeping or pretending to sleep. Some watch the black figures furtively, their heads down. They hope to be passed by. The security guards peer into the faces of those who are half-lying on the chairs. They push apart some people here and there—a few

Roma, for instance. They tap them on the soles of their feet with the tips of their boots. They pick them up by the armpits. The roundup takes place quickly and directly behind the backs of the policemen, who stare curiously through the black windows at the tracks below.

"Hey, old man! You need to go the other way," a black-clad security guard says as he turns a homeless man around.

Then he gives him a swift kick.

The old man is used to it. He doesn't resist. Another man, who's younger and tries to resist, is sent stumbling down the corridor with blows to the back of his head. A third one, thin and short, is literally carried out by his collar.

I do everything short of yanking the cops' sleeves. Staring intently through the window into the darkness, they walk away in the opposite direction.

"What else do you want me to do?" the young commander asks when I come running over with round, naïve eyes and an extended pointer finger. "People must have been complaining about them."

I don't respond. He understands that I understand. No one complained about anyone; everyone just sat quietly, like little mice. Because while the so-called face control was taking place, half the passengers were worrying about whether they themselves would be kicked out. Because the passengers that went unmolested included a lot of those exact same luckless types.

Because of the lie we both recognize, an awkward silence sinks between myself and the young commander.

"You understand . . ." he sighs finally. "I didn't want to say this, but . . . ninety-five percent of the people out there submit to authority, the other five percent we end up having to beat. Over the course of the night, you'll see for yourself what a den of rot this is."

As I'm walking over from one squad to the other, a hungover

twitchy young guy in a tracksuit blocks my path next to the sha-warma kiosks. He furrows his brow and babbles out a request for some food: "Hey, listen . . . I could smash someone's head, but what the fuck for? Buy me some food, won't you, bro? And in return, I'll . . . well, let's exchange numbers. If something comes up, if someone's head needs to get smashed, we'll round up a few guys with bats and smash it. Without money, for free. But only one time! You hear? Scout's honor."

So I bought him some shawarma.

"Ilarion," he says, shaking my hand and laughing.

The name of the patrol commander really is Ilarion—an uncommon biblical name. He's long and lean. Our off-road UAZ groans as it pulls out of the duty station gate for a patrol of the streets of Kyiv's Dniprovskyi District. From four in the afternoon until four in the morning.

"These are streetwalkers," Ilarion immediately begins to narrate the sights.

"Just if we pull up next to them, they'll bite us in the ear," Ivan, the young deputy, adds.

"And you can pick up tuberculosis from one air kiss around here," Ilarion continues.

They both force out laughs. Dmytro, the driver, joins in as well. At first, my presence makes everyone tense, but the longer we drive, the more they relax.

We drive slowly through the streets, but the allotted fifteen liters of gas may not be enough for the entire shift, so we frequently park in courtyards. Next to the Chernihivska Metro Station, a disheveled woman in a housecoat runs up to the vehicle and shrieks, "Why are you standing here? You have corpses lying around!"

"Where exactly?" Ilarion asks impassively.

"Jesus, you don't even know!"

"OK, let's get out of here," Ilarion says with a sigh, and when the UAZ pulls out, he turns to me and explains, "That was one of our specialists."

"Wha-what?"

The crew laughs.

"To be honest, each of them has their own specialty, in something," Ilarion explains. "Our selection of specialists in this district isn't half bad. Right, guys? This one, for instance, collects corpses."

"Yeah," the young Ivan adds. "There's another one who's being shot at by Black people from rooftops. Black snipers."

"And the babushka on the table, remember her? How old was she, pushing eighty? She's convinced her neighbor is trying to irradiate her vagina. So she sleeps on the kitchen table because that's the only spot in the apartment where the radiation can't reach."

"And Mykola Stepanovych?" Ivan reminisces.

"Oh-oh-oh, Mykola Stepanovych! That one summons us twice a week. And sometimes even more than once an evening. You need to come and hear him out. Sometimes for half an hour, sometimes for an hour. You need to nod your head with a thoughtful look on your face, he'll talk his fill, he'll calm down, and then you can leave with a thoughtful look on your face."

"Can't you not show up if you know it's one of the specialists?"

"We need to go every time we're called," Ilarion says.

Ivan nods as if he's in deep thought: "I had to go inspect suspicious-looking balloons one time." A text message comes in on his phone.

"Commander," Ivan exclaims, "our pay's come in!"

"What pay?"

"The horrible one, as always!"

They laugh. We sit in silence.

"Ilarion, why are you in the police anyway?"

"If there had been another job available in the nineties, there's no way I would have joined. But I didn't really want to be a gangster. And now I've gotten used to it. I'll have seniority soon. They're even promising me an apartment in the near future. True, they've been promising me one for ten years already—well, you know how it is."

The calls come rolling in one after another.

The dispatcher says, "There's a fight at the Aphrodite Café. A customer doesn't want to pay."

Ilarion, leaning into the walkie-talkie, responds, "So, I should stop by and pay for them? I'll be there in a sec."

"Make sure that some foreigner doesn't kill you there," the walkie-talkie answers.

Next, racist and homophobic jokes start between the patrols over the air, then an avalanche of general hilarity builds, until Ilarion cuts everyone off because of my presence: "Shut up a little, will ya?"

After settling the matter at the Aphrodite, we respond to a call where a young drunk guy is harassing a young woman in an alley.

"I just wanted to get to know her," the guy whimpers through tears on Ilarion's shoulder. "We were riding together in a mar-shrutka. And she got so . . . she got all . . . all . . ."

"That's not how you get to know women," Ilarion explains, patting the guy's hand soothingly.

"He says to me, 'I'm going to live outside your building,'" the young woman sneers.

We escort the guy away, calling him Romeo behind his back, and we give the girl—so that "Romeo" doesn't follow her—a ride all the way to her building.

"He says to me, 'I'm going to marry you,'" she snorts in the vehicle. "And I say to him, 'Hah, you don't earn enough to support me!'"

After dropping her off, we drive down the paths that run along the metro line in the park because someone was supposedly shooting at train cars.

After this, Ilarion climbs through a third-floor transom window because a woman is locked inside. Her husband, who called the police and an ambulance, is trembling with fear. What if the gas is on? What if her heart gives out? What if she commits suicide?

The firefighters arrive. They bring an extension ladder but are refusing to climb up it.

"Let a cop climb up," a young rescue worker full of self-respect says behind our backs.

A crowd gathers near the building. People are jutting out of windows. Ilarion climbs the ladder.

"Ma'am! Ma-a-a'am!" Ilarion shouts through the transom. Turning around to the rest of us, he hollers, "Everything's fine, she's drunk!"

Then the long and lean Ilarion slithers inside through the transom.

"She disgraced me in front of the whole block," her husband laments.

We drive on.

"And here we have three junkie brothers. Go search them."

We don't find anything on the three poppy-eaters, who are thin as rakes.

"They're decomposing from the inside," Ilarion observes.

"And over there, they're already cooking up some *borshch* for you, commander," Ivan says, pointing at the windows of some other acquaintances, also opiate users.

The third, an amphetamine user, finds the cops on his own. He throws himself on the hood of our vehicle, bat in hand. We brake sharply.

"What happened, carrot-top?"

"There's a guy beating a girl up over there, like this: Bam! Bam! Bam!" the carrot-top says, demonstrating with the bat.

Jumping as he walks, he leads us up to the fifth floor apartment. It turns out that the drunk girl has trashed half the apartment because the guy wants to break up with her. Ilarion sighs and enters. Ivan and I wait outside the door. Carrot-top is next to us on the landing. He can't stand still and is constantly running up and down the stairs.

"My, how much energy you have," Ivan notes in a deadpan tone.

"I play sports!"

"Yeah? What kind?"

Ilarion comes out of the apartment. "She isn't beat up. She's the one that trashed everything, and now she's sitting inside a wardrobe. She says she wants to be single."

Rymma Hryhorivna calls the cops on her own son. She claims that he's beating his bedridden grandma. Ilarion rolls his eyes. He knows this family well. "We call this type 'loyal customers.'"

Rymma Hryhorivna is a rather short, sturdy-looking woman with hair dyed a bluish black. Heavy makeup trickles down her face. Her teenage son isn't letting her into the house; he's standing in the doorway. Behind him inside the apartment with its dark, shabby wallpaper, an old woman, who doesn't appear to be either beaten up or bedridden, peers out. The old woman is trying to thwack her drunken daughter with a cane from behind the boy's back.

Rymma sees Ilarion, familiar and in uniform, exiting the elevator, and that gives her more verve.

"Take him away! He sells drugs!" Rymma shouts and tries to punch her son.

"What happened?" Ilarion asks the son, ignoring Rymma.

The teenager, in contrast to his mother, responds in a calm tone: "Mom's drunk again."

The scene plays out for half an hour. Rymma is a theatrical talent. She alternates between crying, yelling, lunging into hugs, and lunging with fists. Then she complains to the neighbor whose child she woke up.

"Rymma," the young, beautiful woman sighs, standing in her doorway with an infant in her arms. "Why is it there are always cops outside your apartment, but there are never any outside mine? Couldn't you just abide by the law?"

Rymma once again turns to appeal to Ilarion and Ivan. I don't know how the cops manage to look her in the eye during the conversation because I personally have been hiding behind their backs for a while to keep from laughing in Rymma's face.

Rymma Hryhorivna loses it when she realizes that her son won't be taken away. Ilarion sends her down in the elevator to separate the harmonious family. Outside, Rymma rages. Beneath a yellow streetlamp, in the deep courtyard between white multi-story buildings that amplify her voice, Rymma Hryhorivna yells that her mother is a witch, that her son is a drug dealer, that the police refused to protect her, that she's going to file a complaint with their superiors—and when Ilarion ignores all of this and turns his back on her, Rymma Hryhorivna shrieks with all her might, "Cops, go fuck yourselves!"

"We're going, we're going."

But she catches up alongside the car. "Cocksuckers! Pigs! Fine then, I'll insult you! Now, lock me up for ten days!" And, fumbling drunkenly, she starts to force her way into the UAZ.

"Get away from the vehicle!" the driver barks from his seat.

We pull out, leaving her behind. Then Rymma Hryhorivna squats like a hooligan on a tennis court, sticks two fingers into her mouth, and lets out a high-pitched whistle.

"This is how we leave sometimes, to hisses and boos," Ilarion says. "I'm telling you: you can't last in our business without a sense of humor."

He reports over the radio: "We settled the matter. Rymma Hryhorivna is craving human contact."

Ivan starts writing up another report about the actions undertaken by the squad, then, raising his eyes and pointing his ballpoint pen at me, he says to Ilarion, "Take a look at this one, boss. He'll wake up now."

Ilarion says to me gently, "Yeah, I understand. It's unusual, it's interesting." He sighs heavily then continues, "But for us, this is all routine."

Most of the calls are related to family fights, all involve alcohol and are, at first glance at least, funny. Except for one.

"There's a stabbing on Popudrenka Street," comes in over the radio.

"Whoa, now you're going to see some real trash."

We don't encounter the wounded man because an ambulance has already taken him away. A cousin, a proletarian-looking guy with a kind and perplexed face, is waiting to give a witness statement.

The victim, reportedly, went to the house of some people he barely knew to drink. He didn't return home that night. In the morning, he came out of his drunken stupor in some basement with a cut neck and a stabbed stomach. He crawled out through a ventilation window. He started heading home in a marshrutka, all the while bleeding out under his jacket. Feeling that he was about to faint, he got out, convinced a passerby to let him use his phone, and called his cousin.

Ivan is peering carefully into the young guy's face. "And this cousin of yours—it's the same one that cut his veins? Four years back?" he asks.

"No, six. I haven't been around for five years," the cousin

answers, raising his eyes to Ivan. "Oh! So, it was you back then? Thank you!"

Six years earlier, the current victim, in a state of alcoholic inebriation, had cut completely through his blood vessels below the elbow with a broken bottle. Ivan, who arrived before the ambulance, compressed his arm, using a strap from his bulletproof vest as a tourniquet.

"Did you hear that?" Ilarion asks me in a whisper. "He wasn't around for five years. He's also a loyal customer of ours."

"What was he doing time for?"

Ilarion answers with a smirk, "They've got two popular criminal statutes over there on Tampere Street: drugs and apartment burglaries."

Meanwhile, the investigators arrive. Incredibly, they soon find the man from whom the wounded man borrowed a phone. They lead the victim's cousin away a bit, into the grass of a rusted playground, covered with gray exhaust dust, so that the cousin can't hear them comment among themselves, "Apparently, they thought that he had croaked in the basement, but he came to."

The young guy gets a phone call from his aunt, the victim's mother. She's already heard from somewhere. The guy is squatting on the playground and talking into his cell phone: "Aunt Tania, everything's gonna be fine with him. Well, yeah, yeah . . . now that I've gotten to him, everything's going to be fine. I'm going to give my statement right now, and then I'm heading to the hospital to see him. Yeah, I bought it already . . . Everything's going to be fine with him . . . What? Yes. I talked to my boss, and he'll give me a small advance. There should be enough money, don't worry. If need be, I'll give my phone to the pawnshop."

The First

A power-tool duet begins in the apartment below ours. The first one hacks off big chunks of brain matter in a hammer-drill bass: *tr-r-r*, pause, *tr-r-r*, pause, *tr-r-r*. The second one buffs the pinkish-gray crinkles in a polisher falsetto: *ooo-eee-ooo-eee-ooo-eee-ooo*.

The power tools work in harmony. The effect is ideal. It makes you want to hurl your body rhythmically against the wall.

"Schedule!"

"Wha-a-at?"

Yaroslavna is trying to make light of it. She shouts, "I said, we've got a schedule! And they've got a schedule! It's 1 p.m.!"

"But it's Saturday!" Serhii shouts back.

Yaroslavna shrugs. This annoys Serhii.

Their one-year-old son Maksym walks in from the hallway. He moves his legs like a duck—together with his butt. He just learned to walk not long ago. He pokes his finger at the wall and says, "Ooo, ooo."

Serhii squats down next to his son and points his finger at the floor, responding: "Ooo, ooo, rude men. Don't be scared."

And at this the power tools fall silent. It makes you want to take a sharp, deep breath. Silence hangs suspended between your ears. It feels as though dust is settling in your head, between the temples. Serhii clasps his jaw with his hand and squeezes.

"Yarusia," he says to his wife through the fingers of his hand. "Put Masia down. Let's hope for the best."

Yarusia squats down and smiles at Maksym. "It's time for Masia to go to sleep," she coos. "Night-night. *Liu-liu.*"

"*Liu,*" the little boy replies and nods seriously. "*Liu.*"

"What a good little boy we have! He likes to go night-night."

Serhii is making tea when an earthquake starts in the kitchen: *tr-r-r, tr-r-r.* The walls really are shaking; he isn't imagining it.

Then the polisher enters with a pruning-saw aria: *ooo-eee-ooo.*

Serhii groans. He stands up and walks. He peeks into the bedroom. The kid is poking his finger at the wall and crooning "Ooo, ooo."

"I'm going to go have a talk with them," Serhii's lips move.

"Wha-a-at?" Yaroslavna asks in a raised voice.

Exasperation constricts Serhii's throat. OK-OK, let's shout a bit. So that Masia definitely doesn't fall asleep.

"I'm going to talk to them, I said!"

"Whatever you think," Yaroslavna's lips move.

The exasperation rises in a wave. It swallows him, head and all. Again that 'whatever you think' of hers. Her signature catchphrase whenever something needs to be decided.

He turns around.

"Serhii!" Yarusia shouts after him.

"What?"

"Take it easy over there."

He nods, his teeth clenched. He walks out into the corridor, then pauses for a moment.

Thunder is rolling through the stairwell: *tr-r-r-r-r*! You can hear the basses better here. The echo amplifies them. But now the high notes—those are getting drowned out.

Serhii places a hand on his chest and centers himself, stilling his heart, then, slower than he would have liked, goes down a floor. Half the stair landing is filled with bags of construction waste; the floor is covered with a layer of white dust. Serhii presses the doorbell and hears the electric chirping of three tones: *tioo-tiee-tioo*. They didn't hear him; the power tools whir on; he presses the doorbell again and again, trying to aim the chirping into the pause between the two tools. Finally, they hear him. At first, the bass breaks off abruptly, then the falsetto gradually dies down. The door is puffy, padded with cotton wool and covered with imitation leather. When it opens softly, Serhii lowers his gaze: a tiny, elderly man, a head shorter than him and cloaked in white dust, appears in the doorway. Under the construction powder, his face seems brown, like a well-baked bread crust. Wrinkles fan out from the outer corners of his eyes. The man is smiling.

From the appearance of the elderly construction worker, Serhii's anger deflates, the way a children's balloon deflates when you slacken the neck that you're holding between two fingers.

With a gentleness that surprises even himself, Serhii asks, "Good afternoon, are you going to be much longer still?"

Now it seems impossible to raise his voice, to explain by yelling at the smiling little old man that they turn on the power tools every day right at Masyk's naptime. What's more, the kid does eventually fall asleep. It's the adults that want to kill themselves.

"It's Saturday," Serhii says, spreading his arms.

"We're unfree people."

"I understand. I'm like that too. Are you from western Ukraine?"

"Yes."

Serhii peeks over the old man's head into the apartment. The floor covered with white dust has been trampled, the shoeprints superimposed in several layers. On an overturned plastic bucket, with his thin back to Serhii, a young guy sits hunched over and smoking. His spine bulges through the fabric of his light-colored work clothes.

"That's my son," the old man says.

That day, the workers don't drill anymore, but the whirring in his head continues.

Serhii drinks some tea and tries to reset but can't. Melancholy is rolling in; his head is starting to hurt.

He listens: Maksym still seems to be fussing in the bedroom. He and Yarusia call their son *Masia-Teliasia*, Masia the little calf, when he is well-behaved, and when he misbehaves, they call him *Masia-Hivniasia*, Masia the little shit. Though they do so tenderly all the same. Serhii has this feeling that he's now more attached to the kid than to his wife. One time, Serhii and Yarusia separated. Maybe they wouldn't have gotten back together if she hadn't turned out to be pregnant just then. Because the periods of quarrels–reconciliations–quarrels coincided with the periods of the most intense passion, when they would forget about caution.

Today they had been planning to put the kid down and make love, but the power tools woke their son and drove Serhii into a depression. Listening intently to the rustling and whimpering on the other side of the wall, he suddenly catches himself feeling hostile toward the child. He grows ashamed and tries to shake off the hostility. Instead, a memory surfaces that Serhii has assiduously been hiding from himself, like an unsightly wound. About a month ago, he had stayed alone with Masyk while Yarusia went off somewhere for the entire day. Their son was just learning to walk. On top of it, he was teething. The kid whined and whined, whined and whined, whined and whined—and the effect of that isn't much better than that of a power tool. At one point, Serhii grabbed the kid by the shoulder and yanked him. "Enough already!" he hissed. Masia looked at his father wide-eyed. To this day, Serhii remembers that horror in the child's eyes so vividly: my dad, who's supposed to protect me from everything, whom I snuggle up to and whose arms I climb into, is attacking me himself and yelling at me, and I hurt so much.

In the evening, Yarusia was changing the kid and hollered from the bedroom, "He didn't fall when he was with you, did he?"

"Nope, not at all!" Serhii had hollered back carelessly. He was glad that he was in the kitchen at that moment and not next to her, and that there was no need to look in her eyes, and that the wall muffled the falseness in his voice.

"There's a bruise on his shoulder. Maybe he hit himself against something."

"Maybe."

This memory, the wide-open eyes looking at him with love and simultaneously fear, had made Serhii treat the kid with increased tenderness since then. That's why the hostility that stirs in his chest voices itself as pain. It pierces him like a needle threading an insect. Serhii doesn't want to get angry at the kid, but he feels bad, so instead, he begins to get angry at his wife because she isn't able to get their son to sleep.

The pain in his head caused by the power tools now intensifies in the quiet. Inside his forehead, in the superciliary arches, pressure is growing. Serhii raises his eyes: there's a bottle of rum he brought back from Moscow, from his last trip to earn money, standing on top of the cupboard. Maybe it would relieve his head, but Serhii recalls how his father would reach for a stiff drink in any situation he found incomprehensible. Serhii doesn't like his father. And the rum is for his and Yarusia's anniversary next winter.

Serhii hears that the kid is no longer restless, and he frantically tries to shift gears toward lovemaking and to center himself, but can't. The skin on his face has become heavy. Serhii can feel his eyes sinking inward and simultaneously something pressing against his eyeballs from within. He rubs his temples.

The kitchen door opens.

"Finally," Yarusia says. "So, what's their deal?"

"It is what it is."

Yarusia nods. Serhii knows that he shouldn't add anything more, yet throws in with emphasis nonetheless, "Some people need to earn a living."

"Did I say anything? You're the one that wanted to . . . ."

"Shit, some people need to rest too."

Yarusia raises her hand to stroke her husband's hair, but he leans away. This movement angers her a bit. "Do you think I don't get tired?" she asks.

"I didn't say that."

"So, what were you getting at with your 'Some people need to rest too'?"

"It was in response to the, 'You were the one who wanted to . . .'"

"OK, are we bickering? I don't understand."

"That's obvious."

"What's obvious?"

"It's obvious that you don't understand."

"What's going on?"

Serhii doesn't respond.

"What's going on? Are you admonishing me for not working? Because I'm with Masyk?"

"I didn't say that."

"Of course you didn't."

She walks out to check on their son. Serhii feels a wild rage coming on. Now that was fucked up.

Sitting in the kitchen, Serhii mentally scrolls through what he should have said, and a minute later is struggling to remember why they had quarreled in the first place. After each of their arguments, he could barely ever understand what had started it, because each time the reason didn't lie in whatever was being discussed. This time Serhii struck up a quarrel in order not to admit that he didn't want to have sex because his head was splitting. He couldn't have simply explained this because it was so sissy-ish: my head hurts, not now. But he also has no desire to admit this to himself, so he convinces himself that Yarusia is to blame for the argument. First this "whatever you think" of hers, and then the "you're the one that wanted to . . ." And that's how it goes, Serhii thinks, working himself up: first she avoids making a decision, then he makes the decision, and after that she criticizes his decision. Exactly like it is with work, he continues to work himself up. When there was no work, there was no money. That was bad. He found a normal job, so now he's out, and she spends all day alone. That's also bad. You can't make her happy. All she does is criticize. It all boils down to one thing, Serhii tells himself. Some people bust their ass, while others only criticize.

Serhii takes a liking to this phrase, and when Yarusia comes back into the kitchen to make up, his words stop her in the doorway: "It's just that some people bust their ass, while others only criticize."

"Without a doubt."

"Shit. What, isn't it so?"

"Yes. Yes."

Tears appear in her eyes. Serhii immediately feels bad and says, "OK, sorry, sorry."

But he doesn't stand up. He knows from experience: in this state, she won't let herself be hugged.

"OK, I'm wrong."

"Shit, Serhii, sometimes when you say something . . ."

She's talking calmly; only her eyes brim with tears. "It's called, I came to make up, I think."

"What did you want?" he bursts out. "Me to drop down on my knees?"

"Quiet, you'll wake Masia."

"Mm-hmm."

He stands up, walks out into the hallway, crouches down on one knee with a jerk, puts on a sneaker, ties the laces with quick motions, turns, and whispers over his shoulder into the kitchen, "Do you need anything from the store?"

She doesn't say anything. He puts on the second sneaker, takes his bag, and walks out, closing the door roughly and catching it at the last second so as not to wake the kid up with the slam.

He goes downstairs, crosses the courtyard, then walks along the square concrete slabs, stepping on one with each step. Outside, in stark contrast, it's pleasant: crisp but not too cold yet. It makes him want to breathe deeply. It's quiet. The poplars have turned a rusty color. A light breeze stirs each leaf separately. Overhead, a bright blue, transparent sky. It never looked like that in summer. And in the sky drift elongated, rounded clouds of various colors: some white, some beige, some almost black. Depending on how the light falls.

Kyiv is actually beautiful sometimes. If you're looking up.

He and Yarusia had started dating in high school. As a teenager, Serhii had been very bitter, but back then he didn't take his anger out on Yarusia. He had outlets for venting his emotions. He would go boxing. Or to a knife fight. He and the guys, all of them underage, would roam the streets in a pack, looking for adventures and, occasionally, beating up anyone and everyone. This ended badly: two of his former friends are in jail now. Serhii jumped off that train in time; he got out. To this day, he sometimes finds himself thinking about that shawarma seller, a teenager just like they were back then. As they were beating him up, the shawarma-guy shielded his head with his thin veiny arms, which had grossly long black hairs on the forearms.

Serhii also finds himself thinking about that one girl often. They had attacked an Arab couple one day and were beating up the guy, but with the girl Serhii just ripped off her headscarf—he doesn't know what it's called. He couldn't beat her up: even if she was dark-skinned, she was still a woman. But he did cause her pain, and he felt so vile afterward as he walked away, wiping his sweaty hands on his jeans.

Serhii doesn't know what they might need from the supermarket, so he buys sausages, buckwheat, sugar, and pasta, just to buy something. These are "the basics" in their house.

"Exhale," he says to himself on the way back. He exhales, or thinks he does, and readies himself to make up.

But when he enters the apartment, Masia is no longer asleep.

"Surprise!" Yarusia says.

Their son is sitting on the floor, fake-walking a plastic dinosaur and growling hoarsely: "Hugh-hugh-hugh!" It works out great for the kid, and in a normal state of mind, Serhii would be moved by this Masia-saurus. But not right now.

"He's supposed to be asleep for three hours."

Yarusia spreads her arms, and this makes him angry all over again.

"Were they drilling?"

"No."

"Shit."

"His teeth maybe."

"This is called 'getting some rest.' It's the weekend! I'm finally home!"

"Well, shit."

Serhii had been thinking of making up when he returned, but he knows Yarusia well: it would take a long time to convince her that he hadn't been trying to say anything in particular. And he'd have to talk obliquely too, so that Yarusia won't suspect that, in reality, the man doesn't remember what he said that was so problematic. He'd have to compose long sentences, hear out her reproaches, and, most importantly, not let any of the annoyance he's feeling splash out. Because Serhii knows himself too: as soon as they make up, touch one another, embrace—his irritations will dissipate as if they had never existed.

But in front of the kid, who's already begging to be taken into Yarusia's arms, making up like that—substantively—is impossible. Every second, Masia will be a distraction.

Serhii is getting angry at his son for this, not his wife.

Yarusia goes to the kitchen, while he sits with Masia, handing him toys. The kid is shoving the dinosaur in his mouth and whining nonstop. He whines and whines, and whines and whines. Serhii's head hurts. It's becoming unbearable, so, in silence, he dresses Masia, unfolds the stroller, and goes downstairs and outside.

Here again he notices the contrast between the stifling gloominess of the quarrel in the apartment and the bright coolness of the street.

And, as always, Masia stops whining outside. Every time, Serhii marvels at these shifts in mood.

"Masia and his hypostases!" he says, leaning in and turning a button on his son's jacket. "Click-click! The switch from the hypostasis "little shit" to the hypostasis "little cutie pie.""

And that horrible memory of how Serhii once hurt this "little cutie pie" and how the kid looked at him with eyes opened wide in surprise before starting to cry has now become unreal.

He and Masia buy a half-loaf of bread in a twenty-four-hour store and feed the pigeons. Then Masia nudges the stroller in front of him. Then he learns to walk on a curb holding hands. Then to step up on a step and take a step back down.

Serhii picks the kid up in his arms and feels the warm childish palm on his neck.

"Chief!" he hears suddenly and turns around.

"Meidyn!" Serhii exclaims, cheering up. "I didn't know you were in town."

Zhora, nicknamed Meidyn (because he's a huge fan of Iron Maiden), had been Serhii's best friend in childhood, but now they saw each other maybe a few times a year.

"I'm in town, I'm in town. I got fed up with Moscow," Meidyn says. "So, this is your . . ."

"Maksym Serhiovych," Serhii drawls with sentimental deference, stroking the kid's back.

"Maksym Serhiovych. Damn, when will I remember?"

"Not soon," Serhii laughs, "if this is how often we see each other."

"I'm going to have one too soon, you know?"

"Wow, that's great."

"In a month. Listen, Chief, I'm in a rush . . . to her, actually."

"Shit! How are things . . ."

"How's tomorrow? Hey, listen, I actually wanted to ask you to be the godfather. I don't know if it's acceptable to ask in advance?"

Serhii feels himself grinning. "What difference does it make to us whether or not it's acceptable?"

"Exactly. OK, but I'm definitely in a rush. OK, so let's go fishing tomorrow. We'll talk it over there. Everything."

"Mm . . . I have a sort of dad day tomorrow."

"Then let's do it with . . . Maksym Serhiovych. We're not going for the fishing, but just, you know . . ." Meidyn says and bursts out laughing.

"Let's do it!"

"On the shore beneath the electric poles. Where we used to go. Around ten? We're not going to be fishing, just, you know . . ."

"Go on already, go on. Ten a.m. tomorrow! Give my best . . ."

"To Ira."

"To Ira."

Serhii pushes the stroller with his son home. Poplars grow the length of the road. We'll become godparents, go figure. Ira. He grows envious that Meidyn is running home to his wife with such joy. Serhii picks up a poplar twig with a few withered, shriveled leaves and thrusts it into Masia's hand. The kid rolls off like that, his hand with the little branch sticking out to the side, and then says, "Ooo," and points at a poplar. Serhii stops and squats in front of the kid. "Ooo?" he asks.

The kid waves the twig around, then points it at the tree. No, Serhii thinks, he can't understand yet. That can't be.

"You could have told me you guys were going," Yarusia greets him in the apartment.

"Shit, maybe that's enough already?"

The rest of the evening they're both silent, and when Masia starts whining and shoving his fingers in his mouth again, Serhii angrily remembers a past quarrel: how the kid cried, and how he and Yarusia traded shouts over his head. The reason for the fight Serhii, yet again, can't recall; he remembers only sentences being hurled over a toddler's crying. And the kid clutching at their legs.

They go to bed in silence, each under their own comforter, and at one in the morning, Masia wakes up. He crawls over from the toddler bed set up at their feet into theirs. He lies there and doesn't cry, cooing something to himself. He shoves his legs against Serhii's liver and his head against Yarusia's ribs.

The moon shines through the window. Opening his eyes, Serhii watches the translucent clouds glide the length of the whitish lunar surface but are incapable of obscuring it.

Serhii lies there, arching over the edge of the bed to give Masia room. After half an hour, his back starts to hurt. The kid isn't sleeping after all. Serhii rustles his comforter and, together with it, slides down to the floor. In the semi-darkness, he gropes for the throw blanket on the dresser and spreads it out under himself carelessly. The folds poke into his ribs, but he's too lazy to stretch it out smooth.

The moon drifts from one corner of the white nine-story building next door to the other. It's obscured by a few clouds simultaneously: the moon would have shone right through each of them individually, but the clouds overlap in layers, edge covering edge.

"Masia, go to sleep already," Yarusia hisses once in a while.

Each time, Serhii opens his eyes again and watches as the clouds slowly overcome the moon: one cloud moves in on another, until the light barely forces its way through the gaps between them. A plot of the clouds against the moon. A long-drawn-out plot.

"Go to sleep already, Masia!"

A plot of the clouds and Masia.

"Sleep!"

"You're just keeping him awake with all of this!"

Yarusia doesn't respond. A long-drawn-out silence.

He's having a long-drawn-out dream in which Yarusia has become old and homely, and he, the one and only time in their marriage—in Moscow, in another country—cheats on her with some random woman, toward whom he feels both lust and disgust simultaneously, and then it turns out that this random woman in Moscow, after that one and only time, up and got pregnant, and on top of it, it turns out that she knows everyone back home, and everyone finds out about everything, and now he has to pay child support.

He wakes up to grayness outside the window. Nothing remains of the day's bright blue coolness, of the light trembling of the now-reddish poplars. Outside, it's as gloomy as it is in the house. The sky looks knobbly, like the surface of a brain. His back hurts.

Masia is lying there sucking an empty bottle. His eyes are wide open. Yarusia's are closed, though she clearly isn't sleeping. Serhiy gets up and goes to make some coffee. His head feels wretched from not enough sleep. The atmospheric pressure has dropped outside. He can feel the arches of his eyebrows from inside his throbbing temple.

The coffee maker starts to bubble, filtering hot water through the coffee and sugar into the glass coffeepot. Yarusia enters without a greeting. She squeezes past Serhii in a way so as not to touch. Masia pitter-patters in after her. Serhii wants to stroke the child's head but doesn't do it—so that his wife doesn't think he's putting on a show.

And at this point, a hammer drill lets out a hesitant thrum in the apartment below.

Serhii clenches his fists. If these morons are going to drill on a Sunday too, he thinks, I'll grab a knife and go down. Or better yet, for safety's sake, not a knife but a ladle. He imagines himself pushing through the doorway past the old man, feels how his teeth are clenched, and lets his imagination roll: I'll yank their plugs out of the sockets, he thinks, and then I'll tear the plugs off their cords. So they definitely can't turn them on today. And if the young one tries to stop me, I'll shove the ladle into him, he thinks. And in the meantime, Yarusia, squeezing through between him and the kitchen cabinets to the computer on the table, coffeepot in hand, trips over the cord and, in order to not pull the computer onto the floor, leans forward, touching the hot coffeepot against Serhii's right forearm for a second. He throws his left arm out, and the outer side of his half-open hand swings into her face from the side.

"Ah!" she cries in an unexpectedly high-pitched voice and crouches down, placing the glass coffeepot at her feet to not break it, then grabs her cheekbone with one hand and covers her head with the other.

He crouches down and tries to hug her pretzeled body. "What did you . . ."

She flinches, removing his hand. He finds himself wanting her to hit him too, as if that would save him.

"Yarusia . . ."

Without raising her head, she hisses, "Get-t out-t of here."

"I will!" he replies and stands up abruptly, while she remains in a squat, arms covering her head and the coffeepot on the floor between her feet. The pot is half-full of coffee.

His eyes dart over to his son. Masia is raptly tearing off a scrap of artificial leather from the kitchen bench. Serhii puts on his shoes, pulls his jacket off a hanger, and walks out into the common hallway. He goes down two floors. He goes back up. He opens the built-in locker in the hallway. At the bottom, he sees dust-covered tools. A sledgehammer and a hammer. A saw. Pliers. An electric drill with its cord wound round the handle. Serhii takes the fishing rod leaning against the locker wall and a collapsible camping chair. He goes down to the first floor, then outside, and leaves quickly. He stops. He turns back. He walks into a twenty-four-hour shop for a loaf of bread. He holds out the money, then takes the change. He walks out. He goes to the bus stop. Waiting, he stands motionless. It's a Sunday, and there's no trolleybus for a long time. Serhii stands. Then he enters a half-empty trolleybus. It's mostly senior citizens sitting in the cabin; he has five stops to go. He sits next to a window, and the trolleybus pulls out. It accelerates like a rocket. He listens to the electric motor. The public share taxis don't accelerate this quickly. This is a catastrophe. Even if she doesn't leave me, this is a catastrophe.

The trolleybus travels along an old military road made of long concrete slabs. The slabs have been coated with a thin layer of asphalt, yet you can feel the junctures nonetheless. Serhii recalls how he once rode with Masyk and taught his son that the wheels of the trolleybus are saying *shakh-shakh, shakhshakh*, then thinks that when people talk about "staying together for the sake of the children"—men, at the very least—they mean not for the sake of the children, but for the opportunity to remain close to the children themselves. Serhii pictures Masia from the preceding evening, sitting in his stroller, his hand jutting out with the stick, wearing the striped hat with the little green pom-pom, and the tip of his little nose turning red in the cold. She'll leave me.

He gazes out the window wide-eyed. The trolleybus turns off the concrete-slab road. A residential area begins. Houses and apple trees ripple beyond the trolleybus window. The bark of the apple trees is almost black from humidity. Along the sidewalk, an old man and an old woman of a rare but distinctive type are walking: both pushing seventy or more, but they still hold hands. The old man is in a dark brown overcoat, and the old woman in a dark beige one, a shawl the color of withering leaves around her neck. Both are thin. Both stooped, they turn off into an alley, their hands still clasped. Serhii gets out at his stop, the canvas chair under his arm and the fishing rod in his hand. He passes a yard behind a large rusted gate, then a yard behind a large green gate. He walks out onto a footpath between two fences. The Dnipro River is shimmering brown under the gloomy clouds. The old man was petite, but the old woman was even more petite; they've probably been together for fifty years, Serhii thinks. Has he hit her even once? Even one teensy time?

Serhii begins to speculate who among his acquaintances has hit their wife and who hasn't. Meidyn hasn't. Even though he too was in that teenage crew of theirs, with boxing and the rest of it. But Meidyn had hopped off that train quickly. Kokos, another friend of theirs, has definitely hit his wife. Serhii remembered Kokos yelling into the phone at his Tania: "Stop getting on my nerves!" And then he kicked a public trash can. After that, Serhii remembers how he had once seen an alcoholic-looking father in the street with a little girl of about three. The guy was walking in front, the little girl was lagging behind and crying, "Mama! Mama!" and then the guy turned around to her and yelled, "Your mom's gone! Gone! Jesus!" That kind of man definitely hits. And what's more, he hits his kid. Hitting kids is considered completely low-class. Serhii recalls how he had once overheard two hipsters having a serious discussion about how "there's no point in hitting one-year-olds. But two-year-olds, I know, get hit already." He thinks, maybe everyone does, in fact, hit everyone, they just don't talk about it. And after all, he thinks, during my grandfather's time, hitting your family members was normal, no one made a fuss about it. Maybe I'm the only one making a fuss about it?

He wonders, had he hit her hard? Serhii sees Yarusia squatting over the coffeepot, rewinds the reel, and feels his blow. It's not hard, but the movement is learned, trained. A boxer's swing. He can tell her that it was just a reflex. But he dismisses this idea right away. Yeah, he laughs, he got scalded in one hand, and instead of pulling it away, he swung the other one forward.

He grins at himself nervously. It's better not to say that sort of thing. He walks out onto the riverbank. He crosses an asphalt path, cracked in places where the roots of old willows have broken through. Lower, next to the water, there's trampled yellowed grass. Up close, the river seems black. A few greenish-brown apple tree leaves, a dozen or so long willow ones, and one bright-yellow maple one have floated over to the shore like dried little boats. To his right, a transmission tower sprawls its crooked limbs. It's iron and matte. From the tower, wires jump across the river. Meidyn isn't there yet. Serhii left home earlier than he had planned, so he arrived too early. He extends the telescopic fishing rod. Each of its plastic rings clink softly as they snap into place. He molds a little ball from the bread loaf and casts the hook. He wonders whether Meidyn will bring normal bait. Serhii crouches with the rod, feels behind him for the little chair with his free hand, lifts it off the ground, gives it a flap it so that the aluminum legs spread out, and settles on the canvas seat. Had he hit her hard?

The feeling of his knuckles leaving dents in her flesh springs to mind. Fearfully, he suppresses a familiar pleasure and realizes that from now on he'll have to wrestle with this memory. Or maybe with this temptation?

I need to find the time to go back to boxing, he says to himself, but he can't manage to push the tactile sensation out of his head. This pleasure is familiar from childhood, when they went around beating up all kinds of people. It's an acute pleasure, no milder than sex, which had never returned to him before. A hot and soft pleasure. When you hit someone, your body also penetrates and sinks into that other person's body. A fist in a face. A foot in a stomach. He hasn't felt this in a long time. He needs to find the time for sports.

Sports, hah. Serhii pictures the Arab, or whoever he was. And his girlfriend, or sister, or whoever she was. He hadn't been able to hit her. He hadn't been able to hit a woman.

But his own woman—her, he had been able to hit.

But it had been an accident, he reassures himself. A random accident. I'll say to her, come on, think back about how many years we've been together. And in all that time, in all those years, this was the first time, Yarusia, the first time.

A thought floats up to the surface that instead of saying "the first"—because a first anticipates subsequent ones—he should say "the only." But at that moment he feels a bite on his rod and gets distracted.

About a month earlier, Serhii had had a horrible dream.

In the dream, he learned that once upon a time his father had killed his three young children. In reality, his father has two children, and throughout the dream it isn't clear if Serhii and his brother are among those killed, or if they're "new" children.

Serhii went to his mother to question her about it. His mother started waving her hands and scolding him. "Just don't even think about bringing it up with him. Because when someone mentioned it a year ago, he sobbed the entire day."

Holy crap, Serhii thought. She's concerned about the fact that my father was crying and not about the fact that he killed their three children? How did she live with him after that? How did she raise me and my brother? And why does she always make excuses for him, no matter what he did?

And then his mother explained, "Ever since then, your dad gets summoned to court once every ten years. But your dad managed the situation," his mother said with pride, "so that he now only gets summoned as a witness! And for no more than seven days every ten years. He secured that change, officially."

His mother was proud of having such an intelligent husband.

In the dream, Serhii did, in fact, go to his father to ask about it. He sat there, his face fatigued and intelligent, his hair completely gray—grayer than when he was alive. Sarcastically and very calmly, his father replied, "Something like that did happen. In the late sixties or early seventies, during the Brezhnev era."

"But how?" Serhii probed. "How could you do it?"

The father responded, with such indifference that Serhii's hair stood on end, "Well, what? I had been working all day. I was tired. I come home, and they're being naughty. So I, you know . . ."

Horror suffocated Serhii.

"And what about Mom?"

"What about Mom?" his dad repeated dryly. "You know her. She just closes her eyes. She has her own interests . . ."

"Hang on, hang on! You killed the children! And you're trying to drag her into it and put blame on her too?'

"So, what of it?" his dad shouted and stood up. "She's to blame! And you're to blame!"

"Me?"

His father moved toward Serhii, shouting, "You're to blame! You know it yourself! You're to blame!"

He raised his hand as if to strike, and Serhii thought that his dad would kill him again in a second. His dad, his arm raised, was about to lunge forward, when all of a sudden he transformed into a porcelain statue of a Cossack in traditional dress, one of those kitsch little porcelain statues, the mass-produced kind that everyone had in their living room back when he was a kid. But the statue was the size of a person, and Serhii recognized that this was the rebel Cossack leader Maksym Zalizniak. And the porcelain Maksym-dad with the raised hand started to come crashing down on Serhii, smothering him under its weight, and Serhii began to gasp for air and woke with a moan.

Yarusia was asleep. Maksym was too. Even in his own toddler bed. He hadn't come crawling over yet.

Serhii was afraid to fall asleep again. He got up and went to the bathroom. That's crazy, he thought, so this is what I really think of my parents. I didn't even realize that I still hated my dad that much. But why did he say that I was the one to blame? I was to blame for him killing me as a kid?

And then Serhii wondered, why the porcelain Maksym Zalizniak? And he glanced over at the toddler bed and understood. And he again grew afraid, as if back in the dream. He wondered: maybe when his father was transferring blame from himself onto him in the dream, in reality, it was actually he, Serhii, transferring his own blame onto his father? Maybe, in reality, he, Serhii, hated not his father but himself. He feared himself and hated himself.

Serhii had this dream the night after he hurt Masyk. Maksym. Serhii stood in the dark in front of the mirror. He saw only his silhouette.

"I'm a monster," Serhii whispers, staring into the black water.

Circles fan out from the bobber. The bobber rocks gently but doesn't submerge anymore.

"So, where's the kid?" Meidyn asks, sitting down next to him.

I'm Sorry that It Isn't More

We headed to the Kryzhopil region simply because of its melodious name—*Kryzhopilshchyna*. And it turned out to be breathtakingly beautiful there. Uninterrupted fields, just barely green in April, stretched eastward from Yampil, which sits right on the Moldovan border. Not a single village for dozens of kilometers. In the setting sun, you drive past endless rows of poplars with whitewashed trunks. Warm evening light all around. You're having a cigarette, gazing down from the top of a hill.

Now, all you have to do is set up a tent. But amid all the beauty of the fields, it's unclear where to do so.

"Do you see woods anywhere?" my wife Oksana asks, starting to worry already.

The city should be coming up soon.

Finally, right outside Kryzhopil, to the right of the road, we come upon a little grove and pull over onto the dirt shoulder. But three colossal hounds come running at us.

"Arf-arf-arf! Go on, scram, you horrid beasts! We'll see who out-growls who!"

I immediately turn off the motorcycle's engine and begin to

turn it around to set it down quietly. But now, a hunched old man is waving at us from the field, as if to say, Wait up! He walks over to us and shoos away the dogs.

"We're just here for a little while!" I shout to him while he is still some distance from us. "We wanted to spend the night in the woods. Would you mind?"

"Why not? I'm the ranger here," he explains, soothing the dogs. "Drive on over there and go in past the boom barrier. I'll finish up here and will be there in fifteen minutes."

"Wow, really? You don't mind if we put up a tent at your place?"

"Why a tent? You can sleep in the house! What's your name?" he asks and extends his hand. "I'm Vasyl."

For some reason, we couldn't figure out how to get past that boom barrier. It turned out to be fastened with a lock. We're standing there, smoking, waiting. It starts to rain—more of a drizzle than actual rain.

The dogs are the first to appear. Now that the motorcycle isn't growling, they don't take it for a living creature. They wag their tails and even let themselves be scratched behind the ears. In the dogs' wake comes Vasyl, a bit hunched.

"Why are you standing here? I told you to go past the boom barrier. You can walk through the trees here to the left."

I wheel the motorcycle down a steep path to the cabin and start looking around for somewhere to park it.

"Leave it wherever. No one's going to take it here."

"I know. It's just that I'd prefer to put it under a tree. It's going to rain tonight. So, have you been working here long?"

"I've been a ranger for thirty-five years. No, I'm lying. Thirty-four and a half."

"How old are you then?"

"Seventy-two. No, I lied again. Sixty-two. There've been too many years to keep them straight," he says with a soft laugh.

"What's your father's name? It feels awkward to just call you Vasyl. You're older. I should use your patronymic."

"What does it matter? Just call me Vasyl," he insists.

He has this look that's so innocent that it makes you want to cry. I'm already starting to suspect that rangers must be angels incarnate on earth. One time, another ranger saved me and some friends from a storm at the foot of the Chatyr-Dah Mountain in Crimea. It's almost as if all rangers do is rescue incompetent travelers. It's a profession for altruists.

"You can sleep here," Vasyl says, pointing at an old little house. "Sorry that there's no power. It was so windy two days ago! A young oak fell on the roof, as you can see, and shattered the slate shingles. And tore the wires too. Sorry that it isn't more . . . Or, if you like, sleep in my hut. There's at least heating in there. Because there's none here; the stove broke down."

"No worries at all! We were ready to spend the night in a tent."

"Well, I'm sorry that it's such an old house," the ranger resumes his apologies. "I've made an agreement with some craftsmen already; they're going to renovate the place. Look, here are the bags of cement that they've brought. Sorry again. You should make your beds while it's still light out. Because there's no power here. You see, a young oak . . ."

Oksana and I pull the mattress off the bed, worried about bedbugs, and lay a sleeping bag directly on the bedsprings. While we're doing this, another man comes to visit Vasyl. Without even glancing in our direction, the sizable man stomps off to Vasyl's hut. Initially, he strikes us as gloomy, but that turns out to be a misleading impression.

Vasyl hollers over from his hut, "Be here in five minutes, you hear?"

We understand what he was getting at. We gladly pull out whatever we had been planning to have for dinner in the isolated forest and bring it to the table. Some bread and a little smoked, braided string cheese. They have fish and canned meat and fried zucchini. And Vasyl, in the meantime, resumes his usual, "I'm sorry that it isn't more elaborate."

My grandma was like that: she'd feed you to the gills, while apologizing nonstop that it was "so plain and simple."

Mykola, Vasyl's burly guest, pulls a Mason jar out from under the table.

"Moonshine?" I half-ask, half-confirm.

"Cognac!" Mykola clucks with satisfaction. "Well, you know, a homebrew. There isn't much of it. Maybe three hundred and fifty grams. What's that for the four of us?"

Oksana can't stand anything strong, but after a day on a motorcycle in the cold and the rain, she drinks on par with the rest of us.

Within half an hour, we're merry, amiable, and happy. There's a fire crackling in the stove, a radio humming in the corner, and multiple cats rubbing against our legs. Vasyl's hut is literally two by three meters. A stove, a bed, a table—and that's it.

Why had Mykola struck me as sullen? He turns out to be a peaceable and likable guy. He's Vasyl's "forest neighbor"—imagine that. He works as the caretaker of a nearby summer camp while the children aren't there; it's mid-April now. Mykola is forty-two years old, but after a hundred grams, I take him to be a decade younger.

"I raked leaves all day today," he shares. "I kept burning them, and burning them, and burning them. And then in the evening, the wind blew more leaves in from the woods," he says, complaining about his Sisyphean fate.

After the alcohol, Mykola and Vasyl spend the rest of the evening convincing Oksana to quit smoking.

"Oksa-a-ana, you need to quit! You're a woman, you have to bear children," Vasyl drawls, taking drags of a cheap, strong Prima with relish.

Mykola has at least quit himself. So, he works on me a little as well, but badgers Oksana more. Nonetheless, it's all friendly.

"It's better to have a stiff drink once in a while than to fume like that day in and day out," Mykola philosophizes as he fills up his little glass.

They both also turn out to be motorcycle enthusiasts, like us. Mykola—again, a rather sizable man—rides from Kryzhopil to his job in the forest on a tiny scooter. I sit on that scooter later and am stunned: how does a hundred-kilo man fit on it? But he also has a 600cc Kawasaki sports motorcycle at home. "That's just for showing off once in a while, though: it guzzles gas."

He and I go outside to take a piss and are standing next to each other, while he continues to go on about motorcycles.

"It's not the same thing as yours. On a Kawasaki, you have to lie down on the tank. And if there's a woman behind you, she's also lying down, right on top of you. That's good, eh? So, yours is a real Japanese Yamaha?" Mykola asks, zipping up his fly and walking over to my motorcycle.

"Yeah." I zip mine up and walk up behind him.

"This isn't a Yamaha," Mykola says, looking over my Mamayota, as I call my bike.

"It's a Yamaha."

"It's Chinese," Mykola decrees and sticks out his tongue.

We return to the warmth of the hut, where Vasyl has already loosened up and relaxed from the warmth and the home-brewed cognac. He tells us how he used to make it all the way to Odesa on his Jawa in two hours: "There's no place a *durynda* won't lead you to . . ."

"A *durynda*?"

"What? You don't know what a *durynda* is?" the tipsy Vasyl laughs. I'm starting to figure out what it means but want to hear him say it. "Come on, a *durynda*! You know! (To Oksana:) Oksana, cover your ears. (Quietly:) A pussy. (Aloud:) Oksana, uncover your ears. So, the two of you are traveling now, but I'm sure that she's the one leading you around. And you're the one following."

Granted, Oksana didn't completely agree, but whatever. But these two, now that they're drunk, can't let go of this topic. They go on and on between themselves, glancing over at us now and then.

"Hee-hee, they'll manage to make a little boy by morning."

"Hee-hee, definitely!"

Yeah, that's easy to say. Since we've already veered onto the subject, sex on these kinds of trips is, overall, problematic. You spend all day on a motorcycle seat, arrive exhausted—covered in dust, with dried mud splattered all over your clothes, your body sweaty under the clothes—and then, on top of it, hang out late into the night with whoever is kind enough to put you up. It's unclear when, where, and in what state you'll make it to bed. And if you're spending the night in the woods, you're so dirty and sticky that even thinking about it is scary.

Oksana, I see, is already blushing. She seems to be enjoying traveling again for now. So, I try to be supportive of her positive attitude and whisper softly, "See? Where are you going to meet people like this at home? At home, it's always your same old circle. But here, the people are completely different."

"I'm a Ukrainian," Vasyl philosophizes drunkenly, "and I'm very Ukrainian—as Ukrainian as a Moldovan is Moldovan, as they say!"

"Yeah," Mykola adds, his elbows leaning heavily against the table. "When I went to your parts, to Halychyna, they called me a *Moskal*, as if I was Russian. And then I travel a little east of here, and they're already calling me a *Banderivets*, or Banderite, as if I'm some ultra-nationalist Stepan Bandera-loyalist from western Ukraine.

"Oh!" I exclaim, raising my finger and swaying a little in my seat. "My grandfather was from Rivne Oblast in the northwest, and he used to say the same thing! Word for (hiccup) word!"

Vasyl starts telling us how, back during the Soviet days, he traveled around the whole union—back then, the whole country—for work. He's been to all the republics of the former USSR, and even to China.

"What? China too?"

"Yes. I've even been in Afghanistan. I still have three shell fragments right in here" he says, pointing at his side through his plaid flannel shirt.

With tenderness, he tells us about his grandchildren; then with enjoyment, about fishing; and then puckishly, about his youth and *dyrundy*. When we go out with Mykola to look at the children's camp, Vasyl is sitting next to the stove on his bed, looking so old at his sixty-two that I would've taken him to be over seventy, like he had said at first. Yet simultaneously, he's so . . . well, like a child. Or like one of those old Slavic household spirits that hang out by the hearth—a *domovyk*. In thick woolen socks, torn sweatpants, and a cotton quilted jacket. Next to the large stove, he looks outright small. He's talking to his wife on an ancient cellphone: tipsy, his eyes gleaming with kindness, he scratches his almost bald head with his wide hand, muttering something, and starts to nod off.

Oksana and I follow Mykola out for a walk around his camp. The walk ends up being a session of Kryzhopil surrealism. There's something striking about large and completely empty structures in the middle of the woods. From what I recall, it was still drizzling, but I can't be sure because after the homemade cognac, it no longer mattered. We ascend about two hundred meters up a path, then squeeze through a hole in some wire fencing. A half dozen dogs are tailing after us, both Vassyl's and Mykola's. The cats stayed behind with Vasyl next to the stove.

"This is where the children stay," Mykola explains, showing off the peaked-roof wooden buildings with a sweeping gesture like a proud owner. They're large and empty.

Above us, trees rustle. The same ones that force Mykola to constantly rake leaves. A pack of gentle pups follows us. The place feels homey and cozy.

After the hundred and fifty grams, Mykola and I walk arm in arm for better balance. Oksana is trotting around in circles, taking pictures of everything around us in the twilight's long shadows. On a wall next to the hypothetical pioneers' gathering area, there's a mosaic of chess pieces, electrons around an atom's nucleus, spacecraft, and the inscription E=mc2. The wind rocks the crowns of the trees above us.

"Hey, let me show you my moped!" Mykola leads us to a big garage and opens the gate, which has a No Children Allowed sign on it.

"How do you manage to ride such a tiny one?" I ask, sitting down on the scooter.

"It's got such pull that you wouldn't believe it. You want to try?"

"Not at all. I'm drunk. I'll crash it."

"Right," Mykola agrees, instantly calming down.

"I've never even ridden one like that," I tell him a little later, as we walk on arm in arm.

"Woah! And you wanted to start it standing? It would've flown away right from under you!"

"Ha-ha!" I laugh with him, then interrupt him: "What is this?"

"Hang on, let me turn on the lights."

We see gigantic hairless heads and stubby bodies. On the plywood panels where the daily routine of the camp is written out, a pioneer plays a bugle, children do morning exercises with virtually nonexistent arms and legs, and so on. Everything *South Park*-style.

It's warm in Mykola's caretaker's hut. Not from a stove, but from an electric heater this time. An Orthodox icon of Jesus Christ and a red pennant with Lenin, signed "To the best pioneer troop," hang side by side on the wall.

"Hey, let me give you one like that as a gift! Won't that be a keepsake to remember in ten years . . . You can spend the night here too, it's warmer than where you were going to stay."

"That's OK. But thank you."

There's no need to be picky about the roof over our heads, I think to myself.

"Don't wake up the old man. He got a little drunk, and his health was already . . . Well, you saw for yourselves."

We stop by to see how Vasyl is doing one last time. He isn't asleep yet but is dozing off sitting up. His feet dangle off the tall bed in their thick socks. In the hut, together, we each smoke a final cigarette for the night. Half-asleep, Vasyl keeps repeating, "I'm sorry that it isn't more . . . An oakling fell . . ."

Oksana and I go off to our house. We lay down on the bedsprings covered in a sleeping bag, then cover ourselves with another sleeping bag as best we can, pulling it up all the way so that our noses don't even poke out from under it.

The night is very cold. Forget about making a boy!

The Exploitative Realtor

When Oksana was pregnant with our first son, we had to look for a new apartment. After all, once you have a child, you no longer want to co-rent an apartment with strangers.

Like everyone else who's moved to Kyiv, I hated realtors. And our search for a home was proving to be long and anxious. A "neat and clean two-bedroom apartment" is advertised, but when you show up, you find cockroaches, boards torn out of the parquet, bubbles of moisture on the sagging wallpaper, and mold stains on the ceiling. Or, you see a listing that claims a "designer renovation" and find Doric columns made of plasterboard against a pink wall. Beware the "designer renovation"!

Or, better yet, walls full of bindweed. Meanwhile, Oksana's full of hormones.

"I don't know," I sighed. "I'm in a rush, of course. But maybe we can come see it a third time, together? I don't want to decide without my wife, after all—behind her back, so to speak. That would be wrong."

The parquet creaked quietly as I passed from room to room.

They all followed me with their eyes and without saying a word. The landlord, a retired policeman, stood next to the couch in the corner, leaning on the police baton in his hands. His mother-in-law, a sweet old lady who showed me the apartment the first time, was next to the balcony. And behind the old lady was a small woman of about thirty-five, who was just barely five feet tall.

"So, you're the agent?" I asked her.

She nodded wordlessly.

"Inna told me that I was coming to sign the contract already," the landlord said emphatically. "That's the only reason I came."

He waved the baton around in front of him. As if to say, see what an inconvenience this is?

"I know, I'm sorry. Like I said, my wife was unable to come at the last moment."

The landlord looked at me intently, all cop-like. Without blinking. He shifted his body weight, and the parquet beneath him let out a creak.

I started jabbering: "She had her shoes on already but then turned around at the door. Do you know what kind of mood swings pregnant women have?"

I didn't launch into the explanation that an hour earlier, Oksana and I had very nearly rented a different apartment, but then Oksana got agitated to the point of hysteria, saying that she didn't want to decide such an important matter in that kind of state, and I freaked out and came here on my own nonetheless, thinking, fuck, I'll go ahead and rent it and present it to her as a done deal—to finally stop with all of this! But on my way here, I calmed down.

"You can come take a look a third time, and a fourth time too," the landlord said, curbing his irritation. "Just without me. I'll come back to sign the lease. Here, talk to Inna. And where do you live?" he asked, addressing the agent.

"All the way out next to the Chaika neighborhood," the little woman said.

"On the highway heading west, to Zhytomyr?"

Inna nodded.

"Wow! Then ask her forgiveness," the landlord said, turning to face me. "I at least live close by."

"I'm sorry," I said, my eyes wide and my head lowered.

"It's OK," the agent responded with a forced smile. "This is my job."

The apartment was in the Holosiivskyi District, at the opposite end of the Kyiv from Chaika.

"I really do feel bad," I said to Inna after we walked out of the building into the darkness. "When I called you, I was sure that my wife would come."

It was winter. Nine p.m. As we walked, the agent lit a thin cigarette. She took a long drag and exhaled.

"Don't worry about it, I remember what being pregnant is like. I have two children."

I was surprised: Inna was being amicable.

"We have a month and a half left," I started to narrate, in an attempt to smooth over my wrongdoing. "We've looked at a dozen apartments already, but nothing's a good fit. I'm so tired!" I had apparently decided to complain about my plight, presumably to vindicate myself.

"You're heading to the bus stop?" Inna asked.

"I think I'll walk a ways. The metro isn't far from here."

She hesitated a second, then decided: "Well then, let's go. Don't worry, you'll find a good apartment."

She had understood already that I wouldn't be renting this one. I hadn't said it outright, but it had become obvious. After the cop-landlord's "I'm retired, but in our business, heh-heh, there are no former employees, keep in mind that we're going to sign a lease, and, if necessary, I can keep an eye on you, heh-heh."

"Yeah, I know we will," I replied, now feeling almost fondness toward Inna.

"When I was pregnant with my younger one, my husband and I didn't have an apartment or money. And I was seven months pregnant already. But it was OK. I ended up earning enough to both rent an apartment and pay for a hospital child-birth. And two months after my daughter's birth, I was working again. When I'd have to run out for a showing, I'd give the baby to my husband and skip out for two hours. My husband was unemployed at the time."

"What does he do now?"

"He's also an ex-cop," Inna said, waving back in the direction of the building we had exited. "Even now, he still sometimes works gigs in his old district. They've got their own problems there." She gestured with the hand holding the cigarette, and I glanced at her curiously. She noticed the look and hastily changed the topic. "He took the job because they promised to give him an apartment. And then, seven years later, they told him that the building where he was supposed to be allotted one wasn't going to be finished. So there was no longer any point in continuing on such a ridiculous salary."

"So, you rent too?"

"Well, yes. We rented a completely barren place right after the builders left—you know, the "raw materials only" kind. When I arrived from the maternity ward, there was nothing there yet. Just bare concrete walls. Not even a stove. I fell into such a depression then, you can't imagine! And right after giving birth. But it was OK. Gradually, over two years, we bought everything the place needed."

I walked alongside her, picturing everything she was describing. Gray, unfinished walls, no wallpaper, no whitewashing even. One secondhand lumpy futon on which she and her husband sleep. The older, seven-year-old daughter on a little mattress placed on the dark brown linoleum. The younger one in a baby carriage. In the bathroom, the water flushes loudly because the apartment is completely empty and the sound reverberates throughout. Only six months later does a gas stove appear.

"But the rent was very cheap. And the nature out there is incredible! You're surrounded by murmuring pine trees. Our building is right here," Inna says, pointing with her left hand to the left side of the sidewalk, "and here is the forest!" she exclaims, pointing to the right side.

"Where are you from originally?"

"From the Vinnytsia region. Both me and my husband. We've been in Kyiv for seven years now. Our older daughter—she's nine right now—was born back home. But the younger one, who's two, is a Kyiv girl already."

"You're heading to the Akademmistechko Station too, right?" I asked as we entered the metro at the Demiivska Station.

"No, the bus runs from Sviatoshyn Station."

"OK, then we'll go to Sviatoshyn together. Is it far from there to Chaika?"

"Not at all, fifteen minutes or so!" the tiny Inna said with a wave of her hand.

I glanced at her skeptically. Since moving out to Irpin, a suburb twenty-five kilometers outside the capital, I had become well aware how those of us living in the suburbs always mini-mized our travel time when talking to others. For instance, we didn't mention waiting in a long line when you'll only make it onto the third *marshrutka*. We also kept silent about the extent to which we were tethered to the schedule of trams or other forms of public transportation.

"I just need to make it there by ten o'clock, to not miss the last bus," Inna added, confirming my suspicions.

"Do you get calls like this in the evenings often? Because I usually call agents after work and as late as 10 p.m."

"Yes, I'm always expected to pick up and explain everything," Inna replied with a smile.

"Do you work for a large agency? Or for yourself?"

"For my child's godmother. There are three of us."

"And how many apartments do you rent a month?"

"Me?" she asked, then pondered for a few seconds. "About three. On average. If I'm lucky, four."

I counted mentally. If I rented that apartment from the cop, Inna's commission would come out to two thousand hryvnias.

"That's six thousand hryvnias a month—less than two hundred dollars?" I asked, sympathizing with her.

Inna held back a smile and bowed her head a little—as if I had paid her a compliment, and she was pleased but wanted to hide it. "Well, you're counting . . . you know . . . optimistically. In reality, it comes out to three and a half or four thousand."

My notions about rich realtors who were making crazy money off me in the middle of nowhere were crumbling like old dry plaster.

"But if you sell an apartment, then that's a big commission right away," I surmised.

"Well, yes! True, I haven't sold a single one yet," Inna admitted. "They go, look, but no one seems to be buying anything."

Before that, she had explained to me how much she spends a month on transportation. She has showings all over the city. I calculated and couldn't come up with how they had enough to live on. They probably rely on her husband's "problems" in his "former police department," I concluded.

We sat in silence for a while, side by side in the half-empty metro car. The train thundered through the tunnel but didn't interfere with us talking. As if sensing that I was performing arithmetic operations in my head, Inna said, "That's OK, the important thing is to believe that everything will work out in the end."

I smiled at her, and she added this mantra that I find myself hearing so often: "Thoughts materialize into being. If you believe things will work out, they'll work out."

Blessed are those who believe, by God!

She told me about her older daughter, for whom she didn't skimp on anything. About her daughter's hamster and how he had initially lived in a jar, before Inna bought him a special cage with a commission. Now the hamster ran on a hamster wheel day and night. Day and night. They had to insert a pencil into the wheel to have a break from the rattling at least once in a while.

Exiting at the Sviatoshyn Station, Inna smiled at me once more. "I'm confident you'll find a wonderful apartment!"

She ran off across the platform because the last bus was leaving in six minutes.

This Is *My* Home!

"You need to work, not beg. Why, I'm the same age as you and earn money like everybody else. Don't shame yourself . . ." Halyna Stepanivna kept jabbering under her breath, but the other old woman simply walked around her with a blissfully serene countenance. Halyna Stepanivna turned around and continued to mutter over her shoulder at the other old woman's back.

"You wouldn't have *two* hryvnias, would you?" the other old woman addressed a passerby, putting a strong emphasis on the *two* and pronouncing the rest barely audibly.

She seemed to be glowing, as if she wasn't of this world, and that's why she was able to ask so convincingly that the passerby stopped and started looking for the money in his wallet.

"I'm sorry," the passerby replied with guilt and genuine sadness, "I don't have any small bills."

"Would you have a five maybe?" the old woman asked quietly, radiating warmth.

And she received a five. Upon seeing this, Halyna Stepanivna grumbled something indistinct, took her loaded-down handcart, and dragged it in the direction of the metro. The wheels got stuck in the slush of snow and mud. The handcart was heavy from the glass containers piled on it.

Two bearded homeless men were warming themselves between the first and second doors of the metro station. They sat next to the ventilation grill, where warm air blew into the vestibule. One of the homeless men was even smoking up his sleeve, trying to do so unnoticeably. Both men tried to take up as little space as possible, but they got in the way of the passing passengers nonetheless—partly because the air around them was tinged with a sour smell, and the passengers were trying to bypass them without getting too close.

"Could a police officer," a female voice uttered over the loudspeaker sternly, "please report to the support booth immediately!"

The homeless men bent down, picked up their bundles, and hurried to the exit, almost knocking over Halyna Stepanivna.

Halyna Stepanivna didn't like to ride the metro, but sometimes she couldn't find enough recyclables in her own neighborhood: she wasn't the only one who went rummaging in garbage bins.

She, naturally, had a senior citizen's card, entitling her to free rides on the metro, but she bought tokens to not have to interact with the controller at the turnstiles. And so, Halyna Stepanivna took advantage of the fact that the metro worker and the police officer were both distracted with the homeless men. By the time the stern female voice caught up with her, it did so from behind already: "Transporting luggage on a collapsible handcart," spliced scraps of a recording stammered, "is strictly forbidden on the escalator."

Halyna Stepanivna pretended that the recording didn't pertain to her and, without any hesitation, pulled the handcart onto the moving belt. They would probably have let her on regardless, but Halyna Stepanivna was one of those who didn't like to ask.

When she sat down in the metro car, a young woman with

dyed hair stood up and made a show of going over to the next bench. Halyna Stepanivna tried to wash her clothes as often as she could, but you can't really hand-wash an overcoat, and anyway, at the end of the day Halyna Stepanivna always smelled like garbage bins just the same.

She didn't like to ride the metro.

She would've preferred to hide out in her apartment, as usual. Halyna Stepanivna liked to be alone. But Olha, her fifty-year-old niece, had been living with her for several weeks now.

"She sits around all day, not doing a thing," Halyna Stepanivna whispered to herself as she pulled the cart home from the metro. She was bundled all the way up to her eyes. As she breathed in the freezing cold, steam escaped through her knitted shawl and settled on it in a downy layer of hoarfrost.

Olha, it must be admitted, had tried to accompany Halyna Stepanivna to work a few times. However, Olha got winded before even making it to the first garbage bin. In contrast to the skinny Halyna Stepanivna, the fifty-year-old niece wasn't just a little fat but downright corpulent. Olha claimed that this was due to a hormonal imbalance, a disability.

As a physically disabled person, Olha had the higher pension of the two.

The niece first came from Chernihiv for a pilgrimage, and together, she and Halyna Stepanivna had visited the Kyiv Pechersk Lavra—the Kyiv Monastery of the Caves. After a day of waist-deep bowing and reverential kissing of icons and saints' relics, Halyna Stepanivna's knees hurt, but she felt cleansed. Even luminous. So she herself suggested that Olha stay with her for a while. Olha, her corpulence notwithstanding, very much resembled Halyna Stepanivna's late sister. In Chernihiv, Olha was obliged to take care of her son-in-law's pigs in exchange for a place to live. Doing so was difficult, what with her weight and shortness of breath.

"Jesus, Mary, and Joseph!" Halyna Stepanivna muttered in surprise.

She had almost been hit by the building's iron entry door, which a young neighbor had opened from inside.

"Oh, I'm sorry," the neighbor said. "Good afternoon."

"Good afternoon," Halyna Stepanivna replied.

She tried to slip past him to get inside, but the neighbor stopped in front of her.

"Forgive me," he said, "would you mind shaking out the things you have in the corridor? Because my wife and I hear a mouse at night."

"Re-e-eally?" Halyna Stepanivna asked wide-eyed, feigning astonishment.

"Really. We thought that maybe it lives in your bags."

"OK, I'll have a look." To convey her willingness to oblige, Halyna Stepanivna gave two quick nods.

"Thank you!" the young neighbor said, smiling and finally letting her pass.

Halyna Stepanivna headed upstairs even more aggravated. The mouse had gnawed through the bag in which Halyna Stepanivna kept the more decent clothing she found next to garbage bins, had gnawed through the clothing itself in places, and had made a nest out of the scraps of fabric. But, of course, Halyna Stepanivna was unable to catch the mouse.

She exited the elevator and unlocked the iron door that separated the four apartments to the left from the elevator and stairs. That smarty-pants, it turns out, had even hung an announcement inside:

"ATTENTION, RODENT!" it began.

Next, there was a drawing of a mouse with big, long teeth. The mouse was standing on its hind legs, and looked a little like a cunning fox from a fairytale and a little like a Tyrannosaurus.

Esteemed neighbors!
Be attentive and careful when opening your apartment door.
A MOUSE has taken up residence in our corridor.
The pest rustles at night, and one time, we
even saw it with our own eyes!
PLEASE, shake out the items that you have brought from
your apartment outside: since there are no mouse holes, the
little beast clearly lives right here, in your belongings.
Let's drive it out together, or it will end up in
someone's apartment sooner or later—
and then THERE WILL BE TROUBLE!

Halyna Stepanivna tore down the note, leaving scraps of white paper on the iron door along with the tape the smarty-pants had used to affix the notice.

She opened her apartment door and immediately heard a liturgy being broadcast: "We pra-a-a-ay to the Lo-o-ord, our Go-o-od."

A black plastic Chinese radio receiver that Olha had brought with her was playing. The Swedish Elektron-brand TV hadn't transmitted a picture in a long time: even though it would turn on, it only hissed static and displayed grainy wavy streaks that made Halyna Stepanivna's eyes hurt and head ache.

She began to take off her coat and shoes still standing in the corridor, to not track snow and dirt into the apartment. She had left the handcart with the glass bottles outside, on the other side of the door. Next to the bag with the mouse-gnawed clothing.

"Stepanivna, there's soup on the stove!" Olha hollered from the only bedroom without getting up.

Halyna Stepanivna muttered something indistinct and walked into the kitchen. She didn't feel like eating. She sat down at the table and leaned her back against the refrigerator. The old Dnepr-brand refrigerator, smudged by dirty fingers, stood unplugged so as not to use electricity. Even with the bottles and paper she collected for recycling, even with Olha's disability pension, the two women barely had enough for a shared apartment, medicine, and food.

The radio receiver continued to broadcast from the room: "Blessed is the kingdom of the Fa-a-ather and of the So-o-on and of the Holy Spi-i-irit, now and forever and to the ages of a-a-ages! A-a-a-amen!"

Halyna Stepanivna wanted quiet. She found herself thinking about a story she had read in the newspaper *Today* about that grandpa and his roommate. What was his name? Shapiro? Lambrozo? No, she remembered: Lopató. With an accent on the last syllable.

Grandpa Lopató was seventy-six years old, and he was registered at the same apartment as another grandpa—a relative, if she recalled correctly, who was seventy-four. The grandpas were forced to live together, even though their relationship was bad. Finally, Grandpa Lopató's roommate, in an attempt to drive out Grandpa Lopató, brought a third grandpa to move in with them. And then Lopató lost it. He was seventy-six, but he stabbed the roommate with a knife sixteen times. While he was at it, he also stabbed that third grandpa that the roommate had brought to move in twice. The seventy-four-year-old roommate, in between knife strokes, crawled out of the apartment. At first, he did so on all fours, and then he slithered away only on his elbows, dragging his legs behind him. In the stairwell, he bled to death and died. Grandpa Lopató returned to the apartment and fetched a kitchen hammer for flattening cutlets. The grandpa that the roommate had brought to move in was curled up in the corner of the kitchen, clutching the wound in his stomach with one hand. He raised his other hand to protect his head from the hammer. But Grandpa Lopató didn't pay him any attention and took the hammer out to the stair landing. He turned the roommate's corpse face up. He sat down on the corpse's chest. And then he started to methodically beat the face with the hammer for flattening cutlets. Later, the forensic medical examination revealed that all the facial bones had been smashed.

"Holy Lord," Halyna Stepanivna whispered, frightened by these thoughts and crossing herself three times, "lead us not into temptation but deliver us from evil."

Then she stood up and went from the kitchen to the bedroom where Olha was.

The cousin wasn't suspecting anything. "The soup turned out good, didn't it?" she asked. And at this, Olha raised her puffy face and saw the expression in Halyna Stepanivna's eyes.

"All you do is go from church to church while I earn a living."

Olha remained silent, her lips pressed tight. She didn't start defending herself or offering excuses, and it was this that caused Halyna Stepanivna to fly into hysterics.

"All you do is go from church to church while I earn a living!" she repeated, breaking into a scream. "From church to church! While I earn a living! From church to church all day long! While I collect bottles from garbage bins in the freezing cold!"

Olha was still silent, and Halyna Stepanivna was now shrieking. "This is *my* apartment! It's registered to *me*! But you've been living in *my* home for years!"

"What years?" Olha asked, unable to hold back anymore. She had already managed to regroup under the verbal volley, and now her voice was sarcastic.

"This is *my* home! You'd better be out of here by tomorrow!"

"What years?" Olha repeated.

"You'd better be out of here by tomorrow!"

They didn't talk all evening. Halyna Stepanivna stayed in the kitchen, and Olha stayed in the bedroom. They went to bed on the daybeds in opposite corners of the bedroom without uttering a word. In the morning, Halyna Stepanivna, without uttering a word, went to turn in bottles.

Even though it was freezing cold that day, it was nonetheless sunny and windless. Halyna Stepanivna calmed down. She didn't end up having to take the metro anywhere. She turned in the bottles, then took a walk around the neighborhood. She had her fill of alone time. It was quiet and peaceful. There wasn't even any wind. The snow crunched under her feet and under the wheels of the handcart.

I'll have to ask her forgiveness, Halyna Stepanivna sighed to herself. Olha does, after all, do the grocery shopping, she cooks, she cleans the house. She traveled to Chernihiv not long ago and returned with her pension. Olha really does have it hard with that constant shortness of breath. Might as well let her stay. At least there's someone to talk to. And on Sunday, we can go to church together. To ask forgiveness for the quarrel.

Halyna Stepanivna unlocked the door next to the elevator, then took off her coat and shoes in the corridor, to not track in snow and dirt. She left the handcart with the bottles she'd collected over the course of the day outside the door. As always, she turned the twist mechanism on the knob lock so that the door would lock without a key.

She entered quietly because the radio wasn't playing. Maybe Olha was asleep.

Olha wasn't in the bedroom.

Halyna Stepanivna panted, then went into the kitchen.

There was no note either.

In the middle of the kitchen table, a key lay solitary and alone.

Halyna Stepanivna sat down on a stool, her back to the unplugged refrigerator, placed her hands on her knees, then began to sob and couldn't stop.

Feel Unique

He even felt a twinge of jealousy toward that old lady.

The crowd splashed out of the Kyiv Metro into the Akadem-mistechko Station. People flooded the stairs from wall to wall. And that old woman was walking in the opposite direction with an antagonistic look and complaining loudly. "This is a mob! People can't even get through!"

She genuinely viewed herself as separate, as different. As if she wasn't a part of the mob.

He felt a twinge of jealousy toward that lady because he just wasn't capable of that anymore.

Things had particularly deteriorated since he began working as a courier. He spent whole days on public transportation and saw how many people's faces sported superficial expressions. Every other one of them was of the opinion that they weren't like the rest. That he or she was separate, and the crowd was separate.

That antagonistic old woman wasn't the half of it. She even evoked sympathy. Because at least she felt some sort of emotion toward others.

Those who walked, shoving apart the people in front of them

in the metro, were significantly worse. They did so with a look of indifference. They shoved aside with a hand, as if it wasn't people they were shoving, but branches in a thicket, and you just needed to push your way through them. Right through them. He would get the urge to hit those types of people. Even if that type happened to be a woman.

FEEL UNIQUE!

The advertisement beamed from the station wall right into his soul. The girl holding a smartphone in her hand peered deeply into his eyes. And extended the smartphone to him personally.

He had once wanted an iPhone, true, but he had quickly come to realize that "think different" wasn't in a courier's budget. He was better suited to one of the other slogans: all the same stuff, at a third the price.

He hurried to the office for the new orders. He'd have five minutes and could read more about this smartphone online. If they let him near a computer.

In the No to Boredom office, everyone was always bored.

The company sold a variety of games: chess, darts, Twister, go, and poker. Rubik's Cubes, Mafia, The Farmer, and Monopoly. Puzzles, model building kits, and Legos.

When they first arrived on the job, the new hires would try to play the games themselves, but then would quickly return to online crosswords or to the local networking site VKontakte.

"No to Boredom—all the fun stuff," the pimple-faced girl with the nebulous dyed hair pulled back in a ponytail would say into the phone with a forced smile. She viewed herself as the boss because she had been with the company the longest. She believed that a smile could be felt over the phone and insisted that all the other sales managers stretch their lips too. The sales managers, all of whom were under thirty, called the company No to Whoredom among each other on their cigarette breaks. All of them except the pimple-faced one with the ponytail. She viewed this as unacceptable. Her monthly pay was three hundred hryvnias higher than that of the others.

There were five employees in total, counting the courier. Two sales managers sold in Kyiv, two sold outside Kyiv, and the courier delivered the games throughout the city or to the post office.

The office was located in the basement of a five-story Khrushchev-era building, where water and sewage pipes jutted out overhead. In certain spots, they were forced to duck. The basement was lined with prefabricated metal shelving, the racks stocked with game boxes. It was always rather dark there, and it always seemed damp.

"Where've you been so long? You still have five orders today," ponytailed Pimple Face growled as soon as he entered the basement, ducking under the pipe in the entryway. Even with his small stature, he was forced to bend his head. The customers who would stop by once in a blue moon for their orders themselves would sometimes bonk their heads and curse. It was good that the pipe in the entryway was hot water, so it was covered with soft insulation.

On the table lay individually labeled boxes and a list of addresses for the courier. He packed it all up into his backpack.

"L-l-let me at l-l-least have a l-l-look at G-g-google maps," he said, stammering a little from agitation.

"So, the paper map isn't good enough for you anymore?" Pimple Face grumbled, but then turned to the nearest subordinate. "Serhii, let him have yours for a minute."

She never addressed the courier by name. No one did. It was, "The courier will come by" when on the phone with customers. Or simply, "Go," "Here," "Take it," when addressing him directly. Mentally, and with a rueful smile, he referred to himself as "the last person at No to Whoredom."

Serhii, the manager who was supposed to give the courier a turn at his computer, began to minimize and close out links on his monitor in a rush, then cursed quietly, and when he finally gave the courier a malicious glance and stood up from behind his desk, little beads of sweat covered his forehead.

The courier went through the motions of opening up Google Maps and entering one of the addresses off the list, then glanced around and opened another tab. He had remembered the model of the smartphone. There it was. It was a good deal—a super-low price. Twenty-seven different colors to choose from. Four gigabytes of built-in memory, a slot for a memory card of up to thirty-two gigabytes, and an eight-megapixel camera with an LED flash. And oh, those rounded corners and the ergonomic design!

When, later in the metro, he walked past the girl on the poster, who was extending the smartphone out to him, he gave her a smile.

Now he needed to work and save up. And so he once more seeped into the crowd.

At the start of the day, he typically felt amicable toward people. Since he wasn't an angry type himself. True, he had few friends. Probably because he was small and skinny. To make things worse, when he got agitated, he stammered a little. Just a tiny bit, but back in the day this had made him feel like an outsider among the other teenagers. Back in school he was prone to smiling graciously, but by their response the other boys ingrained in him that this was a sign of weakness. He quickly realized that a man, particularly a man of small stature, needed to pretend to be Rambo.

And he learned to put on a tough act, even though he was made fun of for the stammering all the same. He never did befriend anyone at the third-rate college he attended. And it was for this reason that it was hard for him to find a girlfriend after the move. The stammering would start just as soon as he tried to get to know someone and began to grow agitated.

And so, he moved on, alone. He delivered game orders to fight off boredom, bored all the while.

He tried all sorts of ways of combating boredom while on public transit. He took crossword puzzles from the office and finished solving them. This grew old quickly. He tried reading the free newspapers that were handed out on the metro. That was immediately boring.

One time, someone had left a book entitled *The Four Million* in the basement their office was in. He started reading it, thinking it'd be about achieving success, something along the lines of *Think and Grow Rich*. It turned out to be a short story collection. The foreword explained that the title referenced the number of people in New York City at the time of the book's writing. Interesting, he thought. There are about four million people in Kyiv right now too. With the ones that are here temporarily, maybe even more. He read the first story. He recognized the plot of the second one, entitled "The Gifts of the Magi," from who knows where. Cry me a river, he thought with a sneer and didn't read on.

He tried to listen to music, but that just ended up making him sick and tired of his favorite songs. It's impossible to listen to even the best stuff for entire days at full blast in an attempt to drown out the din in the metro tunnels. Right after New Year's, he had grown particularly fond of the then-popular "In the New Year, off a pine, tear a needle of a pine . . ." The "pine" went on to rhyme with "whine," and the "needle" with "wheedle." He would put the song on and listen to it in the metro over and over, until he grew disgusted at that sad joke for the sake of which the whole song had in fact been written: when the never-ending repeat would begin, "My needle's pining, my needle's pining, my needle's pining for you."

He would just smirk and imagine Pimple Face going down on him as his needle pined. Payback.

The urge for payback would swell at the transfer stations. No matter how many times he had to go through one, each time was a shock. Just like no matter how many times you jump into an ice hole, you won't get used to it.

People taking the pedestrian walkway from the Golden Gate Station to the Theater Station would walk clumped tightly into a crowd, waddling from foot to foot like penguins. Elbowing didn't even make sense, but some elbowed regardless.

In the long underground passageway from Khreshchatyk Street to Independence Square, everyone moved in a compact torrent, and the rustling of feet made you think of cockroaches.

In the passageway from the Sports Palace to Lev Tolstoy Station, those who considered themselves the wisest used the curve to bypass the crowd splashing out of the train.

Whenever two trains would pull in simultaneously at some station, it would seem as though the crowd wouldn't fit on the platform and would squirt in both directions—under the wheels of the trains.

He even had the desire to see this. He fantasized about a train chomping on a porridge of bodies.

And most important of all was the fact that the metro overflowed not only at peak times. No, that was the case the entire stupid workday. Who were all these people? Why were they riding around on the metro? Why weren't they at their jobs? They couldn't all be working as couriers.

Thousands, tens of thousands, hundreds of thousands, four million, seven billion. He hears Vasyl Symonenko's poem in his head: "You know that you're human. Do you know this, or not? Your smile is unique, your torment is unique, your eyes are yours alone." My ass.

By the end of the day everyone would strike him as detestable and stupid. Even the conversations overheard in the train car would irritate him.

"The guys and I decided that there's a serious and urgent need for a 'dislike' button on Facebook," some guy on the train says to a girl. He announces his conclusion just like that—with gravitas. The verdict is final and isn't subject to appeal. Dumb ram.

"You need to write to Zuckerberg," the girl replies with a smile. Blind sheep.

"My general opinion is that Facebook should be for close relatives. And VKontakte should be for the rest."

In moments like this, he didn't think about the fact that he too said similarly stupid things. He just loathed in silence.

When he would exit and someone would be dawdling in the aisle, he would purposely walk past in such a way so as to bump them with his shoulder—to jostle them a bit. His tension and aggression grew with each train ride.

When a person from within the torrent would stop in the underground passageway to buy apples from someone's grandma or socks from someone else's aunt, or when it proved impossible to melt into the current, he would get the urge to punch a face.

At the Golden Gate Station, he encountered yet another one of those guys who walked through people like through a portiere. The guy was tall, bearded, and about fifty. The man silently pushed aside the courier with a wide hand and entered the car.

But this time the little courier turned around, planted both feet firmly on the granite platform, and pushed Scruff Face in the shoulder with all his might. Despite being twice as heavy as him, the bearded man staggered.

"Aren't you c-clever!" the courier exclaimed, barely having enough time to start stammering.

He prepared himself for the fact that Scruff Face would come back out of the car in a second, and he'd have to continue what he had started. He wouldn't be able to say more because of his stammering. But he actually wanted Scruff Face to come out. Whatever. He'd slug him. Or get beaten up. Cops. Fuck it all.

But Scruff Face just shook his head and slunk deep into the car, into the dense crowd. Trembling a little, the courier headed off to the passageway between stations.

To calm himself down, he tried imagining people as cells of one organism, of one body. As cells of one city. Or—hah!—of a unified humankind! Every cell thrashing and wrestling with others. He imagined this happening in a human body. It felt creepy.

Wherever he was able to, he delivered the packages on foot, not via public transit. Especially right now, when he needed to save up for a smartphone as quickly as possible. Because he needed to buy it now. It was early spring already, and in May, he would get kicked out of the dorm. In past years it had been possible to stay through the summer in exchange for a small bribe to the dorm mother—under the guise of helping with renovations. But this time, the college dorm was being repurposed into a hotel for soccer fans who were expected from all over Europe. In the face of the EuroCup powers, even the dorm mother was helpless.

He didn't know what he would do for the summer. He'd probably end up having to go to his parents' place to hoe the gardens, hunt down Colorado beetles, and rake away manure. He didn't want to think about it right now. It was better to raise some funds as quickly as possible, buy the phone, and then he'd see.

After mapping out the route, it turned out that he'd need to take a minibus for a few minutes and then get out again. From the cold of the early spring outside to the dizzying heat inside. He'd need to cram himself, in his warm clothing, along with his backpack, into an already jam-packed tin can, then climb out sweaty and run onward all the same. Because he never makes it in time. No, it was better to spend twenty minutes walking at a fast pace, with his jacket unbuttoned to not sweat.

On top of it, the minibus was a few hryvnias wasted each time.

When he was taking the job, the announcement had promised he would be reimbursed transportation costs. Really. At the beginning of the month, Pimple Face issued him ninety-five hryvnias with a receipt as a sign of exceptional trust.

"That's for a metro card."

"And for the *m-m-marshrutkas*, the t-t-trolleybuses?"

"Sorry, friend! We can't foresee all your travel needs, can we? You decide for yourself when to catch a ride and when to walk."

He was obliged to agree. Or do what? Stay unemployed? On the first day, when he returned to his dorm, his legs throbbed with such pain that his ears could hear it. With time, he got used to it. And he stuck to his job: for the preceding few months, he had lived off handouts from his parents, and he didn't want to do that anymore.

And jobs, he knew, could be even worse. One time while job hunting, he had fallen for an ad:

URGENT! URGENT!
Director's Assistant needed!
Education level HS, BA/BS, MA/MS.
No experience necessary.

The flyer was an acid green color. He called the cell number listed on it. He was scheduled an appointment for three days later—and not just anywhere, but at 2 Independence Square, right in the center of Kyiv. That caught his eye: it was obviously a serious establishment if the office was right in the heart of the capital.

The address turned out to be the Trade Unions Building. And the man he had called turned out to be a squat forty-year-old in black slacks, a leather jacket, and a baseball cap. The guy led him into a rent-by-the-hour assembly hall, where there were about a hundred people gathered: the men doing the hiring—or, more often than not, the women doing the hiring—and, around each of them, from one to a handful of applicants for the position of director's assistant.

First, a middle-aged woman in a pink pantsuit walked out on the stage and began talking about the international company that was growing quickly and about how you could earn more in a few hours a day working at this international company for yourself than working full-time as an office slave. But, of course, not all at once. And while climbing the ladder of success, you could, in the meantime, become prettier and healthier by buying the company's cosmetic products yourself.

"And now . . ." the woman in the pink suit said, then paused and clapped her hands, "our EMPLOYEES!"

Energetic music blared from the speakers. The people doing the hiring, who were sitting scattered around the hall, began to clap in time. A rosary of coworkers snaked onto the stage.

His skin began to crawl. They reminded him of cult members.

As a big man on stage described how he had resigned from the police force and was now earning more by simply making phone calls from home to his former colleagues, he slipped out of the hall. He took advantage of the fact that the squat little man who had escorted him there had gotten distracted by a conversation with a coworker.

And so now, as he walked with a full backpack from one point on his route to another, the courier thought, It's better like this.

He was entering heated apartments out of the cold wind of the early spring. Sometimes he would have to wait fully dressed for a rather long time, while the customer inspected the order. Sweat dripped down the length of his spine under his sweater and jacket, making his back itch. His armpits were sticky. He would shrug his shoulders if the customer noticed the scuffs on the packaging or some other defect. He would smile and gently apologize and explain when the customer criticized him for the delay. He needed the tips. No to Whoredom counted on the fact that the courier would partly support himself off tips, and that's why they set such a low wage. And so, he would stand patiently and fully dressed, and then would go out wet with sweat into the biting wind and trek on.

None of the customers ever asked his name. Naturally.

And now he had finally saved up the money. In the middle of the workday, in between stops on his route, he walked into a store and bought the smartphone. From the twenty-seven available colors, he picked an olive-green case. He took the phone out of the box immediately and inserted the SIM card. Right then and there, he ordered a unique ringtone via text for ten hryvnias. It was none other than "In the New Year, my needle's pining, my needle's pining for you." Any way you sliced it, it was a beautiful song.

He walked all day with his hand in his pocket, clutching the phone's ergonomic design. A few times, while heading on foot from point A to point B, he pulled the phone out and played with it as he walked, until he almost ended up under a silver SUV one time that was driving fast on the sidewalk.

And then he plunged into the metro once more. It was 6 p.m., and he was about to head back to the dorm. He had just passed from Independence Square onto Khreshchatyk Street. But then his new smartphone rang.

It was Pimple Face.

"Come to the office for a new batch of orders. There are a lot today."

Then she hung up.

He ended up having to cross back onto the square from

Khreshchatyk via the long underground passageway. He walked through the crowd-packed concrete pipe. The rustling of thousands of steps made him think of cockroaches. He couldn't get rid of this association. At the end of the tunnel, a blind man was playing the accordion to his left, while to his right women were selling clothes off hangers that they held in their hands. Other women were creating a traffic jam by stopping and examining their goods.

He didn't even try to bypass anyone, just walked with the current. He didn't put his new smartphone in his pocket: he went on squeezing it in his hand, seeking support from it, straining with all his might to feel unique.

One Soul per Home

At the entrance to the Zvenyhorod District in Cherkasy Oblast, a sign proudly announces that this is Shevchenko Land. Welcome to the childhood home of Taras Hryhorovych Shevchenko— poet, artist, author of the *Kobzar*, and father of Ukrainian literature. Shevchenko Land makes me immediately wary.

In the village of Husakove, in a bar furnished with plastic chairs and tables, a group of middle-aged men and women drink vodka out of plastic cups. Outside, under an awning of plaited grapevine, another little group drinks. Yet another two have decided to seclude themselves: they're boozing in a wrought iron gazebo on the bank of a manmade rectangular pond.

I try to enter a grocery store with a faded Consumer Cooperative sign and peeling walls. It's closed. A portly older man, who drives up in his noisy red Soviet-era Moskovitch mini-sedan, is also out of luck. He curses and, slamming the car door angrily, drives back to wherever he came from.

On a bulletin board, a fresh white sheet announces that there's a *subotnyk* happening today—a day of unpaid volunteer work on the weekend, in the Soviet tradition. Today, they're going to be whitewashing tree trunks outside the village. In large bold font, in cursive and underlined, the following is highlighted: "The participation of People's Deputies and members of the Village Executive Committee is mandatory." So that the rest of the population takes note that they're working.

At the next intersection, I'm stopped by traffic cops for the second time that day.

"I'm not breaking any rules. Why am I getting pulled over at every traffic police post?"

"Well, there needs to be a check, right?"

In other words, everyone is getting stopped here, one after another, without any pretext whatsoever, with hopes for the best. It's crowded at the intersection: the cops have pulled over a dozen trucks and cars, and even two tractors. People are approaching the traffic cops, their heads lowered, while the cops move pointedly slowly, relishing their power and awaiting propositions from the people they've detained. A fifty-year-old woman in an overcoat and knitted beret walks up to a cop, crying, "We're rushing to the maternity hospital, my daughter feels ill!"

"Why are you telling me?" the cop drawls in a blasé tone. "I'm not the one that stopped you."

Indeed. There are three cop cars at the side of the road, a full crew in each. The woman begs, "They said you're the supervisor here, that I should talk to you."

This woman seems to be let go without a bribe.

Getting a bribe out of me is like milking a billy goat because I'm not in a rush, haven't broken any rules, and am angry to boot. The traffic cop supervisor, filled with a sense of self-importance, and in order to keep the other drivers waiting longer, starts a social conversation with me.

"Aren't you cold on a motorcycle in this kind of weather?"

"Today, no. Yesterday and the day before, I was cold."

"You're what, just traveling around?"

"Yeah."

"From Ivano-Frankivsk?"

"No, that's just my license plate. I haven't lived there since high school. That's just where the motorcycle's registered."

"So where from?"

"From all over Ukraine."

"Where are you driving from, I'm asking."

"I'm not following. I'm driving all over the country."

"Today, I'm asking. Where are you driving from today?"

"Well, I was in Haisyn this morning."

"And what is there in Haisyn?"

"Some beautiful places worth seeing."

"Got it . . . You're heading to Moryntsi?"

"Yes, to Moryntsi, where Shevchenko was born. Where else?"

"Alright," he says, handing me back my license graciously, then dismisses me with a "Go on."

Here, in the Zvenyhorod District of Cherkasy Oblast, Ukraine is archetypical. Like it is in old romantic paintings and in Shevchenko's poetry: smooth sloping hills, poplars bend in the wind in a picture-perfect field alongside the road, countless groves and meadows and orchards all around, and in every village a little pond, white geese on its surface and, above that, green willows bending gracefully.

Right after the Golden Horseshoe of the Cherkashchyna sign, which signals the start of a tourist route that leads through the sight-seeing highlights of the Cherkasy region, the road becomes flawlessly perfect, like a showpiece. In the village of Shevchenkove—the old Kyrylivka, where Shevchenko spent most of his childhood—the tractor of a good-natured gray-haired man pulling a harrow is stuck. After unsuccessfully trying to bypass a white tourist bus parked next to the house that symbolizes the one where little Taras spent his barefooted childhood, the tractor driver, without turning off his engine, climbs out to look for the bus driver. He finds him smoking a cigarette next to the woven grapevine fence that surrounds little Taras's house. With a diffident smile, the tractor driver asks, "Excuse me, I'm very sorry, but could you maybe move the bus a little, if it isn't too much trouble?"

But in Moryntsi, there are no tourists. Instead, kids are skateboarding. I haven't seen anything like that in any other village. Maybe it's only here, on the showpiece roads, that the asphalt is good enough. Though no, there's similarly flawless asphalt in the village of Subotiv, leading up to the Illinska Church, also known as Bohdan's Church and built by Hetman Bohdan Khmelnytskyi in the 1650s, on the tall hill. Immediately past the church begins the wreckage of Ukraine—a wide wreckage, a deep wreckage, with dilapidated farms and leaning fences surrounding peeling houses, and also with a billboard featuring the president's well-fed face.

In a garden, past where the children of Moryntsi skateboard down a slope, obscured by the smoke of burning potato stalks, a peasant family leans over the ground with hoes. A boy of about ten walks along the garden's border, distributing compost by the bucketful from the pile at its edge.

I try to strike up a conversation with this not-so-busy fellow countryman of Ukraine's bard Father Taras, but it doesn't materialize: the boy snaps out a "*pryviet*" in greeting with such overt aggression that I shrink away to the village store. Then he sets out behind me, overtakes me, and says to the saleswoman, "Give me three bottles of vodka."

The saleswoman shakes her head but sells it. He walks out. The saleswoman starts grumbling about "the young people that drink every weekend and not just on weekends." She follows me outside to finish having her say. Meanwhile, that same boy is already standing behind the store and pissing right on that same road on which the children of Moryntsi are skateboarding.

"Ivan! Have a conscience, for God's sake! Turn away at least!"

After my defeat with the drunken Ivan, I manage to strike up a conversation with a group of sober grannies in the neighboring village of Pochapnytsi. This place isn't a tourist attraction, so the road is normal once again—namely, full of potholes. Once again, the peeling houses surrounded by lopsided fences, and old women in quilted tanker jackets sitting on benches rotted from dampness in front of them.

"They've plundered Ukraine!" "They" are the authorities. "There are no jobs, and all the young people have either left for good or become alcoholics. We used to have a sugar factory here, but then it got shut down. You go drive on a little further, and you'll see for yourself. We went on foot to see President Yushchenko in 2014, when he came to Moryntsi for the bicentennial of Shevchenko's birth. We asked for the sugar factory not to be shut down. He so promised us then; he gave such a promise indeed! But the factory was destroyed. Our people now flounder all around the world. All those Yushchenkos, all those Kuchmas, and now this new one, whatever his—it's all the same thing. Breaking is the easiest thing to do. But building something? All they build are pubs!"

"What's your name?"

"What, am I going to get summoned by the authorities now? My name's Viera. I live alone. My children left. And our husbands are all dead. So, how do you live like this? A pension of seven hundred rubles. You pay for the phone, the light, the gas—that's four hundred rubles right there. And after that, live however you like. This is what I have in my old age. You're from the city, so tell me: How does that work? It's the same fields that were always here, but there's no more work. These days, on this street, there's only one soul per home. And there are abandoned houses too. And then there are the drunks that roam the village. They steal metal from the empty houses. There, you see, they're carrying it off."

Two teenagers in shabby clothes walk past us in silence, pushing along an iron cart on two axles. Rusted pipes, old bathroom sinks, and some sort of large springs are heaped on the cart.

"They trade it in over there in the last house. And then they drink the money away. One time, when my grandfather was still alive, we had an antenna stolen. I hear a bang at night. In the morning, I get up, and there's no antenna. And over there, in that house, an old woman got sick, and she was taken away to the emergency room for the night. She came back from the hospital, and there was nothing left in the house anymore. They carted everything away. She went inside, and there were things scattered all over the floor. Everything was tossed around, topsy-turvy. And if she had been at home, she would have gotten strangled herself. So, you go to bed and lie there scared that someone will show up at night and grab you by the throat."

Another old woman, hunched under a bundle of brushwood, approaches from the direction of the forest. I photograph her from afar. I think that she won't notice, but Viera gives me away.

"Hanka! You just had your picture taken!"

Hanka walks up closer and drops the brushwood off her shoulders. Viera says to her, "This man's been asking about how we live here."

"We honor God and live off the fruits of our labor" Hanka quips.

Turning to me, Viera asks shyly, "Tell me, you city types probably know more. Will it be at least a little better under Yanukovych?"

The presidential elections have just taken place. Should I lie to her, or tell her like it is? I look into her clear, bright eyes and have to shake my head. "Nah, I don't think it'll be any better."

"That's what I've been saying!" Granny Hanka jumps in energetically. "What is this Yanukovych going to do? Nothing—that's what he's going to do."

"Ekh. We should've voted for Yulka," Viera says with remorse, referencing Yanykovych's rival Yulia Tymoshenko.

"And under Yulka, what—things would have been better?" Hanka objects immediately.

Meanwhile, I'm looking at her and thinking to myself: there it is, the voice of Ukraine itself, the well of folk wisdom!

But Granny Hanka continues in the same breath: "They all could use a Stalin! They didn't even keep his body in the mausoleum with Lenin, do you hear me? What we need is for Stalin to rise from his grave for two weeks. He'd put all of them in their places immediately. But no, they've got their perestroika restructuring happening there! That Gorbachev—he restructured us into unemployment!"

My hand reflexively wraps around my jaw—in response to both Stalin and the mention of Gorbachev as fresh news. But Viera is listening to Hanka and shaking her head sorrowfully.

Granny Hanka is now ranting and raving. "How many thieves we have in the village! There goes another one!" A woman in her sixties with a visibly alcoholic look and a swollen face walks past us. "It's been a month since she was kicked out of the neighborhood. She and her lover stole a rabbit at night. They skinned it in the woods, we found only the pelt later. And they steal chickens too! They roast them in the woods. That's the kind of neighbors we have. In prison—throw them all in prison! And don't let them out! And make them work! Because otherwise, no one works. Our sugar factory was destroyed! Things were bad after the war, but the factory didn't get demolished. And even when the Germans were here, the factory kept working!"

"Is today Sunday?" Granny Viera asks pensively, now lost in her own thoughts.

"What Sunday?" Granny Hanka asks, throwing her arms up to the sky. "Make the sign of the cross, Viera! Today's Saturday."

"So, I can go to the bazaar tomorrow. Because I went to the

store earlier. Do you know how much they want for onion seeds? Twelve hryvnias."

"Twelve?! They should rot in hell! Might as well take a big rock and head to the bridge. But, just imagine, they've even drained the pond, there's nowhere to drown yourself! This is no life at all. Eke out a life however you can with that kind of pension. But then the people's deputies—OK, fine, let them have a salary of two thousand, even five . . . but no, it's twenty! five! thousand! And how is that kind of man going to believe that I can't afford bread? And why the hell do we need so many of them, those people's deputies? I almost got cross there, but we have a visitor. The whole lot of them should be executed!"

"Hey, did you hear that Yushchenko's house burned down not long ago?" Viera gloats quietly.

"He's not going to get any poorer," Hanka cuts her off and reins her in. "He's got a normal house, and a little house, and a tiny house, and a teeny-weeny one . . . that's just yet another one."

After the torrent of folk anger, I decide to try my luck and ask to spend the night. "I'm happy to pay," I offer.

Since they're in need of money, I expect them to agree and anticipate an evening of listening to their stories. But the grannies recoil instantly, their sensibilities shocked.

"But we don't know who you are," Hanka says.

"I'll show you my passport. And my press credentials."

"No, no. We're all old women, without husbands," Viera says timidly. "You're better off asking Korobko. See that store over there? His wife works there."

I thank them and am about to leave when Granny Hanka gently adds, "Don't be offended. We're single, after all. With how things are these days, your own shirt can scare you. You take it off in the evening, hang it on a chair, and in the morning, it startles you."

Just Don't Laugh

Hey, listen, are you very busy? I don't know who to talk to about this. Just don't laugh, OK? It's about that girl, Maryna. I can't bring myself to describe her as a bimbo, the way we call all of them at school. I thought that Maryna was the girl of my dreams. Hey, come on, don't laugh!

OK, great.

So, anyway, since seventh grade, we've been, you know, friends. It's been three years already. You know what I liked about her? That she wasn't pretentious like those . . . well, you know, bimbos. She isn't all girly. You can have a normal conversation with Maryna. You know, like with a guy. But forget about conversations! She and I once even went shooting together.

So, anyway, I thought at first that I was just friends with her. And then I fell in love.

You know those railroad tracks behind the clay quarry? Yeah, at the edge of town. And there are those big elms growing along the tracks. Or hornbeams, or whatever. One time during summer break, me and Maryna decided to climb one of those trees and bring a bunch of plastic baggies filled with water with us, then toss them down at the train. Yeah, I know, utter brilliance. It was two years ago, we were still kids. We got a bunch of those, you know, disposable baggies. There's a stream flowing down there—OK, so, not a stream, more of a sewage ditch. We filled the baggies with water, tied them up, then loaded the baggies into a big sack.

Maryna climbed up first. And I'm looking up at her from below. Before that, while she was sitting next to the ditch, she had gotten her jeans a little dirty. So, she's raising her leg, and the jeans are stretched along her thigh.

Hey, come on, don't laugh! OK, so, yeah, she's got an ass. So what? She's human. But that's not the point! For me, the fact that those jeans were dirty was somehow painful. Because she could care less, you know? Shit, I almost started crying then. She could care less if her jeans were a little dirty. Well, you get what she's like. That was probably the first time I thought that this was the girl of my dreams.

Obviously, I didn't say anything to her about it. Shit, we were thirteen then. She was fourteen already, true. She had just turned fourteen. Her birthday's during summer break.

I was still scared for another two years after that. Obviously, she saw that I was acting like a fool at times and understood what was going on. But I didn't want us to stop, you know, hanging out together. Well, and maybe she didn't either. So, in short, you could say both of us had cold feet. Like there was nothing there.

We even got used to that kind of frostiness. True, sometimes, if I touched her hand by accident, I'd start shaking even. But she'd pull her hand away silently.

One time, I remember, almost a year after that—well, anyway, it was when I realized . . . We were walking home from school, everything was so green, the horse-chestnut trees were blooming, and I was content as an elephant that summer break was a week away. And Maryna all of a sudden says to me, "You know, I'd like to always be fourteen . . . or even younger."

Meanwhile, she was supposed to be fifteen soon.

"OK, fine," I say. "So, you don't want to grow up?"

At that point, my mind went to sex, naturally, and I assumed that's where her mind went too, and so I stopped talking. And then she says, almost sadly, "You know, I don't know. Do you think things will be any better when we grow up?"

It was like I couldn't speak anymore for some reason. I kept thinking that no matter what I said, it would come out sounding like it was about sex. Shit, well, so we dropped the subject. And later I, naturally, thought to myself: Do I want to always be fourteen? It's like there's nothing to decide. I probably just want time to go slower, drag out a little more. I want to walk with Maryna to school in the morning and back from school in the afternoon. In school, naturally, we were standoffish, otherwise we'd get made fun of. But yeah, I, like, want this to last longer—but to actually grow up in the end. Hey, come on, don't laugh! Shit. That's not the only thing I'm talking about.

So, anyway, I'm scared too, naturally, but the more time passes, the more I want to touch her. She and her parents traveled somewhere for summer break. And then from the start of the next school year, I started constantly telling myself: OK, that's it, by the end of September I'll tell her. OK, that's it, by the end of October. OK, by New Year's for sure. But nah, I just followed her around like a wet rag. I hated myself for it.

Meanwhile, she seemed to grow even more sad. Naturally, I thought it was because of me. Because I was so spineless. I'm walking, my head down, and the whole time I'm thinking: We'll reach the Polish church in a minute, and there I'll tell her. Fine, I missed it, then at the turn onto Mozart Street I'll tell her. Meanwhile, my heart's pounding. And she's not saying a word.

It wasn't as simple to just go and climb up a tree together anymore. Or to go up on the roof—we had discovered one time that the door to the attic in our building didn't lock. But if we were to climb up right then, I'd only have one thing on my mind—were we going to kiss up there? Later, I too started thinking that, yeah, it would be better if we both stayed fourteen forever. Or even thirteen.

So, anyway, the whole year passed like that. The more time went by, the less she and I hung out together. One time, she tells me that her dad is waiting for her. And then she even starts going to church with her mom on the weekends. Go figure! Her mom's been a little cuckoo when it comes to religion for a long time, but in the past Maryna wouldn't get sucked into it. Now she all of a sudden starts letting her mom drag her along. I thought it was on purpose, to avoid seeing me.

And then when the new school year started—this one already—the dance parties started. You know, the ones that Volodia started throwing all the time. One time in the gym, the next time in the community center downtown, another time in the Officer's Club building. Then Lioshka joined him. That's when Lioshka got into DJing. I helped him one time: the two of us dragged that humongous speaker of his from the assembly hall together. We stopped in between floors to rest.

"I can't wait until I finish school and can get the hell out of here," Lioshka says to me.

"Why's that?"

I thought about Maryna, who didn't want to grow up. But Lioshka wanted the opposite: "The sooner, the better. We need to get the hell out of here. I realized a long time ago already that our town is the anus of civilization. Or, to put it simply, it's *zhopa mira*, the 'ass of the world.'"

"Come on," I replied, offended. I like our town.

"Think about it," Lioshka says. "What can you do in a town where everyone knows everyone else? Other than throw school dance parties. You know where I dream of going? New York. Manhattan. That's where you can get serious about DJing and make a career of it."

I thought about it later. Yeah, of course, this definitely wasn't Manhattan. Particularly because everyone knows everyone else. One time me and Maryna, back when we still hung out normally, skipped class in May and went to the river. By the time I got home, my mom already knew about it all because some girlfriend of hers had seen us at the river. Come on, what kind of city is this? Or, shit, this high school of ours, where they've converted one of the classrooms into a Greek Catholic chapel, and the entire school has to sit through the Divine Liturgy, even if only a few times a year. This truly is the anus of civilization. The only thing maybe worth doing around here is going to the school dances.

So, in short, I'm forever going to these dances because Maryna goes. But I'm scared to invite her for a slow dance. God, I hated those school dances, but I went anyway. You're standing there forever, and you've got the shakes as if you're cold. True, it really was cold in the gym. And I'm in just a shirt, you know, to look good. You're shaking, but your armpits are sweaty from fear. And you're already starting to wonder whether or not you stink. And on top of it, it's dark. And from the large speaker, the bass is thudding. You know that feeling? The way it reverberates in your chest? You feel the bass like that, with your entire body, not just with your ears. And that makes you shake even more.

Meanwhile, Maryna's standing against the wall the entire time, like this—almost as if she's propping it up. You know, like a dude. And she's gazing into the void all sad. And in the meantime, I'm gazing at her and hoping that she'll feel it and will look at me. But she doesn't.

She and I were hardly speaking by then.

One time, there was a dance at the former Officers' Club. Volodka had just fallen in love and was constantly playing slow songs. I'm standing there and standing there, and then I pull myself away from the wall and walk over to Maryna.

"Wanna dance?"

She gives me this look, as if I'm about to lead her off to get butchered. Like that—she's looking up at me, with suffering in her eyes.

But she goes. She places a hand on my shoulder, lightly. Meanwhile, my entire body is shaking.

"It's cold in here," I say.

"Yeah, a little," she says.

I don't respond. Like some moron. Shit, and it used to be so easy with her.

And then her leg brushes against mine, with the inner parts of our thighs—and shit, I feel I'm getting hard. Right away, shit! It's good that it was at least dark. I moved away from her a little. And meanwhile, I'm thinking, like, maybe I need to move in closer. Then I can not say anything, and it'll just be clear—hah. But, of course, I'm too much of a scaredy-cat to do that. She and I are two-stepping, the slow song is starting to come to an end already, I'm panicking that I need to say something because otherwise everything will just come full circle, it'll be like it was before, but I'm scared to strike up a conversation, it's like my tongue has gotten stuck in my throat, and then Maryna says, "Come on, let's go outside."

Shit, my heart started pounding so hard that I even stopped hearing the bass from the speakers. This is it, I'm thinking. And I must be the ultimate scaredy-cat if the girl has to make the first move.

So, anyway, we go outside. She's a little in front of me. There's that long cold corridor there. Maybe I can catch up to her here and kiss her, I think. But nah, I'm scared, of course.

Meanwhile, outside, it's cold and dark already. Remember those old chestnut trees that got chopped down a while ago? Maryna sits down on one of the stumps, and I'm standing. Then I sit down next to her. I feel like a stump myself, damn it. I'm sitting there, like a dummy, thinking, I'll tell her in a second, I'll tell her in a second, I'll tell her in a second. And in the meantime, I'm scared to touch her.

And then she says to me, "Sania . . . You're my best friend, but . . ."

And she stops. My blood runs cold. Well, yeah, I think, of course. "But." Fucking "but." And I start getting angry. "But"—you like somebody else?" I ask.

And then this I didn't expect at all: Maryna wraps her arms around her shoulders and starts sobbing. She's crying and crying. And I'm sitting there—well, you know, like—I don't at all know what to do in that kind of situation. She calms down a bit, sniffles, and says, "Sania . . . Sania . . . What should I do?"

Shit, I'm sitting there like a dummy. And she says, "Hug me, will you?"

By now, I don't at all know what to think. So, I place a hand on her shoulder. And I'm starting to get happy: Who knows, maybe I had misunderstood something? Meanwhile, my hand is lying on her shoulder all heavy, as if it isn't mine, like it's made of wood. I don't understand any of it.

"Sania, you aren't going to turn your back on me, are you?" she asks and lets out a sob again. I feel her shoulders shudder. "Yes, I like someone else . . ."

I'm speechless again. By now, I'm still as a rock. Come on, you can't do that to a person! I keep my hand on her shoulder. And I'm like a statue. And she asks, "You know who?"

I don't say anything. Shit, my lips are clenched like a chicken's ass. I don't want to know, but I do. Maryna is silent. Then she says, "Nadia."

"What Nadia?"

"Nadia Moroz. From Class A."

At that point, I grimace. From disgust. My hand flies off her shoulders on its own. Meanwhile, Maryna turns her head and is looking at me from between her hands. I've now grabbed myself by the shoulders and am holding on, all curled up.

For a second, of course, I thought that she said this on purpose, in order to get rid of me. You know, like the chicks that go, "Oh, we're lesbians, we don't want to get to know you better." But then I'm looking at Maryna, at her posture, at how she's all huddled up, and understand that she's telling me the truth.

"But Nadia's a girl."

"No, really?" Maryna replies sarcastically, but with these angry tears in her voice.

I realize how stupid my comment sounded. Maryna hides her face behind her hands again and says, "For as long as I can remember, I've liked girls . . ." And she's looking at me through her fingers. "You aren't going to turn your back on me now, are you?"

"Shi-i-i-i-it. I hadn't noticed."

"Because you only notice yourself," she says with a sigh.

I scowl.

"It's OK, I get it. In your condition and all," Maryna says with unexpected tenderness. "But you really are hung up on yourself, Sania. You, what—really never noticed how I acted when I would run into her somewhere?"

"No."

I was vaguely recollecting a general impression of Nadia Moroz. She was some sort of amorphous creature, one of those affected and childish girlie-girls. How could she like her? Shit, what am I even thinking about?

"I was just standing next to the wall, looking at her. I'm glad you asked me to dance." And she starts sobbing again. "You can at least ask me to dance . . ."

Maryna's talking, and in the meantime, my entire body is cringing. Ever since I learned that there were . . . you know, like, gays, or whatever you call them . . . I've been constantly scared that maybe I'm gay myself. Hey, come on, don't laugh! Even though I had fallen in love with Maryna, I was still constantly scared nonetheless. And here it turns out that Maryna's . . . well, like, a dyke. Or whatever. So, anyway, I'm sitting there on a stump and thinking, shit. And then, all of a sudden: If I've fallen in love with a dyke, could that mean that I'm gay after all? Hey, come on, don't laugh! Shit, this isn't funny.

I'm sitting there with all these stupid thoughts in my head, I'm getting more and more put off by her, and she again asks, "But you of all people won't turn your back on me, will you? I don't know what to do about all this. Who should I even talk to about it?"

"Talk to a therapist."

Maryna sniffles. OK, yeah, that was cruel on my part. Our school had recently hired a therapist, but everyone made fun of her. She was this weird phenomenon: forever spinning some sort of tulle around herself, the translucent kind, meanwhile she herself is this ethereal damsel, to the point that it makes you want to puke, and during her psychology classes she blathers about some sort of torsion fields, rose of the world meta-philosophy, and the macrocosm that will do everything for you if you truly want something. All that nonsense. Well, and, of course, if you so much as have a conversation with the therapist, right away all the department heads, the principal, and, subsequently, your parents know about it. You can have just as successful a conversation with our classroom teacher: that one's forever walking around in red boots, an embroidered blouse, a Hutsul two-piece woven skirt, and a traditional coral necklace, as if she stepped out of some fucking story set in a Carpathian village a century ago, and she starts her Ukrainian language classes with a prayer, crying while she's at it, sometimes even escalating to hysteria. She's an Adventist, or a Jehovah's Witness, or something along those lines; it changes every year. And she makes the kids in the lower grades kneel.

So, yeah, Maryna, just tell anybody in our town . . . In this "ass of the world," everyone really does know everything about everyone. For example, the director of the local museum is gay; everyone knows that. And they crack jokes that you can't have just one gay, there must be two of them. So now, whoever takes a job at the museum, if it's a guy—they point fingers at him and snicker. Which means, when they find out that I'm friends with a dyke, they'll start pointing fingers at me too.

That day the conversation between me and Maryna didn't lead much of anywhere. She got up from the stump, ran inside for her jacket, and went home. I, of course, didn't walk her home. The bass blared from inside, and outside it was dark and cold.

So, now I'm scared. Remember how we had that English language teacher at school, Mrs. Tkachuk? I once ran into this Tkachuk next to Komsomolske Lake and got genuinely scared: she was walking, you know, on straight legs, in this wooden way—and her cheeks were quivering like scraps of rubber hung on a skeleton. And her eyes were empty. So, anyway, a few months later, this Tkachuk hanged herself. You know the story.

But a few days ago, I ran into Maryna in Kirov Park, I looked at her, and with every step her cheeks quivered the same way, but she didn't notice. I got scared, so I walked up to her and said, "Listen, I'm sorry that I acted like that that day. It's just that you were talking, but instead of listening to you, I started getting scared that maybe I myself was ho—kkhm!—homosexualist."

"Like I said, you only think about yourself," Maryna replied.

She started walking away, but I caught up with her. This time I found the courage to take her by the hand. "I won't turn my back on you."

I'm telling you, my whole body was quivering.

I realize that I'm a young, dumb, frightened teenager. Do you think I don't understand that? In reality, I'm very scared. Listen, maybe you at least have some advice to offer? Who can she have a proper conversation with about this? Her mother—well, you know that story. Her dad also isn't an option. I mean, shit, who can you have a conversation with about this in a town where you're forced to pray in Ukrainian literature class and a chapel is set up in the middle of the school—and where everyone knows everyone else and talks about you both to your face and behind your back?

No, I'm being serious. Well, with who? Just don't laugh.

The Gracious Spirit of the Provincial North

These days, Chernihiv brims with beatific goodness, as if out of a story told by Dostoevsky's Zosima the Elder.

"So? Can you feel the gracious spirit of the provincial north?" Pasha asked me with a laugh.

I could feel it. Till this day, there's something of old Kyivan Rus' in Chernihiv. There's something Soviet in it too—in the best possible way. And something of utopian Orthodoxy as well—the calm, the cleanliness. You can't describe it as anything other than *goodness*. Maybe, at most, Sumy or Hlukhiv have a similar ambience. That time in Chernihiv, things of a material nature helped all of us discern this *goodness*. It didn't hurt that the weather was wonderful and calm too. Not too hot and not too cold, a gentle breeze and sunlight that was translucent and warm. We were visiting two locals, our longtime friends Pasha and Sasha.

In snatches, I remember us being in the underground Saint Anthony's Caves. I remember a thin old man with a crazy-long white beard, the kind of man any Ukrainian has seen a thousand times. The sun shining through the delicate May leaves was making him squint. He was watching the wind blow the flaps of a priest's cassock apart. At that moment, the priest was standing next to a brand-new white Toyota, explaining to a woman with bare, shapely legs how to correctly bless her car. Apparently, the blessing of automobiles is an ancient Christian tradition that traces its roots back to Jesus.

Then suddenly, a pretty girl surrounded by girlfriends walked up wearing leggings that enveloped her contours like a see-through second skin. They were all the rage that season. The group was heading into the church above ground. At the entrance, the girl pulled a light, gauzy scarf off her head and wrapped it around her hips. But her friends stopped her: one more hitch before she could enter. One of them handed her another scarf, this one for her hair. Because going to church with an uncovered head is indecent!

As we entered the caves behind them, we heard sweet, heavenly voices crooning something in one of the halls. "The acoustics here are great," Sasha said.

We quietly passed through, trying not to disturb whoever was praying. But when we were returning through this same hall on our way out, there was no one in it. So, Pasha stepped into a niche in the wall and droned, "*Om-m-m-m. Om-m-m-m.*"

Then Sasha stepped into the neighboring niche and chimed in with the Sanskrit mantra, "*Om-m-m-m. Om mani padme hum-m-m-m.*"

Just then, a family of tourists entered the hall, and the mother immediately shushed her noisy son, "Quiet! Look, the service has started!"

After that, I remember us walking through some park. A man was heading toward us with a huge sheepdog on a chain. Suddenly, a yappy little mutt who looked to be a stray lunged at her from the bushes; the mutt was scared to bite the sheepdog but also didn't want to back off. The sheepdog on the chain kept trying to turn its muzzle toward the mutt, despite the fact that it was being pulled away by the neck. Finally, the yappy mutt scurried away from the sheepdog and yapped with all its might.

"Remember what the mongrel said to the sheepdog?" Pasha asked, grinning. Then, in a husky and sultry voice, he quoted the Russian criminal pop song about the free bandit and the nine-to-five worker:

> *Sharik! Like you, I used to be on a chain!*
> *Sharik, I too gorged on the master's grub!*

Till this day, a live orchestra plays in the town square of Chernihiv on Sundays, and the old ladies and old gentlemen dance to songs like "My, my, my Delilah." Sometimes, old ladies dance with old ladies. But never—never!—old gentlemen with old gentlemen. We Ukrainians are strict about that, across all generations.

The day was pleasant and unhurriedly long. It grew dark, but even the evening was warm. We headed back to Sasha's and Pasha's. As we were about to press the floor button in the elevator, a tall young man came running into the lobby and jumped in with us. He was about six feet tall, dressed in a serious, light-colored suit, and had long, fair hair and elongated, aristocratic facial features.

"We aren't overloading the elevator?" Sasha asked jokingly.

"It's OK. If we get stuck, we'll get to know each other," the young man replied genially.

Pasha commented that the elevator had never in his memory gotten stuck. And he had lived there since childhood.

My and Oksana's visit with them was brief because the following morning we were planning on heading to the town of Sosnytsia, not far to the east of Chernihiv. As we were leaving later that evening, Pasha and Sasha decided to see us down-stairs. The four of us got into the elevator and pressed the lobby button.

Ba-boom!—we immediately sensed the chasm beneath our feet.

"A-a-ah! We're flying downward!" Sasha screamed in terror.

"Take it easy," the logical Pasha replied. "If we were flying, we'd be elevated."

In those first moments, everyone felt weightless. But the elevator's emergency brake quickly stopped the fall. All of us, excluding Pasha, managed to shit ourselves. Oksana was white as a fridge.

"But you said that this elevator doesn't get stuck," Sasha said to Pasha.

"This is the first time!" Pasha answered Sasha.

"That guy," Oksana exclaimed, "he clearly knew something! Why did he say, 'If we get stuck, we'll get to know each other'?"

Sasha and I began theorizing that he had been some sort of divine messenger. He was supposed to warn us and did so, but we didn't listen. He had even physically resembled a divine messenger! Tall, with classic-looking features and long hair. But none of us noticed what he had looked like beyond that, so now we started letting our imaginations fill in the rest:

There are those who say beneath his coat there are wings . . .

The elevator doors opened twenty minutes later. Considering that it was a Sunday evening, the fire and rescue service was very prompt.

We went back to Sasha's and Pasha's place for coffee, to wash down the stress, and then headed downstairs on foot, if I remember everything correctly. We were scared to get back in that elevator. The following morning, Oksana and I slept late and didn't leave for the Siveria region until around noon.

Out of nowhere, just past Sosnytsia—in places so vividly described by the Soviet-era Ukrainian writer Oleksandr Dovzhenko in his autobiographical story "The Enchanted Desna"—we found our route blocked by this same enchanted Desna River. The river swashed and sloshed tranquilly over the asphalt road.

Two dozen or so people had already clustered near the water's edge, both locals and visitors. There was even a sixty-year-old woman from Moscow there, with an air of theater about her. You know the type: a slightly melancholy, aging dame with bright, thickly layered makeup and chemically singed hair in shades of violet and flame. With her pants rolled up, the Russian woman was pensively wading knee-deep through the water. The Russian tricolor flag was sewn onto her jacket.

Only drivers of heavy-duty Kamaz trucks and tall minibuses were venturing to drive through the flooded area. And even then, the minibuses did so with reservations.

"Go on, drive through, it's shallow here!" three local boys who were also walking in the water with their pants rolled up thigh-high goaded me.

On the other side of the river, a driver who had moved partly out of the open door of his share taxi stood on the running board and peered down at the murky water suspiciously. Finally, despite the boys' laughter, he found the courage to slowly, slowly inch into the deep part of the water, ready to back up at any moment. The water reached first his bumper and then his headlights. A little deeper and the water would spill through the door into the body of the vehicle—but at this point, the minibus jerked forward and, dispersing waves like a ship with its bow, crossed past the deepest spot.

The story behind all this was *the* Ukraine. They were rushing to have the bridge dedicated to President Kuchma in person prior to some anniversary. And they managed to complete it in time, of course. But the dedication was in August, when the water was low. And so, they didn't get around to filling up the approaches to the bridge. Kuchma came, praised the work, and gave awards to the local officials.

The bridge stood, wide and pretty to behold. In the distance, it rose in an elegant arc. And on all sides, it was surrounded by late-spring waters. The locals call it the Bridge of Fools.

"You have to bypass all this. Head around, to Korop further east of here," a young guy on a scooter recommended to us. "It's better to drive an extra hundred kilometers but actually make it there."

He was undoubtedly right. If the share taxi was submerged, there was no way I would manage to drag a motorcycle across. Neither by rolling it, nor by riding it. But I really didn't want to backtrack that far. Oksana and I were walking in circles, scratching our heads. Then, from the opposite bank, a tall, matte-green ZiL military truck drove across the flooded area. We asked the old driver to ferry us over the water to the start of the bridge for twenty hryvnias.

"I don't have time for that," he responded and waved us off.

And indeed: a uniformed traffic cop and a middle-aged female clerk in civilian clothes climbed out of the truck cab after him. They pulled out tape measures and started measuring the road.

Finally, the cop pointed and said to us, "Head that way, down the dirt road along the riverbank. There are two men sitting under a tree with a six-meter-long launch. Ask them. Maybe they'll take you across."

It had started to rain. We crawled down the muddy road. We found a boat but concluded that it couldn't be the one. It was very small. Then a stout man in a poncho walked out from under a tree and, holding down his hood with his hand, approached us.

"We were told that you could take us across?"

"Why not?" His round face laughed from under the hood. "Let's load it up."

"Onto that?!"

The boat had indeed turned out to be the one. I looked at this supposed "launch" skeptically, thinking, *Oh, we'll sink right along with Mamayota.*

"The motorcycle will definitely fit?"

"Well, we ferried a scooter across one time . . ."

"Ekh, OK, let's do it," I said with a wave of my hand.

If Mamayota sinks, I was thinking to myself, there'll at least be something to remember—for half a lifetime. How we sank a motorcycle in the enchanted Desna. The ferryman's assistant, Charon himself, and I rolled Mamayota over a board onto the boat, grunting all the while.

"Like that, like that . . . More to the center. You," Charon said to Oksana, "sit on the nose. You're going to keep the launch balanced. And you," he said to me, "over here, on top of the back wheel. Hold it, so it doesn't tip over!"

Charon's friend, still on the bank, gave the boat a push. That's how my motorcycle Mamayota set out sailing across the Desna River. We started drifting crookedly, but Charon just chuckled from under his hood. He picked up a single long oar from the bottom of the "launch" and began rowing, as if we were on a canoe.

"So, is this your boat?"

"No way. It belongs to the village council," Charon replied. "They sent us here. There isn't much work in the village right now, so all you do is what they come up with for you once in a while. And today they told me, 'The water's rising, take the launch and go ferry people.'"

Charon didn't stop smiling. He rowed with care, and drops rolled fluidly off the oar into the water. From between clouds, the sun came out behind Charon, tinting the large drops golden, the surface of the water on which these drops fell a bright blue, and the willows over the water a lush, late-spring green.

It was clear by then that no water would seep into the boat so long as we continued to sit straight: with Mamayota and the three of us on it, there were only a few centimeters from the edge of the boat to the surface of the Desna.

We drifted slowly across the sleepy river. A noiseless and sunny drizzle sprinkled us. Frogs and mosquitoes sang their melodies. From the stern of the boat, a good man smiled at us.

The Bazaar Never Sleeps

A short Ukrainian with a graying crew cut clutches with both hands the throat of a bearded Georgian, also graying. The guy with the crew cut is pressing the Georgian against the mound of packing boxes and plastic cluttering the roadside. The Georgian lowers his chin in silence to avoid being strangled.

"I had a standing agreement here," the crew cut says menacingly, trying to claim ground.

"With who?" the Georgian sneers back sarcastically, refusing to yield.

Two groups of supporters gather, one for each man. But no one intervenes. The only thing everyone cares about is the fight ending as quickly as possible: the Georgian and the guy with the crew cut are creating a traffic jam. They're fighting over a parking space. Two identical, black Toyotas stand in the emergency lanes nearby, blocking traffic. The guy with the crew cut loses his grip on his opponent's throat, finally yields to the not-yet-fully-strangled Georgian, and pulls away in his Toyota. Rubbing his neck, the Georgian climbs into his car triumphantly. He parks the swanky car between two trucks

135

covered in nicks and dents. The stream of traffic slowly resumes its forward crawl.

This takes place at 5 a.m. It's rush hour at the wholesale produce bazaar called Farmer in Kyiv's Troieshchyna neighborhood. Trucks of various sizes inch along Elektrotekhnichna Street. Between them, men of various ages, from teenagers to senior citizens, pull platform carts loaded with wooden and plastic crates. It reminds me of a scene from India.

"What are you photographing there?" a young loader stops next to me and asks.

"Just this—a traffic jam this early."

"Hah, as if this is early. This is almost the end of it all." He leans forward at a forty-five degree angle, takes a deep breath to brace himself, then moves fluidly from his spot, pulling his cart by its iron T-bar and weaving between the Toyotas that are clearly popular here, the old Zhiguli four-doors, and the minibuses into traffic.

The string of bazaars that run the length of Elektrotekhnichna Street starts with the well-known clothing bazaar Troieshchyna, which smoothly transitions first into Obrii 2000, then, without a break, into Gloria, and beyond that, without interruption, into Gloria-T. Only past that, facing a gas station and a furniture bazaar, is the produce bazaar Farmer. Unhurried lines of people, with many well-groomed East Asians among them, won't begin to stretch to the bazaars selling material goods until very, very late—not until 7:30 a.m. In the meantime, at the Farmer Bazaar, where people from the Caucasus and Central Asians work alongside the locals, the traffic hasn't stopped since the middle of the night. The frenetic tempo is maintained by the invisible hand of commerce, which spurs people on with its large whip: "Let's go! Let's go! The goods are spoiling!"

In the very early hours before dawn, it's sellers selling to resellers.

"But you always buy from me!" a seller complains as he turns a clear plastic container holding strawberries upside down, displaying its clean bottom. "You know how much you'll charge for them."

The reseller scratches his chin. In the wholesale part of the market, it's not the fruit's cheapness but its quality that impresses. As an end consumer, I've never bought comparable cherries or strawberries. I thought that fruit this perfect only existed in Photoshopped reality. At the Farmer Bazaar at 5 a.m., goods aren't sold by the kilo, only by the crate. And better still if by the utility trailer. Later today, this fruit will be sold at elite bazaars like Besarabka in the center of Kyiv for multiples of these prices. Whatever remains unsold will be sold, far from perfect, to ordinary mortals in a day or two somewhere in the Rusanivka or Borshchahivka neighborhoods. It's June, and the color red predominates at the Farmer Bazaar: garden strawberries, sweet cherries, sour cherries, wild strawberries, and raspberries.

At 5 a.m., there isn't enough space for everyone within the boundaries of the bazaar. Accordingly, commerce is also taking place from vehicles parked in two rows that face a Stopping Is Prohibited sign and a few Tow Trucks Working notices. Policemen meander between the vehicles parked beyond the bazaar's boundaries. They peer at the goods appraisingly. The sellers offer flattering smiles at these "botanical inspectors in police uniform."

Shaih, a fifty-five-year-old who hails from Baku, squints sleepily at the sun as he sits on a stool next to crates of high-end garden strawberries. It's 9 a.m., and he hasn't sold them yet, which means he's now unlikely to sell them.

"By 11 a.m., it'll be dead around here. Tomorrow night, I'll hand them over to wholesalers for whatever price they want, just so that they aren't a complete loss. They won't survive the day after tomorrow."

Shaih is, by local standards, a very small entrepreneur. He leases a plot of land in the Zhytomyr Oblast west of Kyiv, where hired workers grow strawberries for him. He brings the fruit into the capital once a week. He always drives in the strawberries in the evening.

"I didn't sleep all night. I was keeping watch. That's OK, being a little under-slept once a week isn't the end of the world. I mean, you need to do something for a living. I have two grand-children, of course, but you need to do more than just sit around at home with them."

Shaih has been living in Kyiv for fifteen years. He used to be an electrician. For the last eight years, he's worked here. The bazaar has storage units for rent, but since he only has a few dozen crates and it's only one day a week, he doesn't bother renting one. Instead, he asks his fellow citizens of Ukraine for favors, as friends.

"These are all good people here. Everyone's amicable," Shaih says with a smile. "The Azeris, and the Georgians, and the Arme-nians, and the Ukrainians, and the Russians, and the Moldovans too—irrespective of nationality."

I envy his optimism because I've been hearing an earful since early morning. While Shaih and I are talking, a repurchaser dis-satisfied with a price is shouting at his neighbor: "He came onto my land, and now he's going to push me around!"

A woman selling hand pies, upon noticing that I'm buying foreign shawarma, opines, "Oh, it'd be better if you bought from your own kind . . ."

And Yura, who has a monopoly on selling umbrellas and canopy tents for retail locations, advertises his merchandise as he pushes his cart through the crowd like this: "Attention, atten-tion! Every Moldovan who buys an umbrella receives a residency permit in Ukraine!"

Slavik, a young loader, reminds me of a small predatory animal in his behavior. When I find him at our agreed-upon location, he's dozing on his cargo cart, shielding his eyes from the sun with the crook of his arm. It's a scene from an early Maxim Gorky story. Sensing my presence, Slavik instantly wakes up, leaps next to me, and doesn't stop moving for even a minute after that. He moves jerkily and unpredictably, like a small cobra. Slavik has a shiner the size of half his face.

"Oh, you and I are going to concoct one hell of a story! Psst! Just give me a minute to . . . Say, if we bomb this bazaar, how much do you think we'd get paid for that?"

"Umm . . ."

"Or, better yet—you should hire yourself out as a loader with me! You'll make so much in a week or two that you'll forget all about your writing! I've already made three hundred eight hryvnias today. But when you first start, you can't sit like I was just sitting. You have to walk, walk, walk the entire time. Because no one knows you here."

At that moment, a portly salesman yells, "Hey, I need a wheelbarrow!"

Slavik trots over to him with his cargo cart and loads his crates of cherries with exaggerated vigor and enthusiasm. We've just met, but Slavik gives me his jacket to hold. "There's money in there," he says. "Take good care of it."

As I watch him move, I notice that, in addition to the shiner, he also has shallow cuts all over his neck and shoulders.

"Forty," he says to the salesman.

"We had agreed on thirty!" the salesman shouts at Slavik.

"No one agreed on anything with anyone." Then, after a pause, he adds, "OK, fine. You can't blame me for trying."

The cherry salesman hands the money over not to Slavik, but to the customer who's just bought the cherries; the customer is supposed to give it to us when we unload the crates at their destination. Together, we pull Slavik's cargo cart to a minibus at the entrance to the bazaar (I'm a "cousin" new to loading). As we're leaving, another cargo cart rolls up to the customer, and it turns out that he had, in fact, agreed on thirty—just in advance and with another guy. But Slavik has just accidentally intercepted a client who didn't bother remembering who he had made an agreement with. Slavik twitches, then snarls at the dissatisfied cries of the competitor from whom he's just stolen earnings. He laughs.

After we unload the cherries into the minibus, the buyer gives Slavik the money from the seller, and Slavik hands the money over to me right away, under the pretext that he has no pockets. He's demonstrating his trust in me. Only half an hour later does he finally find a pocket somewhere on him, so I give him back his money. Slavik boasts about how easy working at the bazaar is. He shows up in the evening, pays fifty hryvnias to rent a "wheelbarrow," and earns, as he puts it, "Thirty hryvnias in just fifteen minutes! You saw it yourself!"

We spend the next two hours wandering around the bazaar, hollering, "Wheelbarrow! Wheelbarrow!" but no one else hires us. There's no shortage of loaders at the bazaar.

"In the past, you could have some level of job protection, it was fine. But these days, whoever wants to just shows up and works."

Slavik claims that most loaders at the bazaar have done time. I don't know. I honestly don't know. That may be the case, but Slavik looks to be the most criminal of them all.

He spends most of the hours we're wandering around the bazaar spewing out one startup project idea after another. "Do you know how to melt metal? No? That's OK, we'll figure it out. We can melt and produce wheelbarrows ourselves and rent them out to others."

Then he tells me, "So, that Azeri in the yellow T-shirt over there, he's a local boss. He works with pallets. He smokes crack. I'm thinking about moving up the ranks and working with pallets myself."

It turns out that you can pick up and resell the wooden pallets that truck drivers lose or forget. You just need to work your way into the business in a way that you don't find yourself getting beat up. You need to establish contacts. Because otherwise, "the Azeris might even butcher you. They're Muslims, after all. They do, however, have noble principles."

Next, Slavik asks whether I know any realtors. He knows of a foolproof money-making scheme that involves real estate.

After that, he asks if I know anything about search engine optimization, in case he ends up working in website promotion.

"But for now, you come at night. We'll work together. I'll arrange a wheelbarrow for you. Oh, hey, listen! There's this awesome place I want to show you. It's called The Lake. Come on."

Slavik starts leading me out of the bazaar, down a road flanked by two concrete walls that ends in a commercial zone. As he clarifies where we're heading, the awesome place transforms from a lake into garages, where a wheelbarrow boss is supposedly waiting for us. I look at the cuts on Slavik's neck, at his twitchy mannerisms, and gently shy away from the offer.

"Ah, you think it's sketchy, I get it. No worries," Slavik says, instantly slowing down his gait. "Fine, let's forget about the garages if you think it's sketchy. Let's just work with one wheelbarrow for now. I need the money. Come back at midnight."

"Yes, yes, of course. I'll be here."

As the strawberry farmer Shaih had predicted, the wholesale produce bazaar grinds to a halt by eleven o'clock, but over these few hours, the retail produce market has revved up. The goods at this one are less exclusive, more aimed at ordinary people. A line of women holding pails and bags stretches down a concrete-slab path that runs between the garages outside of the bazaar toward its entrance. Some are here to visit "their" sellers specifically.

Lida, Olia, and another Lida have been selling produce together for a long time. They tell me that all three of them are the same age, each fifty-seven. That's just how it worked out. All three of them have been selling produce since Soviet times. All three are from the Sokyrianskyi District of Chernivtsi Oblast in western Ukraine. They work for themselves, with no boss.

"We noticed in the morning that there weren't a lot of strawberries today. So, we decided not to let the wholesalers have ours. I hope we didn't miscalculate," one of the Lidas says.

Housewives from the Troieshchyna neighborhood buy strawberries by the bucket or basket for jam. When I ask the three saleswomen why they have such a long line, while their neighbors don't have any customers, the women beam with pride. "The same customers always come back to us. Everyone knows that we don't under-weigh. On the contrary, we'll sooner give a customer two hundred grams extra."

Olia and the two Lidas sell seasonal produce. They rent a room in Troieshchyna for the three of them. Sometimes they pay the landlady part of their rent in fruits or vegetables—for canning.

"You won't sell two and a half tons of strawberries in a day in Chernivtsi. It's good that this bazaar exists because there are no jobs back home."

Right next to Olia and the two Lidas, the olive-skinned Tania sells her goods. She specializes in flowers from the Zakarpattia region in western Ukraine; that's where she's from. But the spring daffodils are already done blooming, and the chrysanthemums won't bloom till September. So, while the chrysanthemums continue to grow, Tania buys cherries in bulk right here at the bazaar and resells them to retail customers in order to earn her rent and not lose her spot. Renting a stall at the bazaar is more expensive than renting a room in Troieshchyna.

Olia, the two Lidas, and Tania are glad that they have profitable work. Paying additional fees to the police is no longer necessary. They're satisfied with all of it—well, except that they dislike the "blacks."

"The ones who work here all the time are normal. But then there are the ones who come for only a season. Those sometimes beat people in order to set their own prices."

This hasn't happened to the women, but everyone's heard about it happening. A young man from the bazaar's administration will further confirm these "episodes with the transients." I had spoken to him in the morning, outside his office because he wouldn't allow me over the threshold, but the following night, he'll stop me himself under a lamp out in the street. But the administrator won't clarify from which national minorities these people are, instead lumping them all into one shared category of miscreants.

From three in the afternoon, the bazaar's rhythm grows increasingly sluggish. The market's invisible hand has grown tired and lowered its whip till the evening.

An ethnic Tajik from northern Afghanistan describes to me how he escaped from the Taliban. His parents are still in Afghanistan.

Valia, who pushes around a mobile buffet cart, fantasizes to me about how much she could make on coffee if she were allowed to work for herself and not the administration. The drinks and food sold to bazaar workers are more expensive than they are in the city. There's a monopoly. If you don't like it, you're welcome to head all the way to Troieshchyna.

The pensioner Raisa Leontiivna, on the other hand, works for herself, selling sunflower seeds to the bazaar workers. Every day she commutes on discount buses for senior citizens all the way from Obukhiv, fifty kilometers south of Kyiv. "What, just because I'm a senior citizen, I eat less than you?" she asks me. "You can't survive on a government pension, but sunflower seeds are a favorite of both Ukrainians and foreigners." Raisa Leontiivna is one of the few people here who uses the neutral word "foreigners" when referencing non-Ukrainians, as opposed to more emotionally charged words. She claims that no one bothers her at the bazaar. "One time, this man came up to me," she says. "He was handsome, in uniform, and he tells me, 'I gave orders that no one should lay a finger on you, old woman.'"

The bazaar comes alive again after the afternoon lull, closer to nighttime. By midnight, it's once more full of people, this time in the light of lanterns. The entire area is brightly lit. At midnight, there are more mobile coffee shops and snack bars on wheels than during the day.

Women with onions and herbs stand at the bazaar entrance, outside the gate. Each of them has only one or two bags, which they brought over on foot, not by vehicle. These women are constantly being chased away by the guards, so that they don't get in the way of the cargo vehicles passing through. Each time, the women disperse, but before long, they flow back together like water.

The most aggressive wholesale buyers have been here since the evening, on the prowl. "Maybe someone will bring something good, then I'll be the first to buy it," one of them tells me.

Trucks keep arriving and arriving. In the harsh glare of their headlights, the veins in the necks of the male loaders bulge from exertion.

Slavik has been calling my cell phone since the evening. I don't pick up. I try to keep my back to walls so that he can't approach me unnoticed. As I dash from one spot to another, I look around furtively.

All around, deep night sets in in Kyiv's residential neighborhoods. But here, at the bazaar, the marketplace wheel of samsara unspools faster and faster.

Just Pay Your Taxes

A little drunk already, Serhii Tkach goes out onto the balcony for a smoke. Even though we don't smoke, Vadym and I follow him. The balcony is glassed in, and Vadym, the owner of the apartment, opens one of the windows. The side wall of the balcony below the windows is lower than is standard in Ukraine, only reaching to mid-thigh. Serhii Tkach stands closest to the edge of the balcony, to blow the smoke outside.

It's cold and wet. Below us people walk around in overcoats and warm jackets. Serhii leans out and, from the tenth floor, makes a hand gesture like that of some emperor or prophet.

"Just pay your taxes," he proclaims in an undertone to the people below.

He turns a little, and, with a Moses-like gesture, continues: "Just pay your taxes. And you. You too. Just pay your taxes."

"You can make that into a religion," Vadym notes. "The one and only commandment is . . ."

"Just pay your taxes," Serhii says to us now, this time more forcefully.

"Yeah, the only commandment," Vadym repeats. "But if you don't pay them, nothing bad will happen."

"There's no such thing as not paying them," Tkach contradicts him gently but firmly. "As to what'll happen, that's none of your business. You just pay your taxes."

"It's the same thing, just from different viewpoints," I say. "Vadym's cult has a more humane interpretation of the doctrine, while Tkach's cult has a stricter one."

"Dear citizen, you may interpret things however you like," Tkach insists, "but please be so kind as to submit your paperwork by the twentieth of the month."

I laugh and feel a pang of jealousy: now this is a man with an imagination. Only later do I remember that Tkach recently got a job in the tax office. He's smoking and looking down. His face is elongated, his chin is wide, and his black hair, which is short and wiry, sticks out like little horns. His eyes are filled with a constant and sad irony. Serhii resembles a little devil, but the kind from a nativity scene. If he's even capable of harming someone, it's more likely to be himself than anyone else.

"Shit, Vadym, you've got such a low balcony," Tkach says, leaning out the window and over the side.

"Just don't jump, Tkach!" Vadym exclaims, his lips stretched into a forced smile but actual fear visible in his eyes.

Vadym has known Serhii Tkach for much longer than I have. Serhii and I met when he was typesetting a certain glossy magazine that I was proofreading, and Tkach, for me, is first and foremost a talented designer. But he changes jobs often. During the Orange Revolution in 2004, Serhii Tkach worked in the campaign headquarters of the pro-Western candidate Viktor Yushchenko. When Yushchenko won, Serhii accepted a position in the president's administration, but after only a few weeks, he quit. This is how he justified it at the time: "It's one thing to work for the Messiah and another to work for the authorities."

"I respect you a lot for that, Tkach," I say to him now on the balcony, referencing his work in politics. "But still, why did you quit back then?"

Serhii looks at me with that sad-yet-mocking look of his.

"I couldn't picture myself in the administration for some reason back then." He pauses, then tacks on, "I found myself later, in the tax office."

Vadym and I laugh. "It's OK, Tkach. I don't think you'll stay there for long either," Vadym reassures him.

"Thank you for the support," Tkach replies, exhaling smoke and leaning over the edge again.

Vadym is also a former civil servant from the presidential administration. Once upon a time, he had predicted that he'd become a "typical functionary in an official Ford, with official boils on my ass," but before long, he too quit, unable to stand it. "The people who hang out there are the ones who know how to create work when there is none and come up with crafty schemes, like our H., a snake who bites her own tail . . ."

"And gets a kickback while she's at it," Tkach quips.

We burst into laughter again.

"I wonder," I say, "was that joke actually funny or are we just drunk?"

"I think it was actually funny," Vadym replies.

Tkach isn't laughing though. The more he jokes, the more pain is visible in his eyes. And the sadder he grows, the more caustic his irony becomes.

Vadym continues: "I look at my former colleagues and think how good it is that I failed. This one owns a plot of land in Kyiv's historic Koncha-Zaspa neighborhood, that one's bought himself a McMansion in the chichi exurb of Bezradychi . . . I can't really bring myself to judge them, but I'm glad I didn't have those kinds of choices to make. Because if I had been told, 'Oh, Vadym dear, you just got married, your kiddos will grow up and leave soon, here you go, take a plot of land for your troubles . . .'"

"A plot of public land," Tkach interjects.

"Mm-hmm . . . I don't know how I would have responded. I think that often they don't even do it for themselves, but for their loved ones."

"And before you know it, your arms are up to here," Tkach says, pointing to his shoulder, "in shit. Forever."

"And that's why I won't become an adherent of your tax religion," I say with a snicker.

"So, don't. But the requisite paperwork better be on my desk by the twentieth."

"But our Mr. Mytsyk believes that taxes should be paid punctually," Vadym notes pensively.

"Mr. Mytsyk has just been living in Great Britain for too long," Tkach, the taxman, says. "But here, our taxes go straight to Yanukovych's lavish Mezhyhiria Residence."

"Mr. Mytsyk says that it's none of your business where the taxes go. You . . ."

"Just pay your taxes!" we finish the sentence in unison.

"And don't think about anything," Tkach adds. "The important thing is not to think about anything."

"Yes, Tkach. Come on, how much can you smoke?" Vadym jabs at him. "Let's go inside already. I'm cold."

"Hang on, one more. Shit, Vadym, the wall of your balcony is so low . . ."

A Fancy Send-Off

I had left Luhansk at three o'clock in the afternoon and driven southwest once again down the highway that leads to and around Donetsk. I assumed that I had passed the city a long time ago because I had been pushing on the beltway for fifty kilometers already. But no.

"Donetsk is right over there, a kilometer from here. I live in the city and walk to work."

The gas station attendant is younger than me. He works six days a week, twelve hours a day.

"I don't know. Yeah, I guess it's a lot of work, but what of it? I feel sorry for you though. What, you like riding in the rain like this? You really do like it? Ha-ha! OK then. What matters is that your soul is satisfied. I'm ignoring my soul for now. I'm better off spending the money on my kid."

"You've got kids already?"

"Yeah, my son's a year old. You don't have any yet? It's actually better that you wait a bit because kids are a pain in the ass. What's going on in your part of Ukraine—in Ivano-Frankivsk?"

There isn't even a shadow of hostility. I smile. To this human being, I'm another human being and not some generic ultra-nationalist "Banderite." That boosts my spirits. Too often, people from the east view everyone from the west as a blind and mindless follower of the WWII anti-Soviet Ukrainian hero Stepan Bandera.

"Good luck, brother!" this guy from Donetsk calls out, raising a hand in a wave as I pull away.

The "Donetsk steppe" begins immediately past the road junction. Every time I encounter this here, it amazes me: massive urban agglomerations and between them nothing but empty fields. No villages, not even a gas station. Only the occasional hawk swooping above the steppe. Before long, I leave the hills behind me. The narrow road, straight as an arrow, runs into the horizon. A high-voltage power line whirs along its length.

It's growing dark, but I don't want to stop.

I've driven eighty kilometers without encountering a single population point, which is why my map doesn't help me figure out where I am. I'm heading in the right direction—more or less. But what oblast am I in? Still in Donetsk Oblast? In Zaporizhzhia Oblast already? Or maybe that little corner of Dnipropetrovsk Oblast that juts between them?

There's nothing but steppe and more steppe all around me. And I begin to appreciate why in these lands—precisely here—governmental authority hasn't been acknowledged as such. The Zaporizhian Cossacks came this way on horseback centuries ago. It was also here that the revolutionary Nestor Makhno advocated anarchy during the Russian Civil War.

The drizzle grows constant. I turn on the headlights because I can't see much in the moist twilight. My legs are wet up to my thighs. My raincoat has soaked through, and I can even feel that my T-shirt is getting damp. But my mood is wonderful: you can breathe so freely here in these steppes! And with each passing kilometer as I approach Makhno's hometown, I imagine my motorcycle transforming into a horse-drawn cart. If only I have enough gas to make it to Huliaipole. What an appropriate name for a town in this steppe vastness: *Huliai, pole*! "Dance, field!"

In another thirty kilometers it becomes clear that I hadn't been riding through Pokrovsk, as I had imagined, and therefore, there was no way I could have been in that little corner of Dnipropetrovsk Oblast. When, following the signs for Huliaipole, I had turned onto a tertiary road a while ago, I had unknowingly taken the route through Velyka Novosilka.

As soon as I reach Velyka Novosilka, my first order of business is to find a gas station. I've made it there on fumes, as they say. I start asking a man a little older than me how to drive through the town without getting lost. Incredible! Just as had happened yesterday in Luhansk and a few days before that in Donetsk, this Donbas native offers to lead me through town. He gets into his Zhiguli and waves toat me. "Follow me, I'll show you the way."

I adore the communication style of Donbas. People have an abrupt, somewhat naïve directness. They speak with their eyes wide open, choosing very serious words. They have a desire to help and a simple yet slightly coarse, though no less pleasant, friendliness. I like Donbas.

"Who the f-fuck are you?" a voice drifts toward me from the darkness. "Take off that f-fucking helmet, s-so I can s-see you!"

Right off the bat, I encounter a completely different communication style, a completely different charm. A forty-year-old blond guy is standing beneath the overhang in the doorway of the village store. I walk up closer to him. The man has a mop of dirty blond hair parted down the middle and an elegant face. He's leaning on a cane and swaying.

"Take off the f-fucking helmet, I s-said," he slurs.

"Hang on, it's raining," I reply, then hide under the store's overhang and take off my helmet.

"W-why don't I kn-know you?" the dirty-blond guy asks, irked.

I find him amusing and I'm touched by him too, but I have no desire to get involved with a drunk, so. I walk past him inside. He staggers in after me, swaying and leaning on his cane.

"Can I have a coffee?" I ask.

"Sure. How many sugars do you take?" a pretty young sales-girl asks with a sweet smile.

"Two." And while she's pouring the powders into a cup and pouring boiling water over them, I say to her, "Go figure, thirty kilometers from Novosilka, the first village in the Zaporizhzhia Oblast, and you hear Ukrainian right off the bat. It's as if I've crossed a border."

"It's because we're Ukrainian. And over there, they're Muscovites."

My smile congeals a little on my lips. After a pause, the girl hands me the coffee with a giggle. "So, why are you dawdling?" she asks.

Whereas in Donbas you have proletarian directness, here there's endless jabbing. Picture Ilya Repin's painting of Zapor-izhzhian Cossacks, laughing as they write an insulting reply to an ultimatum from the Ottoman Sultan.

The dirty-blond man with the cane is, in the meantime, looming behind me.

"Lionia, give the man some peace," the girl says to him.

I turn around to Lionia. He's reminding me more and more of someone: both physically, with his elegant face and the parted mop on his head, as well as with his "Who are you? Why don't I know you?"

"Your last name isn't by chance Makhno, is it?"

"What f-fucking Makhno? F-fucking Bandera!"

"OK, OK," I say, raising my hands in acquiescence. "You just look like him." I turn to the girl. "So, do you guys still have anarchists here in the Huliaipole area?" I ask in an involuntarily ironic tone.

The girl doesn't quite understand what I'm getting at, but she says proudly, "Freedom—that's what we love most around here."

I smile again, because there's no getting by without a smile, and go outside to have a cigarette with my coffee. Lionia latches onto me again, and I brush him off mildly. He and I are standing under the overhang. Suddenly, the girl comes out and presses three hryvnias into my hand. I take them, thinking maybe I forgot to get my change. After the long bike trip from Luhansk, I'm so out of it, so freaking out of it. But the girl says, "That's what you paid for the coffee. It's on me. Because determined people deserve help. I envy you—in a good way."

I simply melt. Not because of the three hryvnias, of course, but from the gesture itself.

"Sh-she's my relative," the drunk Lionia boasts.

"Yes, you're embarrassing me. Lionia, stop bugging the man already," the salesgirl repeats to him in that same playful tone.

"It's OK," I reassure her.

It's true, a minute later I end up having to disentangle myself from him with determination and, ultimately, to abruptly run away. Because all of a sudden, he wants me to give him a ride home on my motorcycle. "It's j-just a k-kilometer. C-come on, give me a r-ride!"

He'll probably fall off along the way, I think as I roll-start the motorcycle. Meanwhile, Lionia is clacking with his cane, hobbling after me like a zombie.

I reach Huliaipole at half past ten in the evening. I'm wet and tired, but happy. I have this immediate feeling of home, even though I don't know where I'm spending the night yet. The rain that had started outside Donetsk is still coming down as I drive slowly over potholes. Water pools in my shoes, but something pushes me on.

"Take a left, then a right, and you'll see a hotel there," I'm told by a woman at a twenty-four-hour convenience store, whom I tear away from her TV.

"What's it called?"

"Natalia," she replies quickly.

The hotel is called Lidia. A forty-five-year-old woman—Lidia herself—opens the door for me. After putting my things in my room, I go back down to the lobby and ask her, "Where can you park a motorcycle overnight?"

Lidia explains how to get to the only parking lot in town with a guard.

"You won't get lost? I'll lock up in the meantime, so no one comes and steals me." Yes, Lidia also likes to joke around. A second later, she adds thoughtfully, "Though for some reason, no one's doing any stealing these days . . ."

At the parking lot, I'm told that without my own lock, they can't guarantee the bike won't get stolen. "So, are you leaving it or not? Why are you standing there like that! You're spoiling my whole view!"

The following morning, the rain is still falling.

I decide to visit a museum, which I normally don't do on the road. But this is Huliaipole, so I treat myself. For the soul. To see with my own eyes Makhno's black flag with the skull and bones and the words, "DEATH to all who stand in the way of freedom for the working people." As is to be expected, I find the working people more interesting than the museum.

My initial impression that people here are constantly joking around is confirmed. Not everyone, of course, but nowhere else have I encountered such a concentration of banter in a single conversation. One man in his sixties, upon noticing a billboard against corruption, says to his wife, "Check it out, they put it up as a reminder to themselves." On the porch of the town's Social Security Administration building, a group of men hides from the rain under an awning. One of them can't resist and runs out into the downpour. "It's so fine! Like tiny seeds!" he exclaims gleefully. One of his friends responds from the porch, "What's the matter with you? What do you need an umbrella full of holes for? You're bald either way!" This humor is abstract, on a different level already from the usual kind of banter one hears.

Outside a pharmacy, I meet Baba Shura, who is seventy-five.

"What is there to dream about? I support three families with one pension. I give my son money for his alimony payments, and then my granddaughter asks me, and when I tell her, 'I already gave your dad money,' she gets offended. And all I keep thinking is, Just let there be enough left to bury me. Lie down in a coffin, and at least you won't need supper then. That's the sort of fancy send-off I'm saving up for."

Baba Shura spent her entire life working as a milkmaid. She has tattoos on both her hands. I'm too shy to ask how a Soviet peasant woman ended up with tattooed hands. And Baba Shura, as it turns out, is definitely Soviet:

"You know how that song goes? 'Ukraine and Russia are together forever.'"

"They've supposedly separated already," I reply, allowing myself to contradict her, which I do only very, very hesitantly.

"Well, yeah, the west of the country doesn't want to be friends with Russia. Look at how long they were still fighting after the war," she says, referencing World War II and the decade of the Ukrainian Insurgent Army's partisan activity as if these were recent events. "We need to finally reconcile. Because otherwise, there'll be war."

Baba Shura never stops smiling, even when she's talking about something sad, like that fancy send-off of hers. Periodically, she adjusts her scarf. She looks at me kindly. She's waiting for the rain to pass. She's worried that she'll get drenched on her bicycle in the five kilometers she has to ride home.

In Huliaipole, there are a lot of people on old bicycles, ones from the Soviet era. The tallest buildings in town are three stories. The vernacular is close to that of western Ukraine. And there's an unhurriedness characteristic of the steppe—a dignity without fuss. In half a day, I make it around the entire town four times and can't stop delighting in its people. I keep thinking to myself, How beautiful these steppe dwellers are. How open and noble-looking and honest their faces are. Some of them seem to be right out of that Repin painting of the Zaporizhzhian Cossacks. I notice that the alcohol tumbler of a mustached and serious-looking older gentleman in a Puma zip-up sweatshirt is adorned with a slice of lemon. How pleasantly worldly.

An amiable woman in her forties offers a succinct and worried response to my question, "What do you dream of?" "Getting married," she says. She has short auburn hair, brightly painted lips, and delicate features. She's very pretty. I recall the pensiveness with which the hotel owner Lidia had said the day before that "no one is doing any stealing these days."

What towns like this live off of remains a mystery to me. All they have here is basic commerce, utility services, and the monopolist telephone operator Ukrtelecom.

"Yes, it's very difficult," a young woman in the street agrees. "Especially if only one person in the family is working, and for minimum wage on top of it. I'll probably head to Moscow for a while to earn some money. But I need to wait a bit because my son is little."

"Yeah, I guess you could say that there are no jobs," an older woman patching the asphalt in the center of town says to me. "The farm machinery plant isn't operating; nor the shoe factory; the chemical plant over there isn't operating either. Just us utility workers—we're the only ones working."

Each time I ask about anarchists, I'm told about a music

festival sponsored by the chief of police and about the young partygoers that attended. There—they've found me some anarchists. Yet they do remember Makhno with respect.

"Nestor Ivanovych was, as they say, cruel but fair. He's heading somewhere and notices that some family is poor: 'Here you go, have some of what I have!' That sort of thing doesn't happen these days. If you're poor, if you're not poor—no one gives a . . . fuck." At that last word, the gray-haired man in his fifties leans toward me and lowers his voice so that his old mother can't hear him.

His eighty-year-old mother adds, "In the past, there were landowners, and now, there are businessmen. It makes no difference. Guys like him," she says, motioning at her son, "toil for their benefit for nothing."

"We're called Makhnovites around here, the same way that you guys are called Banderites in the west," the son says, starting to get worked up. "But why *not* call me a Makhno follower? I don't have any formal education myself, but I'm well-read, as they say. Makhno did everything right. Everything he did was for the poor. It's only now that the politicians berate first these guys as Banderites, then those guys as Makhovites, and those other ones as "'Donetsk-types.'" It's profitable for the politicians to pit groups against one another. Meanwhile, things are probably the same everywhere, right? There's no money to be had! You've traveled all around Ukraine: You tell me, what have you seen?"

The Two Antons

The café was called From Dusk till Dawn. When I asked the waitress about it, she laughed and said that she had asked the owner about it too. It turned out that the owner had never heard of the vampire movie; it's just that the café had been an evening pub until not long ago. A busy highway passed through there at the time. Then a new road was built and traffic decreased, so the establishment began to operate during the day, but From Dusk till Dawn remained.

The bartender had the right look for a café with that name. She was a tall and slender woman of about thirty, with a narrow waist—the kind Ukrainians call "wasplike"—and attractive, wide hips. She sported a vamp-ish look: a pale face, long and straight black hair, and beautiful thin lips. Only one thing didn't fit the image: exiting the café behind me, she started to cut the daisies growing around the bar. "I grow them for myself," she explained. "I love daisies . . ."

The bartender offered some advice about my itinerary from Tokmak to Vasylivka, noting that I was taking a long and roundabout route. I'd be better off going through Molochansk—through the villages.

"It's true, the road here in Tokmak isn't great. But you'll drive it quickly."

Well, I didn't. The road really did turn out to be not great. I smiled wryly when I saw the sign: the recommended speed was 50 km/h. Meanwhile, I was driving 10 km/h in first and second gear, trying to avoid at least the biggest potholes.

And holy crap! Just as I was mentally updating my rating—Tokmak ranked second for awful roads, after Svitlovodsk—I heard a rattling noise below me, and then my motorcycle lost thrust and slowed down. I got off it with resignation to have a look. The chain had ripped into iron scraps.

I was standing up to my knees in a deep pothole. The chain hadn't simply "ripped": several misshapen links were dragging from the rear. And that meant there'd be nothing to rivet back: the chain wouldn't have enough length.

I silently rolled Mamayota forward because it had stopped at the only spot in the road where it was possible to pass. A traffic jam had started forming behind me.

I pulled out a cigarette. I'm standing there, thinking. I look up at the sky. I think some more. The railroad passes through Tokmak. I keep thinking. I can push the motorcycle to the station and try to ship it home by freight train. Waiting in Tokmak for multiple weeks for a new chain to arrive didn't make sense. I was sure by now that this would be the end of my trip around Ukraine.

Dunts-dunts, dunts-dunts!!!

A yellow Zhiguli, covered in the dust of Tokmak's roads, braked next to me. Loud music blared from inside the car. Two young men peered out the window. They were ordinary young men, sporting buzz cuts and track suits. There were a lot of young men in Ukraine that looked like that.

"What happened?"

"This," I said, showing them the chain that I'd already managed to remove.

"That sucks," the first young dude observed sympathetically.

"I'm gonna give Vasek a call," the second young dude said, reacting instantly. "What model did you say it was? . . . Listen, Vasek," he's already saying this into the cellphone. "There's a biker that broke down here. You don't have a spare chain, do you? You don't? OK, thanks . . ."

"Hey, listen! I've got an old one from Minsk in the garage," the first dude remembered. "Maybe we can try it? On the off chance it fits?"

Meanwhile, I was standing there, listening, and was stunned. Human kindness—even after so many iterations—was still capable of astonishing.

"Just we won't be back for half an hour or so," the young dude warned me. "Because we live far away, at the other end of town."

I called Vitalik, who was waiting for me in Melitopol, and gave him a heads up that I wouldn't be arriving that day. No, that's not actually what happened. In the first attack of panicked pessimism, right after the chain broke, I had already phoned Melitopol and said that it was all over, that I wouldn't be coming at all. The trip had ended, life was nothing more than decay and pain. Now I called Vitalik again and said that I would, in fact, come, but that I didn't know when.

The young dudes in the yellow Zhiguli came back.

"Well, Tokha?" one of them said to the other, who was already fitting the chain on the sprockets of my motorcycle. "Does it fit?"

"Your name's Anton?" I asked the first young dude, surprised.

"Yeah, and mine too," the second young dude replied for both of them. "We're two Antons."

"And I'm an Anton too! A third one!"

"Well, the monkey in the middle gets to make a wish."

I made a wish that the chain from the Soviet MɪNSK would fit my Japanese Yamaha YBR. And—voilá!—the chain fit on Mamayota's sprockets perfectly.

"Everything looks right," one of them said. The two Antons weren't surprised. "You've actually got a Minsk, just a Japanese one."

However, the chain did turn out to be too short after all. Damn! The two Antons measured, knocked the misshapen links out of my chain, then knocked a portion of the links from theirs. They riveted both together. They did it all by hand. And I had been taught in Kyiv that riveting required a special tool. Hmph.

The first Anton started cutting off the head of one of the links with a file. He missed and cut his finger. As he was sucking his bloody finger, the second Anton took over the job. In the meantime, I'm just standing there and watching stupidly. I'm an intellectual, after all, ha-ha. The two Antons threw a board on the ground, then placed a hammer on the board, then a nut on the hammer, and then a link on the nut. Inside the nut, they knocked out the pin from the link. Then they took off the nut. And then they riveted it back on the hammer. Done!

In the end, I had to phone Melitopol a third time. I apologized for being a nuisance: I would, in fact, arrive that day.

As they worked, the two Antons told me about how their car had once broken down in the middle of a field and no one stopped to help them. And then, another time, someone had promised to come back just like they had, but never came back. They told me about their work too. They work together. For themselves. They go looking for customers, then forge grating for fences and fireplaces, or grilles for doors and windows.

"So, Tokha, we have an intimate relationship with metal," one of the Antons said, pointing at my chain.

"You have no idea how grateful I am to the two of you. And here I had thought that my trip was over."

"We'll add it to our list of good deeds," the second Anton said, laughing off my thanks.

"Let's at least take a picture," I proposed. "We are the three Antons, after all."

"Ha-ha! OK, let's do it in front of the motorcycle."

We squatted down to be able to fit in the frame.

That picture was taken with a self-timer from the hood of a yellow Zhiguli out of which music was pumping. The picture has no artistic value. It holds value of a completely different nature.

Faulty Presuppositions

Vitalik, my contact in Melitopol, turned out to be a thin, swarthy guy. He wore large brown horn-rimmed glasses. We only knew each other through the Internet, and not all that well at that. Upon meeting me in person, the first thing that Vitalik did was to declare that Melitopol was a multiethnic city. The second thing he did was to note that historically, it was a "Jewish town." And from that point on, he didn't stop spewing ambiguous jokes about Jews. I never did figure out whether he was an anti-Semite or a Jew himself.

Vitalik gave me a heads up that we were going to his friends' house, and not his, because his "wife doesn't understand all this stuff." As twilight set in, we spent a long time wandering around the sandy streets of the city's residential district, looking for some side street, be it Second Komsomol Alley or Seventh Parallel Alley. It was growing dark, and beyond the fences, the cherries looked black. I was pushing my motorcycle awkwardly over the sand so that Vitalik and I could stay at eye level and so that the engine's noise would not interfere with us talking. We didn't manage to find the road on our own. In the end, after a call on Vitalik's cell, Valerii Velantynovych came out looking for us in the sands amid the night-cloaked cherry orchards.

"See, Vitalik? This means you haven't visited us in too long," he said by way of greeting.

Lidia Pavlivna, Valerii Valentynovych's wife, first sent me off to shower and set the table for everyone in the meantime. When I emerged from the bathroom, Vitalik and Valerii Valentynovych were already engaged in a lively argument. I sat down to listen. Right away, Valerii Valentynovych showed me a photo album of Russian paintings. Out of politeness, I flipped through it, without stopping at any one page. Vitalik and Valerii went on with their discussion.

"You guys eat, or it'll get cold," Lidia Pavlivna kept interrupting.

"What are we supposed to do, just stop talking and gorge ourselves?!" Vitalik finally replied, banging his fist on the table.

Lidia Pavlivna then turned to me: "You eat, you eat. They're going to be at it for a while. They love this."

". . . and nonetheless, I'm a Russophile!" Valerii Valentynovych continued in the meantime.

"The important thing is to not be a Ukrainophobe," Vitalik snapped back.

Valerii Valentynovych didn't respond immediately. After a long pause, he indignantly started on about how the previous president awarded the World War II-era nationalist leader Stepan Bandera the title of Hero of Ukraine and now the new one couldn't seem to annul the title, no matter how hard he tried. He then, of course, moved on to the topic of "forced Ukrainianization." Vitalik interjected: "And while we're being pitted against one another with the help of the TV, while we're arguing over extraordinarily important problems, like what language to speak or whom to recognize as a hero, we continue to get robbed." Vitalik paused and smiled sarcastically. "You, Valerii Valentynovych, are a victim of capitalist propaganda."

"There's no need to make a victim out of me," Valerii replied, pouting half-jokingly though half-seriously too.

"Have some mushrooms," Lidia Pavlivna coaxed to defuse the situation.

Jabbing his fork into a honey mushroom, Valerii Valenty-novych began to repeat his views about friendship with Russia. Vitalik interrupted him swiftly and, with an oversized shot glass in hand, proclaimed, "The Ukrainian people have three faulty presuppositions. First: that Russia is the successor to the Soviet Union. That's not the case. Russia is a capitalist country just like Ukraine . . ."

"What are you, a communist?" I asked, raising my eyebrows.

"More about that later." Based on his unpremeditated reply, it was clear that Vitalik would revisit it later with pleasure. "The second faulty presupposition is that the unification of Ukraine and Russia would mean the revival of the Soviet Union. That's also incorrect. And for the same reason—because both Russia and Ukraine are capitalist nation states. And, finally, the third faulty presupposition: Valerii Velntynovych, are you not con-fusing today's Russia with memories of your own turbulent and romantic youth?"

In response, Valerii Valentynovych slurped the juice out of a pickled tomato.

"And now, to return to your question . . ." Vitalik really did have the gift of gab. "You've probably figured out by now that I'm not exactly a communist. I'd be satisfied with any political system that would be effective and would at the same time ensure the wellbeing of at least fifty percent of the citizens."

"Go on," Lidia Pavlivna interrupted, "eat, eat."

Vitalik jabbed a few pieces of fried potato with his fork, only to wave them around in the air as he continued: "A friend and I wanted to join one of the political parties after university—any one of them. We wanted to do something for Ukraine. Well, everything was clear from the get-go with the Yanukhovyches and the Tymoshenko Bloc. That's why we joined the Communist Party. We figured, all of the old farts would die soon, and the party would need new blood. And there we'd be: ta-da!" Theatrically, like a dancing Roma, he clapped his hands, then spread his arms wide, the fork still in one hand. "But almost immediately, we saw that these guys weren't at all communists. They were the same sort of capitalists as the rest—just operating under a different brand name."

"Another gherkin?" Lidia Pavlivna asked, leaning over to me.

"And regarding language," Vitalik continued, glancing in Valerii Valentynovych's direction, "I adore that new film about that Civil War–era anarchist revolutionary, Nestor Makhno. They addressed the matter of language perfectly, in my opinion. Whatever language someone started talking in, they served in! And that included Surzhyk . . . Like that machine gunner who, according to legend, thought up Makhno's *tachankas*, the horse-drawn machine gun carts. Note, he wasn't a Ukrainian *kulemetnyk* or a Russian *pulemiotchik*, but a Surzhyk *kulemiotchik*—a hybrid of the two. 'You wheel these machine guns on a cart and then take them down to take up a position. It's . . .'—Oh, how I love this word! —'It's *duristika*!' *Duristika*!' Vitalik repeated with delight, 'Stupid madness! First off, you're wasting time. And second, you can't maneuver.'"

When Vitalik had gabbed his fill and left—"the wife's waiting"—Valerii Valentynovych started telling me about his "turbulent and romantic youth," as it had been previously dubbed. Till this day, Valerii Valentynovych is a "trekker," as he put it—something that has stayed with him since his teens. After finishing—or rather, not finishing—school, Valerii Valentynovych traveled to the Russian port city of Murmansk because, "you know, the sea and the North," and took a job with a fishing fleet there. "How wonderful all of it was," Valerii Valentynovych sighed nostalgically. "Even though it was hard. When you have to gut three fish a minute in the freezing cold, but your fingers are curled stiff and aren't obeying. Or when you have to clamber up the boat rigging to chip off the ice that's frozen onto the ropes and is threatening to tear them. The wind is swaying you on the mast, your hands are frozen to the bone, an icy crust is forming on that beard and mustache of yours that have just started to grow, you suck at that crust while hanging on a rope, from up high you look at the tin-gray waves crashing against the ship, causing dirty-white sprays of crests to fly higher than the bulwark, an albatross whinnies over your head, and right above the bird's body, grazing the tips of its wings, dark clouds move, dropping oakum onto your shoulders while you hang on the rigging in the piercing wind, soaking wet and shivering from the cold, but you're young and happy!

"Ekh . . . and after that, they want us to part ways with Russia!" he concluded, making a logical turn.

He rested his temple on his palm, his elbow planted on the oilcloth-covered table. As he chewed on a gherkin, his gaze grew distant and languorous.

Rehabilitation

As Tom Waits put it, "Now, George was a good straight boy to begin with . . ."

Anton and I met in our first year at university: both of us had tested into the highest-level English language course. Anton was a very likable guy—one of those that girls describe as a "pretty boy" and either really like or really don't. Symmetrical features on a still childishly round face, skin just barely tanned, dark wavy hair, thick eyebrows, honey-colored eyes, and slightly plump lips.

Anton smiled often and generally wore a good-natured and faintly ironic expression. We were somewhat friendly. One time, I even hung out at his house. I didn't meet his mother. Anton's father was the owner of a company that made gold ornaments for churches. He had contacts in Orthodox circles.

When his father left the house, Anton and I smoked a joint on the balcony. It was my first time. After, I lay on the couch, trying to discern whether or not it had kicked in. I kept closing my eyes. I was under the impression that there would be some sort of hallucinations. But all I kept picturing was my own red throat. It was burning. Then the red heat shifted lower, into my stomach—and that was the entirety of the effect.

Anton was saying something, but I couldn't understand him. He was laughing a lot. I got up from the couch and went to the bathroom. As I was coming back, I spotted a religious magazine on a coffee table in the hallway—a Protestant one, I think—with "*Isus liubyt vas*," "Jesus loves you," written on the cover. I walked into the living room and blurted, "*Isus liubyt kvas.*" Jesus loves *kvass*.

"And fish," Anton replied and started choking with laughter.

I started laughing too. I can't say what struck me as so funny, but we kept looking over at one another and laughing, then we would seem to calm down, breathe deeply to catch our breath, and then catch one another's eye and again start laughing.

We finally calmed down and went out on the balcony for a smoke. An ordinary one this time. After that, back in the living room, Anton turned on some music, and I felt the vibrations passing through my chest, shaking my ribs, changing my heart rate.

"What is this?"

"The band Massive Attack. It's spot on, no?"

I nodded.

We didn't start hanging out more often after that, but whenever we'd cross paths in the university courtyard or in lecture halls, we'd nod to one another with genuine friendliness. At the time, I felt a greater or lesser degree of antipathy toward the rest of the guys in my year.

From Anton, I learned about the British band Portishead and the British musicians Squarepusher and Aphex Twin. Whenever I would run into him in the courtyard, next to the statue of the Ukrainian philosopher Hryhorii Skovoroda, or in the subway passages, Anton would almost always be wearing large, obviously high-quality headphones. He loved music.

Anton would go to all-night raves and then would spend English class nodding off. Other times, conversely, he would arrive after a night out with bags under his eyes but more cheerful than the rest of us. Those times, he wouldn't be able to sit at a desk. Our instructor, an American from the Peace Corps, was a more laid-back educator than the Ukrainians—but even he would sometimes comment when Anton would spend half the class drumming two fingers on his desk, unable to stop.

Anton and I smoked up together a few more times, and then our paths gradually diverged. One time, he invited me to try some sort of speed, but I got scared. "It's not my thing. I'm a nervous Nelly as is."

I went on having a joint on my own once every few months, like everyone around me. OK, so, once or twice, I tripped on hallucinogens too.

Over our years at university, Anton changed. Our final year, whenever I saw him in the courtyard, he'd rarely smile at anyone. He seemed exhausted. Under his pretty eyes, not-so-pretty bluish shadows appeared. His tanned skin acquired a yellowish tint. His face lost its childlike roundness.

After that, I traveled to America for a year and a half and, accordingly, didn't see Anton at all. At one point, I heard from someone on Facebook that he had gotten seriously hooked on amphetamines or something like that, and that his father had committed him to a religious rehab clinic.

When I returned to Kyiv, I got involved in community activism, specifically, in the Save Old Kyiv movement. We were protesting the erection of new buildings in Kyiv's historic areas. There was one case in particular when a large Orthodox church started to be built in the only square in a certain neighborhood of Kyiv, next to the historic Karavaievi Dachi district. It was the standard scheme: first, they put up a tiny chapel; then, a year or two later, they'd build a little wooden church; and from there, they'd erect a large edifice that took up the entire square, complete with a parking lot and a clergy house. All of it, of course, under the personal protection and blessing of the Lord Almighty. At one of the demonstrations against this illegal development, a few members of the protest painted a hammer and sickle on the fence, which led to a quarrel between them and the rest of us: most of the members of our group couldn't stand this symbol. And the locals protecting the square clearly had no interest in the hammer and sickle either. But I'm telling a story about Anton. A day later, an article appeared on a Protestant website that, based on the graffiti on the fence, logically concluded that it was satanists and Marxists opposing the godly construction.

The article proved lethal. Its killing power lay first and foremost in its seriousness—in the absence of even a hint of humor.

Sure, our group had a laugh, but I turned my attention to the author's name. The last name was familiar. At the next demonstration, I walked up to a former classmate—because once puberty was firmly over, many of the guys toward whom I had felt antipathy in university unexpectedly turned out to be wonderful people, and a few of them were now also a part of the Save Old Kyiv movement. "Have you read the article about the satanists?" I asked.

"Yeah," my fellow classmate laughed and adjusted his glasses.

"So, the author of the article—is it *that* Anton? *Our* Anton?

"Well, yeah. In the clinic, he got . . ." and the classmate paused, searching for the right word. "Rehabilitated," he finally said.

A few years later, I ran into Anton at an international conference on religious studies. I had been hired to do simultaneous interpretation. The conference was taking place at my alma mater and primarily focused on how Orthodox doctrines differed from Christian ones. During the first break, in a panic, I went in search of someone who could tell me how to translate the Ukrainian term for "the trial of the soul" into English and explain what it even meant. Anton saved me. He also wrote out some additional terminology for me on a piece of paper.

We didn't find any time to talk more that evening. On the second day, we bumped into each other next to the buffet table during a coffee break. Anton no longer had hollows under his eyes. Conversely, he had become rounder. He was even starting to grow a little paunch.

I took a cluster of grapes from the table, while he picked out a tiny canapé with cheese and an olive.

"I've thought about you at times," I said. "Do you remember: Jesus loves *kvass* and fish?"

He looked directly at me, his gaze boring into my forehead. "No."

I even felt the firmness of the period after this "no."

Anton started talking to an American that was passing by and walked away from me.

When the signal was given, I climbed into the glass booth at the back of the auditorium and pulled on my headphones, preparing to continue interpreting. I exhaled. My partner, who had been hired because she knew one of the conference organizers, was a lousy translator. I already knew that I would have to do eighty percent of the work myself; my partner would only give me a chance to catch my breath at the least important points of the lectures.

Anton, meanwhile, took up his spot as the moderator.

Take Care of Yourself, *Bratishka*

"What fucking Soledar? Sh-i-i-it. You missed the fucking turn, buddy. Now you have to fucking head twenty fucking kilometers back. Sh-i-i-it."

In that first moment, the density of his forcefield makes me recoil. But Valera has such a good-natured expression as he says all this, and he's smiling so gently, that I muster the courage to respond. "What do you mean?" I show him my atlas. "The road through Soledar to Lysychansk is right here."

"Sh-i-i-it. Don't waste my fucking braincells, boy." Valera pauses and merrily scratches the crown of his unwashed head. "Where the fuck are you trying to get to? Ultimately?"

"Well . . . through Lysychansk to Luhansk."

"To Luhansk? Sh-i-i-it. That's a whole nother fucking matter. Go all the way to the fucking fork in the road, and then take a fucking left. Then you take the fucking highway, and there's that stripper club. But that Soledar? Sh-i-i-it. What the fuck do you need it for?"

"Well, here, take a look . . ."

"There's nothing to fucking look at there. There's nothing fucking there, buddy!"

"And from Lysychansk through Sievierodonetsk—that's going to be a left?"

"What fucking left?" he asks, smiling even more kindly. "Why the fuck are you going to go all the way through Rubizhne? Sh-i-i-it. Take a fucking right, straight to Luhansk."

I get used to the density of his forcefield rather quickly. And beyond the forcefield, I can see clearly a good-hearted person with a rather particular way of expressing himself.

While Valera and I are conducting this refined conversation, a man with gray hair, a gray mustache, and in a gray Jeep pulls up alongside us. "Excuse me," he interrupts politely. "If you don't mind my asking, is this the right way to Debaltseve?"

"Yes, that's correct," Valera replies with unusual restraint, his taut voice almost quivering. "Just stay on the highway the entire time. Don't turn off, please. Just take it till the very end. That'll get you to Debaltseve."

And not a single expletive. When the Jeep pulls away, Valera glances at me sideways and adds sarcastically, "Sh-i-i-it, you could quit your fucking job and set up a paid fucking consultancy over here. So, why are you going to Luhansk anyway?"

"Well . . . I'm traveling. I want to ride around all of Ukraine."

"Ah, you're traveling? I'm traveling too over here." Valera lovingly pats the side of his dirty-white truck. "But why alone? Where's the wife?" he asks, screwing up his face.

"My wife traveled with me in the beginning. And then she refused to. She says it's very difficult."

"That's what mine says too," Valera responds. "'What the fuck kind of job is this you have? You sit around all day doing fucking nothing.' So, I took her along one time. At first, she's turning her head this way and that way: everything strikes her as interesting. And then, after a couple of hours, she doesn't know what to do with herself anymore. Her legs are like this, her shoulders are like that, and then she climbs into the back. She's clearly miserable. And I ask her, 'Well, how is it? Because you're not even doing shit, you aren't behind the wheel, you can move around however you want. It's easy, right?'"

"Can I ask you something?"

"Sure, but nothing vile."

"What is it you dream of?"

"Sh-i-i-it. What do we all dream of?" He scratches the crown of his head again. "That we all get to live a normal life. It's just that those motherfuckers upstairs don't let us live."

"And what does Ukraine mean to you personally?"

"Ukraine? It's a homeland for everyone. Ukrainians—they're fucking everywhere. There are even Ukrainians in Africa. But then, sh-i-i-it, they start dividing into east and west. Who the fuck needs that? It's all for those motherfuckers upstairs."

"Do you mind if I take a picture of you?"

"What the fuck—why not? Go ahead, take my picture." Valera stops talking, looks into the camera, then hollers, "Hey, boss! Come here and get your picture taken too!" He's yelling across the road to a fat man, who's fumbling with a tire next to another truck. "Maybe you'll end up in a magazine!"

The chubby boss wipes his hands with a rag as he approaches. "So, where are you from?"

"From the Ivano-Frankivsk area."

"I don't hear a dialect on you."

"That's because I was talking in Russian. When I'm talking in Ukrainian, everyone notices it right away."

"Exactly!" the boss exclaims happily. "You guys from the west have this way of talking: you talk as if you're almost singing," he says, also switching to Ukrainian. "But it's all the same to me which language we use. There are really good people out where you're from."

"Yes," Valera agrees, scratching his chin seriously. "There are good people in Halychyna too."

Valera and the boss fondly reminisce about the hospitality with which the people of Halychyna welcomed them. All of a sudden, Valera stops short, glancing around. "Look at that!" he exclaims. "He's already fucking gone off with his ruler. Sh-i-i-it." A few dozen meters away from us, a traffic cop is starting to measure the dimensions of a truck he just stopped. "I would have sent that cop to hell. What is this, a fucking inspection? Call in an inspector from the city if you need but stick to your fucking job."

When I leave Valera for a few minutes to listen to a conversation some other people are having at a nearby gas station, that same traffic cop is being discussed at the gas station, only this time philosophically and calmly: "Well, he's just that kind of cop. What're you going to do? Just let him have his fun."

Then Valera calls me back. "Hey, dude! Come here! There's a neighbor of yours here—from Ternopil."

"No, I'm just driving from Ternopil now," the truck driver explains. "I'm actually from around Kyiv."

"Aaahhh . . ." Valera drawls disappointedly.

"Listen," the Kyiv long-hauler says to him. "One of my wheels made this horrible sound yesterday. Look," he says and reveals a completely torn tire. "Worst of all, it happened on a level part of the road! Here I am, driving, and then I hear, *Ba-a-a-bakh*! Fuck. Well, look, there's still thirty percent of the tread, right?"

"Yes, more."

"That's what I'm saying. It wasn't bald. Why'd it do that? And the load's only eight tons . . ." Then he notices my motorcycle. "How many cc's is it?"

"A hundred twenty-five, it's small," I answer and lower my eyes self-consciously.

"My son wants a motorcycle too. Only he wants a Yamaha Fazer 600. What do you think?"

"Well," I frown and pretend to be an expert. "In my opinion, the 600 is a bit much for a first-timer. A friend of mine switched from a JAWA . . . to this same Fazer, actually, and crashed the bike on his first ride."

"That's what I've been telling my son. But no, he wants a Fazer. I was offered a contraband one for five thousand dollars. So, now I'm debating . . ." my neighbor says dubiously. "How fast does yours go?"

"Only ninety. It won't pull any faster, it doesn't have enough power."

"What the fuck do you need faster for?" Valera cuts in. "I generally don't drive over seventy kilometers an hour. It's better to, say, get here from Kyiv an hour and a half later. Why the fuck am I going to get all banged up on some incline somewhere? Sh-i-i-it."

"That's also correct," my neighbor from outside Kyiv concurs. "And don't you speed either," he instructs me. "Drive slowly."

The boss agrees.

Valera shakes my hand firmly in farewell: "*Berezhy sebe, bratishka.*" Take care of yourself, little brother.

This *bratishka* of his made me feel bright and warm and happy.

Less than three years later, at that very same spot outside Artemivsk where I met the trucker Valera, some dudes will forcibly disarm Ukrainian servicemen. A crowd of them will meet a truck with "People" painted on its side on the highway. They'll unload Kalashnikovs from the truck into the trunks of private cars. I'll watch the video taken on a cell phone with pain. My eyes will search to see if Valera is in there somewhere. I try to see if I can feel his dense forcefield from behind the footage. To which side of all this did you get carried, my friend? Take care of yourself, *bratishka.*

Did You Fall Off the Moon,
or What?

"This train won't stop in Svatove!" the female conductor announces, dumbfounding one passenger after another.

"But I've got a ticket!"

"Did you fall off the moon, or what? There's war there!"

"But I was just there just two days ago!"

"And that was two days ago! We're heading to Kharkiv now, and then on through to Lozova. Be grateful that the train's at least running that far," the conductor snarls. "Because we could strike. Why should we work where bullets are flying?"

A passenger named Auntie Liuba, a dumpy village woman of pre-retirement age, is traveling to the Troitske District in the northwest of Luhansk Oblast. Like me, she was supposed to get off in Svatove. She and I sit down next to each other and begin considering our options. Overhearing us, a freckle-faced university student named Yaroslav, who's in a similar situation, joins us. We end up deciding to spend the night all together at the train station in Kharkiv.

"Because it's very scary alone," Auntie Liuba says, pressing her clasped hands to her chest. "With what's going on these days."

My heart twinges. It turns out, however, that she isn't talking about the war, but about thieves. Auntie Liuba is a quarrelsome, thickset woman with short gray hair. She describes to me how the Ukrainian army drives around her village on armored personnel carriers, and all the village women go out to feed the "naked, barefoot, hungry boys."

"It's because of *them* that there are tanks in my village, and now because of *them* I can't even make it home. Dogs. Bastards. And that's not all!"

"What else?" My heart skips a beat again.

"There's been no rain in over two weeks!"

Auntie Liuba, Yaroslav, and I are ready to spend the night on our bags, but at midnight, by some miracle, we find a ride. The husband of a young woman in our railcar who was also heading to Svatove has come to pick her up from Kharkiv.

"Speak Russian, to not attract unnecessary attention," he advises me, before switching back to Ukrainian Surzhyk.

I inquire why it is that separatism hasn't taken root in the northern Luhansk region where they live, in contrast to the south of the oblast. But I don't hear any patriotically pro-Ukrainian pronouncements.

"Where we live, every separatist needs to first milk four cows before doing anything else," Auntie Liuba grumbles.

Yaroslav laughs at her answer and adds, "And also, by the time you make it to where we live, your wheels will fall off. Even if you're in a tank."

Auntie Liuba spits poignantly to indicate her agreement.

During our drive to Svatove, which takes half the night, we pass three Ukrainian army checkpoints in our old boxy sedan. Out in the steppe, we almost run over three foxes that leap out in front of our headlights one after another, their greenish, luminescent eyes flashing. And our wheels really do almost fall off.

"Svatove's a big city these days!" Auntie Liuba mutters bitterly as we approach the unilluminated town through purplish hills in the middle of the night. After the separatists captured Luhansk, the administration of the entire oblast flocked to this district center.

Auntie Liuba and Yaroslav drive on to Troitske further north. Meanwhile, I wait for daybreak at the Svatove bus station in the company of three drunk women, scared to go out into an unfamiliar city with what's going on these days. The women sit around a radiator pouring alcohol into plastic cups. They aren't snacking on anything. They offer me a drink too, but I decline. Instead, I take a nap, my back leaning against the radiator.

Finally, a dewy morning dawns, and I venture out into the "city."

For a better understanding of the newly minted city's flavor, it's worth noting that there isn't a single building taller than three stories in Svatove. Actually, no, that's incorrect. There's a four-story white concrete district administration building, which, in view of the circumstances, has temporarily become the oblast administration building. Old bicycles and scooters from China, which are sold on credit here, predominate in the town. The most common car is the boxy Soviet-era Zhiguli sedan, behind the wheel of which is typically a guy with a long Cossack-style mustache that extends almost from mid-cheek to mid-cheek.

So, here you are walking at seven o'clock in the morning through the center of a well-swept and quiet town, bathed in dew. You're finding yourself moved by the welcoming calm and serenity of provincial Ukraine, when suddenly you realize that from under a kiosk, from ground level, the barrel of a machine gun is aimed at your chest.

The machine gunner shifts both his barrel and his gaze away, and lets you pass. He isn't alone here. In the square in front of Svatove's House of Culture, there are a few dozen of them. All of them are just the way you—having spent your entire life in a peaceful country—always imagined "armed to the teeth," with under-barrel grenade launchers, bazookas, bulletproof vests, torsos strung with metal, grenades in plain sight, and about a dozen magazines per Kalashnikov rifle.

The town is tiny; everyone can see everyone and everything. To ensure that you, a visitor, aren't misunderstood when you're encountered again, you go to the local authorities to introduce yourself and to get the phone numbers of the higher-ups just in case. The windows of the first story of the police building are barricaded with sandbags all the way to the top. Dozens of people with machine guns keep you from walking up too close to it. The town hall is locked and unlit. On the roof of the white concrete government administration building, the black figures of machine-gunners loom along the entire perimeter. In front of the building, dozens of buff men in body armor over black T-shirts sit in black jeeps and SUVs.

"Our police force is unreliable," they explain to you in the administration building. "But the Ukrainian army has gotten them back in line."

Right now, the oblast police force is headed by that same general who, only a month earlier, was a "people's policeman" in the self-proclaimed "people's republic." He's now switched to the other side, having calculated that it would be more advantageous for him. Among the people, this police general is known as Tolik Zhelieziaka, or Ironman Tolik. The nickname is supposed to reflect his character, as well as the fact that he protects the semi-legal scrap metal market in the oblast.

"Hey, Kyiv guy, come here!" the mayor of Svatove calls out to me.

He already knows about my presence. The mayor is sitting

outside the locked city hall on a bench between the white cedars and the spruce trees—the same bench where the local drunks were hanging out earlier in the morning. Even now, some of them are still sitting nearby. The head of the town is a short but husky man with a proletarian look about him. He's wearing a tight-fitting T-shirt and a cap stretched tight. The only thing he seems to be missing is a soccer ball under his arm. Based on his appearance, you wouldn't guess he's the mayor. I walk up to him. Tolik Zhelieziaka drives past us in a black SUV, guarded by machine-gunners.

"The big boss," the mayor laughs. "In terms of rank, as well as in terms of . . ." And he makes a big-belly motion with his hand.

When I begin to ask him questions that are awkward to answer between the white cedars, in front of the locals, the mayor leads me inside the town hall. He simply unlocks the door with a key that he pulls out of his pocket. It's so strange, so commonplace. The first floor of the town hall is dark because the windows are barricaded on the inside with those same kinds of sandbags as are outside.

The mayor in the cap tells me the patriotic story, well-known among Ukrainians, about how the people of Svatove and Starobilsk supposedly stood shoulder to shoulder and didn't let in the separatists, but his is a less dramatic version. In reality, separatist militants spent time in both Svatove and Starobilsk. It's just that they managed to address everything through negotiations with the local authorities. "You guys are normal dudes, and we're normal dudes too." They didn't even tear down the Ukrainian flag in the town square.

"You aren't going to go and plant potatoes in asphalt," the mayor explains. "You need soil that's been prepared for planting. Whereas in other regions the 'people's republic' was welcomed as liberators from the 'Kyiv junta,' let's just say that here they didn't encounter a rejoicing crowd."

Nonetheless, a so-called "referendum" on the autonomy of the "people's republic" did get held in Svatove—again, in contradiction to the moving story about this "outpost of Ukrainianness of the Luhansk region." The "referendum" was held without precincts, on those very same benches next to the white cedars where drunks sit today. And then what happened? In the end, it wasn't the militants that entered Svatove, but the Armed Forces of Ukraine. It was this governmental order that decided where the locals were "separatists" or passively pro-Russian, and where the people were "patriots" and an "outpost of Ukrainianness."

My lengthy conversation with the mayor in the cap ends when the coordinator of the provisionally "pro-Ukrainian"—everything here is provisional and in quotation marks right now—self-defense force arrives. The self-defense force consists of those same guys with the Cossack-style mustaches that I had seen all over town earlier.

"We have almost a thousand willing fighters. But you can't fight Kalashnikovs with handguns and pistols. 'Give us Kalashnikovs,' we tell the authorities. 'No,' they say. They don't want to. Fine, then let them blame themselves."

"A clusterfuck started when they just handed out Kalashnikovs to whomever," a young guy tells me, grabbing his head. "I'm actually for separation from this pederastic government of ours. It would be better, of course, to become a part of Russia. And if not, then to at least have autonomy. But, you know, it's good that the Ukrainian army was brought here. Because that militia of the People's Republic—it's too much! At first, I was supportive of it: here you go, people are fighting for what's theirs. But when they started looting? It'll be better here if the Ukrainian army sticks around."

There are many paradoxes in the views of Svatove's residents. It's a rainbow of various hues. People here aren't divided, as they are in bad books, into the good and the bad, the black and the white, into the die-hard Bolsheviks versus the ardent monarchists, into blue-and-yellow sincere patriots versus tricolor *Russkiy mir* supporters. Nowadays, many people in Svatove hate the separatists but simultaneously don't recognize the new Ukrainian government.

I overhear women arguing at the bus station: "Liudka's telling me, 'If we vote in their presidential elections, we'll recognize their rule by doing so.' And I say to her, 'OK, so what are you proposing?'"

There's a transportation collapse in the region. The driver of the Kharkiv–Sievierodonetsk bus explains to his passengers, "Today, Svatove is the final stop. Yesterday, it was Kreminna."

"And past that, what?"

"Past that there's war."

A gaunt old grandpa, who looks much like my own grandpa, learns he can't make it home from the city, so he walks away from the ticket office, grumbling, "They proclaimed all these people's republics, but they don't give a shit about the people themselves!"

A middle-aged man with a Cossack mustache spits and sums up the "militia of the people's republic" with one word: "riffraff."

People from different parts of the surrounding region are gathering at the bus stations, both from the Ukrainian side of the front and from the other side. Everyone's angry, even the people who are managing to retain a sense of humor. In one station, a heated criticism of "them" begins, but during the conversation it suddenly becomes clear that the views of the people talking differ by several shades of gray—and that, for one person, the bad "they" are the "Kyiv junta," for another, it's the far-right and paramilitary "Right Sector guys," for a third, it's the "separatists." They're "terrorists" and "guerilla militants," for one person even if for someone else they're "defenders."

And suddenly, it becomes impossible to speak other than in quotation marks. Such seemingly ordinary words like "our own," "our guys," "they," and "those guys" are, as a general rule, pronounced particularly distinctly, with emphasis and elongation. Only *we* is never in quotes.

When the views of the people talking happen to not to differ, a common language is found:

"'They' divvy up power and money among themselves, meanwhile we get crap," the men complain angrily.

"When will 'they' finally finish so that we can rest?" the women sigh.

And then the eyes of everyone there run the length of the column of military equipment nearby. "I'd willingly crawl on my knees first to one side, and then crawl on my knees to the others, begging them to stop," someone says.

A young guy from Kadiivka, further south in the oblast, describes how he's on his second day of trying to make it home by a combination of hitchhiking in private cars, catching rides on Kamaz trucks, and, as a last resort, walking on his own two feet. "At one point," he says, wide-eyed, "I even walked right up to a Right Sector checkpoint outside Starobilsk. Thankfully, they let me through."

Two hours later, after squeezing into the only public minibus for the day and successfully passing a few roadblocks in the steppe, I find myself in the lair of these same Right Sector guys.

When I first arrive in Starobilsk, I'm greeted by what feels like a nonsensical game: There are taxi drivers that are "ours" and those that are "not ours." Getting a ride from one of "not ours" isn't allowed, even though the entire city knows where the battalion I'm trying to get to is located. I finally get set up with one of "our" taxi drivers, a guy named Andrii, who has gold teeth and who insists that I not pay him anything. I climb into his car, then call the battalion's command post. "Just have him flash his headlights," Ivan, my contact in the battalion, instructs over the cell phone. "And he should drive up very, very slowly."

We drive out of Starobilsk, then on through a village. Past the village, we turn off into the woods. At a crawl we drive down a roughly cleared road through the forest. Young saplings brush against the sides of the car. We see a concrete fence overgrown with ivy. Andrii flashes the headlights, then comes to a stop. I climb out and walk forward slowly. I'm met by a man in a bandana, holding a Kalashnikov, but I know his call sign, so I'm allowed to proceed past the barricades. For now, the battalion doesn't have a brand name, like Donbas or Azov, just a number. In response to my question of how they can *not* have a resonant and memorable name at a time like this, they answer solemnly, "Because we focus on our tasks. PR is of no use to us."

True, the day after this conversation, the battalion will, in fact, come up with a brand name, which will become one of the most infamous in Ukraine.

The battalion is housed in an abandoned sausage workshop. It's a striking place. No less striking are the volunteer fighters themselves. Men and women of the battalion live together. Some sleep on the premises of the workshop, others in tents outside. They cook their food on alcohol burners and open bonfires, and dry their undergarments on ropes strung between trees. I'm fed a brothy fish soup out of a cauldron. The whole place smells of smoke. All of it together reminds me of Sydir Kovpak's partisan army from WWII—with the addition of portable internet and smartphones. Like true partisans, the battalion was formed in the woods. Prior to the battalion being organized, its volunteers had no military experience. Most of them are young people from the area.

The volunteers call the battalion commander, a retired army man, simply by his patronymic Petrovych—with intimacy and affection. This Petrovych will become very well-known in a few months, after threatening the staff of an international human rights organization with torture.

"Meanwhile, we don't have a single Right Sector guy in the battalion," says a young man in a striped Russian military undershirt, with a Kalashnikov over his shoulder. "The Right Sector is decaying from the inside from immoral behavior."

As befits partisans, the battalion's relationship with locals is complex, despite the fact that, in contrast to Kovpak's army or the Ukrainian Insurgent Army generations ago, the volunteers don't force anyone to put them up or feed them.

"They roam around the village with machine guns," an old lady laments, peering out from behind her face. "Meanwhile, our children are walking to school."

"They walk around with weapons, but who are they exactly? Ours? Not ours?" a young woman complains to me at a bus stop.

"The battalion is now under Ukraine's Ministry of Defense, so this is now 'our army' protecting us," a young man in an old car who's giving me a ride through the checkpoint into town says sarcastically and screws up his face. A big "separatist" orange-and-black St. George ribbon, a Russian military symbol, hangs from his rearview mirror rather demonstratively. "Sometimes they protect us, other times they shoot at us themselves."

All of Starobilsk is on edge because of several incidents that occurred the preceding day. The main national TV channels depicted the events as "shooting on the part of the separatists," because of which the entire town immediately stopped believing Ukrainian television. In reality, this is what happened: A few dozen provisionally "pro-Russian" Starobilsk residents blocked some military equipment, specifically, two empty Kamaz trucks. And then a few dozen provisionally "pro-Ukrainian" locals—the difference of a few shades of gray—tried to talk their godfathers/in-laws/brothers into letting the trucks go. The negotiations were progressing sluggishly: no one wanted to fight people they knew. But then partisans from the volunteer battalion arrived in jeeps and, without asking too many questions, arrested the four most vocal "separatists," thereby angering even the "pro-Ukrainians." Commander Petrovych orchestrated an impromptu military prison in the sausage workshop, having decided that he had the right to do so. Worse than that, during the arrest, Petrovych's fighters opened fire and wounded one of the local "separatists" in the leg. They did, however, immediately dial the emergency number 112 and also loaded the wounded man into the ambulance themselves.

"It's complete Makhno-style anarchy!" a taxi driver who witnessed the ordeal exclaims. "So, how is it that the normal army is stationed in a pioneer summer camp nearby, and no one says a negative word about it?"

That very same evening, whether out of misunderstanding or out of panic, a driver started pulling away from a checkpoint after he had been told to wait, and the partisans started shooting at him one after another. The worst part was that there was a pregnant woman in the car. She was shot in one of her kidneys.

Despite all the conflicts with the battalion, the locals, irrespective of their political convictions and the shades of gray in their views, are afraid of the withdrawal of government forces. "So, Ukraine will leave, and then we'll be enemies of the 'people's republic,' right?"

Over the course of my few days in the region, a half dozen people completely independently of each other mention the Soviet musical comedy *A Wedding in Malinovka* to me. It's about a Ukrainian village during the Russian Civil War, where power alternates almost daily between Soviet and Ukrainian nationalist forces. The villagers, never sure who's in charge, continually adjust their behavior and dress. In particular, the famous hat-changing scene, "Again power is changing," is quoted by various people in various places—from the semi-unemployed actor in the district drama theater to the umpteenth Cossack-mustached hunter I encounter, who waves his arms and complains about "Fucking Somalia" being in his region.

"The militia came and left, and now we're all separatists according to Kyiv, right? The Ukrainian army came just now, it'll leave in a while, and then what? For the militia, we're already their enemies. Hello, welcome to our wedding in Malinovka! But then where are we supposed to go, huh? Power is changing hands, but we're locals, and we'll stay here like shit on a colander."

An Average Schmuck

"Liberated" Sloviansk has been appropriately painted in blue and yellow for the Independence Day of Ukraine. It's just that here and there, on top of the fresh paint, there is even fresher graffiti that screams "NATO out!" Some of the billboards that read "Thank you to the Ukrainian Army for the liberation of Sloviansk" have already been spattered in red paint.

"Has your city also been painted blue and yellow?" an overweight woman in her forties asks into her cell phone. "Incredible!"

She and I are standing on the highway, at a bus stop at the turnoff to the bombed-out Semenivka, and when I tell the woman that that's where I'm heading, she verbally accosts me: "What did you come for? All you guys do is walk around and walk around! You show up, smile a bit, take some pictures and videos of our misery—but there's no point to any of it! How have any of you helped us?"

Her name is Lena. After calming down somewhat, she spends half the day showing me around Semenivka, a residential settlement in the north of Donetsk Oblast.

"I'm sorry that I barked at you," she'll say later, in Ukrainian. "It's just nerves."

Lena takes me from one set of acquaintances to another: everyone in the neighborhood knows her. Many of them have had their homes damaged by Ukrainian shelling because the guerilla militants had set up camp in the psychiatric hospital in the middle of Semenivka, and they were getting shot at. The psychiatric hospital has been bombed thoroughly, as have some of the private houses near it.

"Many residents won't come back," Lena tells me. "The settlement's heating plant isn't working. We're waiting for winter with fear. But let's go walk around the settlement and you can ask people for yourself."

Liubov Andriivna Pechalna is the only resident left in a two-story building with eight apartments. Liubov Andriivna used to work at the psychiatric hospital that stands destroyed by bombing nearby.

"Today is supposedly a holiday, but I'm in mourning. My house is empty, my yard is empty."

The roof of the house is wrecked. The windows are boarded up with sheets of plywood.

"We need help—roof shingles, windows. OK, fine, forget the windows, but there should at least be a roof. Some activists from Kyiv came, claiming they'd be back. What do you think?" she asks me, her eyes hopeful. "They seemed to be sensible kids."

Most of the settlement hasn't even heard about either the activists or any planned aid. I listen as they talk.

"Some Germans came at one point," one of the women whose home has been damaged is telling another one sarcastically. "They asked me for my address. And then they sent rolls of toilet paper for each of us!"

"No house, but at least your asses are clean!"

Half of the residents of Semenivka speak in Surzhyk.

I knowingly provoke them once or twice, just to see their reactions: "Some people are saying, 'Why help them? They supported the separatists.'"

The women almost push me off the stairs for this.

"If that's what you think, then it's best if you leave now. Go on!"

"The separatists were doing their own thing, and we were doing our own!"

"And what would you do if people with assault rifles showed up in your town?"

"Those who ended up supporting them were already on their side when they entered Semenivka! Yeah, of course, you say hello to people if you know each other. What else are you going to do? But I ran away on the first day they started shooting."

Lena, who's taking me around the settlement, turns out to be a joyful and cheery woman, despite having "barked" at me initially. She's a stereotypical chubby optimist. As she waddles along in front of me, she describes how she fled to stay with relatives in Zhashkiv in the Kyiv region after the shooting began.

"They would call me a separatist there. But whatever. I worked in a bakery. I even found myself a lover. He also called me 'my little separatist,'" Lena says with a giggle.

She takes me into a bombed-out preschool in the neighborhood. Before the war, Lena worked as a nurse there. We step over fragments of concrete and broken glass.

"Of course, they had to name the preschool *Belochka*—The Squirrel," Lena laughs, switching from Ukrainian into Russian again. "You call a taxi and say, 'Please send a car to The Squirrel.' 'Where is that?' 'Right next to the mental hospital.' And they hang up."

Next, the two of us go into the destroyed psychiatric hospital.

"I haven't been here since I've been back. I was scared to go alone. Come with me?"

Theoretically, the place has been demined, but following Lena is nonetheless scary: a brick fence, large and abandoned grounds, smashed buildings, trees with all their branches cut off. Lena and I walk right down the middle of the asphalt paths that connect the buildings, careful not to veer toward the bushes on either side. Half of Semenivka can tell you the story of how a team of electricians visited the psychiatric hospital, which was considered demined. One of them made a careless movement and got his arm blown off.

"We're scared to walk along roadsides in general. The mines probably haven't been cleared there. The scariest are the trip-wires," Lena says cheerfully as we crawl under some wire. "A girlfriend of mine went to pick some leaves and grass for her parrot. Her foot caught on a tripwire. It's good that it stretched, because she was able to carefully remove the wire from her foot. She called the sappers. They found six mines!"

As she's telling this story, Lena heads inside of one of the hospital wings. I'm too scared to refuse to follow her. All of the internal doors of the psychiatric hospital are missing handles, but Lena, who managed to have a job here as well at some point, opens them deftly with an improvised picklock. We find ourselves in the pediatric unit, where we encounter pencil drawings and toys strewn around the floor with construction debris, against a backdrop of walls riddled by shelling and heaps of collapsed concrete in the corners where the walls meet.

"Great. Have you seen enough? Let's go to my house now. My parents stayed here the entire time. The old people didn't flee."

While Lena's mother walks back and forth between the kitchen and the living room, setting out boiled potatoes with sliced sausage and glasses of homemade fruit *kompot* for me, Lena's aging father Tykhon Borysovych talks. Grandpa, as he calls himself, has a single gold tooth and is always laughing. He's thrilled to have only had a few windows knocked out. One time, a mine fell on the asphalt right in front of the gate to his house, but it didn't explode.

"Why would I run away? I'm going to die soon anyway," says the eighty-two-year-old Tykhon Borysovych, laughing again. "Grandma and I wrote out a list of phone numbers," he continues and shows it to me. "And each time the shelling started and we climbed down into the basement, we left a note that said, 'We're in the basement,' and this is a list of who to call if they were going to be digging us up." This too strikes him as very clever. "What else am I going to do? I've survived two wars— World War II and this one. It's just that during World War II, everything made sense . . ."

Here I thought Grandpa was going to start talking about politics, but he was referring to military tactics.

"Back then they would bomb, and then the infantry would launch an offensive. Everything was clear. But now? One side bo-o-o-mbs," he says, raising his hands, "then the other side bo-o-o-ombs! And that's it. They bomb a bit, and then no one touches anyone else. What was the bombing for then? It just causes destruction for us locals."

I find myself troubled by another one of his theses: "Come on, what kind of war is this? In the entire settlement, only four people have been killed."

Tykhon Borysovych refers to the Russian-backed separatists as "let's-call-them terrorists" and to the Ukrainian army as "let's-call-them our guys."

"Now this is what's interesting. Even if in the beginning someone did support the let's-call-them terrorists, later the attitude changed, and everyone started hating them. Because OK, so it didn't work out for you, just accept it and leave. Don't torment people." Tykhon Borysovych winks at me and continues, "But when they say on TV that the . . . let's-call-them our guys don't use Grad multiple rocket launchers? That's a lie. They shot at Semenivka's residential area three times. I'm a former mortarman myself, and I'm telling you, you won't hit anything with that kind of salvo from mortars. It was impossible to count the explosions, just boom-boom-boom-boom-boom." Tykhon Borysovych laughs merrily, showing his gold tooth.

I chew *kovbasa* in silence.

"I understand," Lena says, leading me on through the residential area. "The Ukrainian army was given a square to bomb, and so they bombed it. But that doesn't make things any easier for the civilian population. And why did they miss their targets by so much? Why was there no reconnaissance? Just come under the guise of a civilian and ask us. Instead, it felt like a naval battle."

Lena points at a collapsed building three hundred meters from the psychiatric hospital and repeats, "A naval battle, I'm telling you. 'An A-5! Did it hit the target? No, it went past it!' Meanwhile, what is it? It's actually a Zh-9!"

As we reach Lysychanska Street, one of the epicenters of the destruction, women in housecoats are gathering for a meeting. Incidentally, walking around outside in housecoats worn over naked bodies is accepted here. At the moment, housecoats in a large purple-flower print are quite popular.

The women are gathering because they've heard that "some people's deputy from parliament" is supposed to arrive. This piece of news is traveling by word of mouth, and not everyone in Semenivka has had a chance to hear it, yet one to two hundred women gather nonetheless.

"Maybe this one will at least do something to help," one of the women says to another. They're all talking in Surzhyk.

Before long, a certain Vadym Anatoliovych, the director of a boiler and mechanical plant, arrives in an SUV. However, it turns out that Vadym Anatoliovych didn't come to help, but, conversely, to have the victims help him. Vadym Anatoliovych wants to become the secretary of the Sloviansk City Council. This would make him the acting mayor of Sloviansk while Nelia Shtepa, the city's former mayor, is under separatist arrest for refusing to fully cooperate with them. Vadym Anatoliovych needs the residents to help him "unblock the city council building" on Tuesday, because money is being allocated to the city for repairs, but, without a boss, it's impossible to claim the money. If and when Vadym Anatoliovych comes to power in Sloviansk, he'll claim the money and help Semenivka—as soon as possible, if not immediately.

What Ukrainians call a *srach*, or "shitstorm," in the comments of a Facebook post begins in the crowd:

"One group 'protected' us, another one 'liberated' us!" one of the women shouts, "now a third one is going to 'help' us!"

"Here's yet another one that wants to make money off our misery!"

"They all make promises and then they leave!"

"And then the militiamen will come again, and the Ukrainian army will start pounding us for it again!"

At the edge of the crowd, one woman says quietly to another, "In short, it's clear that we'll be rebuilding our houses ourselves . . ."

As Lena, pulling me by the sleeve, steers me away, she asks, "Well? Have you heard the voice of Donbas?"

"I've heard it. Thank you, Lena. I'll come visit again. Let's stay in touch."

"Let me give you my number."

My friend Ivan, at whose house in Sloviansk I had spent a night a few years earlier, was forced to emigrate to Russian-annexed Crimea. He had spoken too openly and loudly against the new regime. Though he didn't particularly support separatism either, having managed also to spend some time in a prison basement of Igor Girkin's separatist militants. While there, he had shouted things like, "How can this be? I'm a local, after all." And they, as he describes it, beat him begrudgingly—so that he wouldn't disturb the sleep of the other locals in the basement.

"I've got this one guy who still supports the militiamen, even now," Ivan tells me over the phone. "Want to talk to him? OK, but just to warn you, he's a little nuts about Orthodoxy. I'll text you his number in a sec. His name's Viktor."

Viktor turns out to be a young man with a black beard. He arrives at the spot where we had agreed to meet on a bicycle and immediately leads me deep into the park close by.

"Let's just do this," he begins the conversation. "I trust Vania, therefore, I trust you."

"Is there any reason to be afraid?"

"Friends of mine have already been hauled off with sacks over their heads."

Meanwhile, schoolchildren in embroidered shirts and little girls with blue and yellow ribbons in their hair are dancing in Sloviansk's main square. Merry music is playing. The Lenin monument in the square has been dressed in the colorful, billowing pants of Ukrainian Cossacks. Blue and yellow balloons are being released into the sky. They're celebrating Ukraine's Independence Day. Couples, mothers with strollers, and families with children are walking around in the park.

"It's all amorphous," Viktor says in reference to them. "If we became a part of Russia, they'd celebrate Russia Day."

He's hoping for the return of the militiamen and thinks that it's possible: "You know, something along the lines of, 'Remember the mysterious tactical technique: we're actually going forward when we retreat.'"

Viktor didn't join the separatist militia himself only because he's physically disabled. And now he isn't leaving Sloviansk because he can't abandon his old sick mother. Viktor is intelligent and open-minded, which is why, throughout the conversation, he says things like, "the militiamen are against the army" and "the people's republic is against the government." Not a single time does he use words like "junta" or "Nazis." Viktor talks very calmly. As someone with a higher education, he often quotes philosophers and claims that his views are built on pure logic. "There's this parable," he tells me. "After coming up with the rules of logic, Aristotle sacrificed one hundred bulls to the gods out of joy. And ever since then, cattle have hated logic."

Viktor reminds me of a friend of mine who, with a similar reliance on logic, joined Petrovych's battalion as a volunteer, then rationalized the need for victims among the civilian population and also the necessity of torture. Everything was based on pure logic for that guy too. Because everything in life begins with some basic assumption, and from there you have, "If A, then B." For example, Viktor knows perfectly well that there are even Serbian monarchists among the militiamen currently fighting in Donbas, but he doesn't see anything wrong with this. "Well, if we proceed from the unity of the *Russkyi mir*, then . . ." Indeed, the only question is what basic assumptions to start from.

As Viktor and I talk, the "amorphous"—that is, the civilian—population of Sloviansk continues celebrating—some because it's Ukraine's Day of Independence, and others simply because. Late in the evening, over a dozen cars start pulling into the square in front of the train station, all honking nonstop. A crowd of onlookers comes closer, while others, just to play it safe, shuffle off until they can press their backs against whatever wall they come to first. Others start to grow visibly agitated. Still others start to run chaotically around the open space. Anything anyone might be trying to say is drowned out by the cacophony of car horns. The cops that seemed to be there moments ago have suddenly receded toward the train station building, disappearing behind its white columns.

Who is that coming? The let's-call-them terrorists? Or the let's-call-them ours?

As the cars pull in, a single letter becomes visible on the side of each car. The car horns keep blaring, alarmingly.

"M . . ."

Everyone strains to make out the message.

"M A R . . ."

The rest of the cars arrive, and with them the rest of the letters, and everyone in the square relaxes and laughs with relief.

"MARRY ME."

Six months pass.

"We're not against Ukraine! We're not against Ukraine!" the forty-three-year-old Lena shouts, drunk and beating her bulging breasts. "But we're against this government! And that's not just me. I'm telling you what the people are saying. This is the voice of Donbas!"

Over the past six months, new ideological stamps have been affixed. Now, you're either a "patriot" or "anti-Ukrainian," you're either a "nationalist" or "pro-Putin"—as once upon a time there were the "builders of communism" and the "anti-Soviets." In the discourse of the mass media, the entire world, from the Netherlands to Somalia, has separated into the pro-Ukrainians and the pro-Russians without realizing it. Even though no one admitted this outright, the Ukrainian army had lost to Russian weapons in Ilovaisk, and then again at the Donetsk Airport and in Debaltseve. Internal refugees spread throughout the country, and we Ukrainians learned to refer to them correctly as resettlers. We also learned to hate one another, if not for the differences in our addresses, then for the differences in our views.

Lena and I have met up so many times over these six months that she jokes with mild sarcasm, "Won't your wife be jealous of me?"

Sometimes, she calls to tell me about the newest local scandal. For instance, an international organization actually allocated money to the bombed-out Semenivka so that its residents could replace broken windows, then the local official calculated everything at the highest price but installed the cheapest windows. What can you say? It's "the Ukraine": everything just as we expect it and like it.

I know Lena's parents well by now and have gotten used to Tykhon Borysovych's odd humor. I also know Lena's estranged teenage son, who's growing like the steppe grasses: I never do manage to squeeze out of her where the child was while Lena left for Zhashkiv during the shelling, but definitely not with her. I've heard stories about her lovers, but apparently not about all of them.

Today, I once again traveled through the "liberated territories," having just returned from Kramatorsk to Slaviansk, and Lena and I are having a stiff drink with *pelmeni* and pickled mushrooms in the restaurant Slavhorod.

"All these years, we've been told by Kyiv that Donbas 'had fallen asleep.' That they wanted to 'wake us up.' Well, we're awake now. Is Kyiv happy?" Lena snickers.

The attitude of the civilian population of the "liberated territories" to the parties of the conflict can be summed up most accurately by the Shakespeare quote that I heard from a friend of mine from Donbas: "A plague on both your houses!" Or by the following, which I heard on a sleeper railcar from female resettlers who didn't notice I wasn't asleep on the top bunk: "These are the goats that sit in the cities, and those are the goats that bomb the cities."

The unavoidable question of "who fired" is rarely, if ever, decided in favor of the Ukrainian army. It sometimes reaches the point of absurdity. When Ukraine hadn't yet lost Debaltseve, one local woman kept trying to convince me that Ukraine's National

Guard, which was stationed in the city at the time, was "battering and battering and battering" Debaltseve themselves. "They were battering themselves?" I asked, and the woman shut down. She was offended. Or she had stopped trusting me. By contrast, whenever I talk to anyone from the army, I'm told none of them ever shoot at residential areas, of course. In these conversations, it's the militants shooting themselves. According to the army, none of them shell the cities; all of them are simply shooting at the coordinates they've been provided, without any idea as to what's located at these coordinates. Likewise, none of them shell the residential areas; all of them are simply "responding" to the militants that are shooting from there. Nothing is connected to anything else, and nothing affects anything else.

And in the meantime, the residents of these "liberated territories" laugh resentfully at the very phrase "liberated territories." "Who did any liberating? *They* left on their own."

I hear my fill of different variants of this sentiment, even from the most "pro-Ukrainian citizens." And not only from citizens. "The most offensive thing is that no one fired at *them* when they were leaving," a Syrian named Muhammad tells me. "Why not bomb Girkin's column of separatist militants as it's retreating from Sloviansk to Donetsk? Now they're getting it in Donetsk . . ." Muhammad, incidentally, had fled the civil war in Syria a few years earlier to stay with friends in the Donetsk region. He knew where to flee to.

Many people feel uncertain. "You best remember whose territory you're in," a female controller admonishes a *marshrutka* driver in Kostiantynivka. "Don't say, 'Rightsec,' say, 'Right Sector.'"

And one of the people who puts me up for a night—one of the most avid pro-Ukrainians I speak to during my stay—makes an awkward request in the morning: "Could you . . . could you maybe not, you know, expose me like that? These are troubled times."

Rumors are constantly circulating that the "people's republic" will return to the "liberated territories." The rumors intensify at specific points: after the withdrawal of the Cyborgs from Donetsk Airport, after the loss of Debaltseve and Vuhlehirsk, after the shelling of Kramatorsk with Grad rockets.

"If you listen to the Ukrainian mass media, every single person here is a terrorist!" That's what one of the *marshrutka* drivers in Konstiantynivka tells me. Others around us nod in agreement. They've gathered in a circle, waiting for the next train to transport people to the "occupied territories." As a reporter from Kyiv, I have their sympathy: "We understand. If you write the truth, you'll get summoned by the Security Service of Ukraine right away." And they pat me paternally on the shoulder.

In a café located underground, in the darkness behind a partition, a bald and buff guy is quietly telling another guy about a businessman friend of his who was first held captive in a militant basement prison and was later buried in the ground up to his neck at the military airfield by Ukraine's intelligence services. Beaten up and morally shattered, I've recently been released from an interrogation that involved torture due to a suspicion of espionage. I don't know what to think now, so, ready to believe anything, I sit behind a partition in the darkness, drinking heavily, listening to the muffled voices, and plagued by turmoil: What's going on with my country?

During one of my visits to Semenivka, Lena leads me around the settlement, passing me off as her nephew, and purposely strikes up conversations with neighbors so that I hear what they have to say. All I hear from all sides is, "these people are in Rostov" and "those people are in Moscow."

"Militants took over my house and lived there," a young guy tells us from the roof of his house, where he's doing repairs. "They left more trash and litter after themselves than pigs would."

"When will you move back in?"

"In the spring. I'm staying at my aunt's in Mykolaiv right now."

"And what about the M family? Are they coming back?"

"The M family? Ha! Maybe if the DPR returns here. But it'd be better then to not let the neighbors come back."

"Ha-ha, exactly!"

The M's, a mother and son, are the local rich. They own three apartments in the settlement. These apartments weren't damaged by artillery, but the M's have left forever, as have a few other families.

"Whoever felt any guilt is no longer here," Lena explains. "And those who didn't feel any guilt are now the ones getting caught."

The questionable legality of the actions taken by Ukrainian law enforcement officers who are "fighting terrorism" is a known fact. One of the sources of this knowledge is collective: the residents of Semenivka openly identify by name the locals who initially disappeared and then were magically "found" under arrest. One such local is Dima, a social outcast and the town fool, who has ended up in the district police station on more than one occasion for drunk and disorderly conduct, fighting in public, theft of scrap metal, and the like. When Igor Girkin's militants seized the police station where Dima had been beaten by cops so many times, he showed up and watched with schadenfreude. After that, he lived quietly with his family, got hammered as he had before, and didn't take part in the ensuing political events. After the "liberation" of Sloviansk, when Girkin left and government forces entered, Dima disappeared. A month later, his relatives found him under arrest in the Kharkiv region. Another local was also picked up by the cops for nothing. Neighbors claim that the cops let him go after his mother paid a ransom. Semenivka's third "terrorist" was an old alcoholic who most likely got picked up to look good in their reports to superiors. He disappeared for good because none of the locals showed any interest in him.

I hear about similar situations from a police officer from Kramatorsk, who appeared to insist on a meeting with me precisely for this reason. "There are a lot of people in the city without insignia, and the police operate on the brink of unfairness, if not outright illegality," he tells me.

"What are you surprised at?" an old friend of mine, who's now close to the leadership of the local security service, says in response to my question about the matter. "The cops always beat people, even when there's no war going on. But they do catch real separatists. The cops are doing their jobs. Well, OK, you also have the ones who nab people just to look good in front of their superiors. You've seen the news about how "'so and so many subversives'" were caught? It just means that the mission arrived. The cops need to submit reports to their superiors. Now the local SBU guys are making a stink because one of the "'subversives'" was an agent of theirs. He was spying on someone, baiting them in order to catch a bigger fish. And then the cops showed up and wham-bam, that was the end of that."

According to this friend, the cops let the small or wrongfully detained fish go after a beating, addressing the issue of the small fry's potential future "recruitment" by separatists in a very interesting way: "They make them say, 'Putin is a dickhead,' on camera."

Incidentally, "What about Putin?" is one of the most astonishing phenomena in the region. The vast majority of locals are, to one degree or another, "against everyone" right now. Yet at the same time, they hate Kyiv fiercely, feel half-hearted disdain toward the "people's republics," and mention the role of Russia in the war at most in passing. Why? I pose this central "What about Putin?" question to everyone I trust enough and whose trust I'm not scared to lose.

"Personally, I'm surprised by it," says an engineer from the New Kramatorsk Machine Factory, who strikes me as an intellectual, with a laugh. "Sometimes you get this impression that it isn't even about the politics, but about personal charisma. It's something Freudian. Middle-aged women, from about forty-five to sixty—those women in general all seem to want him."

But most other people just scratch their heads in response to my question about the lack of criticism of Putin. The idea of the Kremlin's influence on the development of the conflict seems still to be new to them. What do I mean exactly? Everyone in Donbas is perfectly well aware of the role that the annexation of Crimea, and the propaganda in Russian mass media, and the presence of volunteers from Omsk and Tomsk and wherever else, and the omnipresence of Russian weaponry and so on have played in the conflict. Yet they only reference these things as technical details at most. Just like the presence of far-right groups on the Maidan in 2014 is only mentioned as a technical detail in Kyiv.

On the day that Lena and I go drinking in Slavhorod, she had just finished taking tests at the employment center in Semenivka because she's been practically unemployed since the preschool Bilochka where she worked was bombed. Based on the results of the tests that day, she describes herself to me as, "An average schmuck. Not all that smart, but not too dumb either."

She continues munching on *pelmeni* between sips of vodka while I delight in her self-deprecation: if nothing else, she isn't average in that respect.

"I don't know who among my acquaintances would venture to describe themselves like that," I say to her. "Everyone tends to feel self-important. Including me. Lena, let's have a drink to modesty!"

We drink some vodka infused with black pepper and eat some *pelmeni* sprinkled with vinegar. And finally now, half a year after we've met, Lena confesses to me that one of her lovers was a militant of Girkin's. Not the lover in Zhashkiv who called her "my little separatist," but the one before him, in Sloviansk. This lover didn't tell Lena that he was joining the militants, but she figured it out herself when he returned from a "business trip to Moscow" with brand-new camouflage, a weapon, and a new smartphone with a communication encryption program.

In response to her new openness, now finally, half a year after we've met, I venture to admit to Lena that I'm not actually from Kyiv, but from Halychyna in the west. Lena freezes for a moment.

"There, you see?" she exclaims after a pause. "We should have just talked and not started firing at each other! We understood each other perfectly well, like friends!"

Now, Lena wants even more that I, a westerner, "understand Donbas."

"I think I've felt it," I say after everything and stab a pickled mushroom with my fork. "There's just one thing that I don't get at all."

"What?"

"I fully understand what makes you not like official Kyiv. That's perfectly clear. Why you hate that Poroshenko is also obvious. But, as you said yourself, everyone is well aware that Russia ignited and is stoking the conflict. So why is no one criticizing Putin?"

Lena sits absorbed in her own thoughts for a long while.

"You know, you've stumped me," she finally says.

My Daughter Still Doesn't Understand

"Could you please point me toward the resettlers' camp?"

"We have one of those here? Really?"

"Yes, right around here somewhere."

"It's the first I've heard of it."

Spring is running late this year. It's cold. It's mid-March, and there's wet snow on the ground. I pass a factory for reinforced concrete structures and an abandoned industrial zone but still don't see the camp. It doesn't even have an official address yet.

"Excuse me, you don't know where there's a resettlers' camp around here, do you?"

"Are you heading there? Do you need anything maybe? We have a couple of blankets."

" . . . "

"But I don't think there's any more room at the camp."

"Aaahhh, so you thought I was a displaced person?"

"Well, you're looking for housing, so I thought . . ."

"Do I look like a displaced person?"

"Hmmm. What does a displaced person look like exactly?"

"Indeed."

"You ask around if they need anything there. We have warm items we can give."

The modular housing camp turns out to be in the middle of a field on the outskirts of Kharkiv; it straddles the highway that leads to the airport. The closest permanent housing is five hundred meters away. The fenced-in area is crammed with metal-and-plastic trailers that house four hundred people. Facing the trailers, across the road, is a wasteland overgrown with weeds that's been claimed here and there by Kharkiv residents for impromptu vegetable gardens.

"This place is a palace for us," Liudmyla tells me.

Despite everything, her lively, joyous nature is palpable. The plump, young Liudmyla brought three children with her from the so-called "Luhansk people's republic." The middle child, Maksym—or "Maksymka," as she's forever calling him—has Down syndrome. Wherever the mom happens to go, wherever she stops or sits down, five-year-old Maksym plants himself next to her and embraces her sturdy leg.

Back home, in Antratsyt, the family lived in a two-story building, made up of several apartments, that resembled a long barracks. Half of the apartments were empty even prior to the war. Antratsyt wasn't renowned for its prosperity. They used a wooden outhouse. The town had no water supply system. They carried water from a well up to the second floor in buckets. They heated their home with coal. The town got its name from anthracite, also known as hard coal or black coal. That's what was issued to the miners—not clean coal. To heat their apartment in the cold season, Liudmyla would pick through four buckets of raw fossil fuel every day by hand. You threw away the slag, then burned the anthracite coal in an iron stove.

"But in the camp in Kharkiv, we even have a shower! Granted, it's in the next building over. Well, and you have to wait a bit in line. But we do have one!"

Liudmyla shows off her palace housed in a metal-and-plastic trailer. Whereas most of the people in the camp live dormitory-style—a long corridor with doors to numerous cubbyhole-sized rooms on either side—Liuda with her husband and three children managed to get allotted an entire two semi-detached rooms. Fifteen square meters! That's owing to Maksymka, with whom the other children sometimes have difficulty sharing the same space: Maksymka occasionally has fits that devolve into hysteria. Meanwhile, the older daughter has homework to do.

Liuda sits on a metal chair in a housecoat. Maksymka hugs her sturdy leg, whimpering now and then. When he does, she strokes his head. Fluorescent lights, white walls, iron beds, metal lockers like in a school or gym. And emptiness. There's nothing even with which to fill the small space because they left in the middle of January, in a GAZelle minibus, with all of a few bags. Plaid oilcloth bags are practically a symbol of Ukraine.

In order to buy tickets for the GAZelle, they sold their cellphones and household appliances for whatever they could get. They traveled through Russia because Ukraine had closed the checkpoints along the entire demarcation line with the militants at the time: Liuda left right during the battle for Debaltseve in early 2015.

"I thought I'd lose my mind. The checkpoints were closed, and we couldn't get passes made: you need to spend some time in Ukraine for that. We drove for days. With a disabled child. The driver would stop when we needed him to. He was kind. But it was, after all, a minibus full of people like us. We didn't want to be a burden to anyone."

From Antratsyt, they headed east, to Russia—through Kamensk-Shakhtinsky, Voronezh, and Belgorod—then back into Ukraine.

"I almost cried when I finally saw a Ukrainian flag at the border. We had made it."

And that hadn't been her first attempt to leave. As soon as "all this started" (the resettlers talk about the war cautiously: in euphemisms, obliquely, without value judgements), Liudmyla traveled to Kharkiv without the children. But she was unable to find any housing that time. She had to return to the just-proclaimed "Luhansk people's republic." Incidentally, when "all this started," Liuda initially supported the idea of an autonomous republic: as she understood it at the time, it was about decentralization. Well, and, like most of her neighbors, Liuda watched Russian TV and saw the torch-lit marches of the "fascists" on her screen, the coming to power of the "junta."

"And then the militants showed up in Antratsyt, and it started . . ."

In the end, Liuda's family didn't leave as a direct result of the hostilities. It's fairly calm in Antratsyt; there's no bombing. Instead, what began was looting, extortions, forceful taking of apartments and cars, and perpetual internal clashes among the militants. That and an overall increase in poverty.

"Life became unbearable."

Liuda's first husband, the father of her two older children, abandoned her five years ago, right after Maksymka's birth. At the time of Liuda's departure, he was "serving in the militia." Her second husband, Yevhen, worked in a bootleg coal mine back home, for which he received, in addition to money, that same raw fossil fuel for heating the apartment. Yevhen came here with Liuda and the children. The entire time that I'm in their trailer, the man lies in silence, his face turned toward the wall. That time, Liuda says that he's sick; half a year later, when I return, she'll confess that Yevhen has been depressed for several months. There's no money, and no one's hiring the "Donetsk-types" from Antratsyt or wherever.

"There was a sign announcing a security guard position in the hypermarket next door. He shows up, and they immediately check his domestic passport to see what kind of registration he has. 'OK, we'll call you.' A day later, they call and say, 'You're not a good fit.' And off the record, they add, 'The owner said not to take displaced people. He said he has nothing against your personally, but you're unreliable: in a month, you might quit and head back home.'"

Yevhen would come back from his job hunting, lie down with his face to the wall, and not talk.

Don't start feeling sorry for them. Don't start personally living through other people's stories. There are a million displaced persons. And a million is just a number. Each of them individually is a person. But a million is just a number. The important thing is to perceive them as numbers, not as people. It's easier like that.

An emotional aloofness is even noticeable among the volunteers, notwithstanding the active compassion. It's self-protection. They're bureaucratizing aid. The director of the volunteer organization working at the camp tells me, "We have a psychologist for the resettlers, and now she needs a psychologist herself. The majority of our volunteers are displaced persons themselves, and I'm constantly telling them, 'Issue items to people per the list, but there's no need to ask them about anything, and by no means should you get close to them. You won't be able to stand it.'"

She shows me a picture of a five-year-old girl on her phone, who's just been rescued from an area under active shelling. It's impossible to look into the child's eyes even in the photograph.

Svitlana works as a cleaning girl in the administration's trailer when I visit the camp for the first time. Very timidly, she asks me to change seats a few times so that she can wash the floor under the chairs. She's received instructions to make the place spic and span: the camp is expecting a visit from none other than the deputy mayor of Kharkiv.

I suspect that she's simply been forced to have a conversation with me—that she feels it's her duty to. Like she does with the cleaning. It's the price she has to pay for living here.

Svitlana's name suits her. She's *svitla*, "light" and "bright": her face, her eyes. She's a young, pretty, even-tempered blonde with freckles, who smiles as she talks. Svitlana's a single mother from Vuhlehirsk in the Donetsk Oblast. I remember Vuhlehirsk well from when I rode all over Ukraine on my motorcycle. Contrary to its name, which in Ukrainian conjures up images of coal mines and craggy mountains, the town turned out to be green, peaceful, and welcomingly cozy. I remember the brick five-story buildings, the dense shade of the trees that lined the streets, and the patches of sun on the warm asphalt here and there.

Svitlana left Vuhlehirsk with her seven-year-old daughter and her mother, who had had several strokes. Back home, Svitlana worked as a pastry chef. She spent years saving up money to buy an apartment. And finally, she had saved up enough and bought one. A few years prior to the war.

"In the fall, the fighting seemed to have ended, and Vuhlehirsk looked like it was remaining in Ukraine. Real estate prices fell, so I bought a garage for cheap from an old lady I was neighbors with. I didn't own a car yet, true, but I was taking the long-term approach," Svitlana says, smiling at her naivete. "If only I had known it'd be better to have the actual money on hand."

A few months later, it became clear that the Donetsk and Luhansk "people's republics" were beginning a joint advance on the strategic city of Debaltseve. Anticipating that Vuhlehirsk would end up in the combat zone, Svitlana packed up her things in advance.

"My daughter's teacher kept saying, 'Why, nothing's going to happen here. Who needs our Vuhlehirsk?'" Svitlana narrates, a defensive half-smile on her face.

They managed to get out on one of the last trains. Within a

few days of their fleeing, railway service ceased, and, before long, fighting began. Vuhlehirsk ended up getting bombed harder than Debaltseve itself.

Svitlana watched what was happening to her town on the news, both on TV and on the Internet.

"One time, I stumbled on this YouTube video. It was the middle of winter, and two homeless-looking people were leaving Vuhlehirsk. They were walking and pulling something on a handcart. A reporter walked up to them—you know, to get a comment from them. I look, and it's my nephew and his first cousin!"

Svitlana's laughter sounds like little bells.

As it later turned out, these boys—her relatives—had hidden from the shooting in a cellar for the night. In the morning, someone with a car was supposed to drive them out to Ukrainian territory for a fee. But out of fright, the boys weren't able to fall asleep till morning, until the shooting had stopped. And in the morning, they overslept. The driver drove up right under the building and kept honking, but they didn't hear him in the cellar and didn't come out. So, the car drove off. They ended up piling as much of their belongings as they could pull onto a handcart and set out on foot in the direction opposite where they were originally headed, toward Yenakiieve, deep into the "Donetsk people's republic," just to get away from the line of fire.

"And here I had taken them for homeless people. Their faces were all dirty from the cellar." Svitlana smiles again. "But I looked closer, and they were my kin!"

She tells her story slowly, in detail, and with a continual half-smile. She says that when she came to the social welfare office in Kharkiv, she happened to be assigned to a kind-hearted woman who, on her own initiative, had brought some beds she owned to some communal office. There, in that communal office—among the civil servants and visitors, amid the constant bustle of someone else's workday, in a cubbyhole of a room—is where Svitlana's family lived until not long ago, when the modular camp was opened. Now, Svitlana has a room that she shares with her daughter and mother in a dormitory trailer.

"My daughter still doesn't understand that we have nowhere to return to," Svitlana says with that same shadow of a half-smile. "She's forever saying, 'Well, when we go back . . . Let's go mushroom picking again, OK?' She reminisces about her toys . . ."

Svitlana is silent for a long time, then says, "It was such a quiet little town. I adored it."

And, to her own surprise, she begins to sob, covering her face with her hands, and can't stop for a long time. She takes jerky breaths several times, trying to calm herself down, falls silent, then tries to speak again and again breaks into sobs.

Meanwhile, you're sitting beside her—still and very erect, with this sensation as if you're trying to swallow a rock. A person is trembling from weeping right next to you, and you don't know what to do or what can even be done. If you were a woman, you would at least give her a hug, but as it is, you find yourself just stupidly mumbling something along the lines of, "There, there . . ."

The Apolitical Wunderkind

"These are from my first book," the sixteen-year-old Ivanna motions toward the photographs on the pink wall with a careless wave.

Her last name is the most well-known one in all of Ukraine and also a common one, which is why she doesn't precede these words with anything else. Ivanna is tall and thin, with long, straight, dirty-blond hair and a pleasantly shaped and longish oval face. Her slightly short upper lip makes her even cuter, even more endearing. Today, she is dressed in a modest long dress and high heels. She stands erect, and speaks confidently and loudly. It's evident that she's used to speaking in front of an audience.

Everyone moves to a different hall of the exhibit.

"Altogether, Ivanna has published five photo books already!" announces an employee of the private gallery where the girl is exhibiting.

"Five or six, I can't remember exactly," the girl clarifies and shrugs her shoulders. "But those are just mine. There are the ones that I've co-authored too."

"Yes, altogether eleven books—at her age!" the gallerist's voice rings. "Ivanna's also won the grand prize at several competitions, including Crystal Spring, Silver Marvel, and Guelder Rose Branch."

It grows quiet for a while after this statement. All seven or eight of us attending the exhibit move from photograph to photograph. The gray carpet mutes our footsteps. You can hear the fluorescent lamps that are mounted on the drywall ceiling, just barely droning. The gallery is located in the basement of an apartment building. It was opened not long ago.

"And this is from my four-volume photo book," Ivanna breaks the silence. "My father and I initially wanted to publish just one book from this trip, but we realized that there were simply too many wonderful photographs! And so, we published four."

The gallerist smiles. "Yes, Ivanna has traveled around many countries with her parents. She publishes a book based on each of her trips."

"This over here is from an expedition through US national parks," Ivanna explains. "My parents and I rented an SUV and drove across the whole country. My older brother and his girlfriend were also with us. This photograph over here," she says, pointing, "is the view from the highest paved road in all of America. When we travel somewhere, my parents and I always rent a car and plan out the itinerary together—to not spend two nights in the same location. We drive to one location, spend a few hours there—you know, spend the night—and then drive three or four hundred kilometers to the next location."

While she talks, new guests approach.

"This is Viktor, an author," the gallerist announces. "Meet Ivanna, our young talent."

"Nice to meet you."

The gallerist presents the next one: "Volodymyr, a painter."

And another one: "Valerii, a poet."

There's also another category of guests:

"This is Yulia. She's a successful lawyer."

"Oleksandra, she's . . . you work in HR?"

"Yes."

Ivanna's behavior is dignified. She looks people straight in the eye and shakes their hands. She understands that there are too many guests now to continue giving a group tour, and so, she walks away to the center of the hall.

"Ah, support has arrived." The gallerist motions toward the door.

A boy the same age as Ivanna walks up and pecks her on the lips. He looks a lot like Kim Jong-un. A pampered face, plump pouting lips, and cheeks that beg to be pinched. His scornful eyes give the impression that they've seen hard work or poverty only from a distance. His black hair is slicked back and slathered with something for sheen. Only, this young man isn't in a tux, but in jeans and a sweater that scintillates in different hues under the fluorescent lamps. Designs shaved with hair clippers decorate the back of his fleshy head.

Ivanna and her boyfriend look around, grab their jackets from the entrance hall, and exit in a hurry.

The attendees continue to behave politely. They smile at one another. Everyone walks the length of one wall after another, without lingering for long next to any one photograph.

"And here are the parents of our young talent!" the gallerist announces to everyone.

The parents glance around, their eyes searching for their daughter and not finding her.

The parents turn out to be very pleasant people. The mother is dressed in a dark blazer and a straight business skirt, with a chunky red coral necklace around her neck. The father has a long and bushy, traditional, Shevchenko-style mustache and the nationally typical Ukrainian belly. You keep expecting him to break merrily and heartily into an old folk song.

It's obvious how proud the parents are of their daughter. They honestly believe in their child's gift, and they aren't ashamed of it.

The girl sincerely believes in her own talent too. She's returned with gum in her mouth. She kisses her parents on the cheek, up against their necks. The boyfriend gives Ivanna's father a firm handshake.

"So, then, shall we start the official part?" the gallerist asks the girl's father and points toward the first hall, where chairs are set up in rows. "We expected more guests, but maybe people are still on their way. We're waiting for spring to finally arrive, but it's still snowing!"

The guests present take their chairs. Ivanna goes off into the corridor for half a minute, then finds her spot—without gum now—in the front, facing the hall. She seems not to get nervous at all in front of an audience.

"I've been working with photography for a very, very long time," the sixteen-year-old Ivanna begins. "Here you can see landscapes from my travels. I know how to photograph people too, of course, but I enjoy photographing nature more because it contains intrinsic beauty that you don't have to contrive. I find nature inspiring."

The gallerist, who's standing next to her, smiles pleasantly. Ivanna continues: "My creative work is quite well known already, though mostly among my own age group for now. And, of course, I'm known on the Internet. It's difficult to be a celebrated photographer at age sixteen. But, at this age, few people can produce such beautiful photographs. I myself don't even know how I do it. I simply take photographs, and then I look at them on the computer and think to myself, 'Wow, awesome!'"

A few adults in the audience laugh awkwardly. Ivanna looks a little ill at ease.

"And now, a word from the mother," the gallerist announces.

The mother smiles the entire time she speaks and holds her hands in front of her like an opera singer, fingers interlocked. She describes how her daughter would make her husband stop the car in particularly pretty locations in America's national parks, and then would run around with a tripod.

"And now the father," the gallerist says. When he hems and haws, she insists: "Come, now, say a few words! You're an artist, after all!"

The father makes an impression on everyone in the audience with his modesty and honesty. Four years earlier, he had given Ivanna a single-lens reflex camera. One day, after a trip to a festival in Kamianets-Podislkyi, he decided to clean up the photographs she had taken. "And we were surprised to discover that there was a lot worth looking at there!"

While Ivanna was abroad on vacation, the father orchestrated a gift for her. "We picked out photographs, compiled them, and printed a book. It wasn't that expensive."

When Ivanna returned and saw the photo book, she immediately asked, "Can we make another one?" That's how her success story began.

The father, as can be deduced from his account, didn't grow up privileged. He comes from an ordinary provincial family and hasn't lost touch with reality.

"I realize that a professional camera won't materialize in the hands of every talented child," he says, "and that it's imperative to work for talent to have room to develop. That's why I'm constantly telling Ivanna, 'Work, study.'" He turns to his daughter and continues: "I'm always telling her, 'It's not nature that inspires you, it's laziness.'" Then, in the direction of the audience, he says, "Here I am driving her to places that are beautiful at first glance, so that she'll have something to photograph." Then again, he turns toward his daughter: "But you need to go out in the street and photograph people, experiment with different styles of photography. And that takes a lot of work." The father concludes with a sentence befitting a teacher of language and literature: "Creative output requires painstaking work."

Ivanna is obviously angry at her father's public pedagogical display. Her eyes open very wide, and her face grows stony. You can almost see she wants to roll her eyes, but people would see.

After the parents of the young talent, the audience, which turns out to be a hand-selected crowd, is invited to speak next. I'm shamelessly a part of the crowd. During one of the speeches, an intelligent-looking man with a familiar face enters the hall. Where have I seen him? Where in the world had I seen him? Then I remember. This is the youngest people's deputy of the current convocation of the Verkhovna Rada. He's a member of Ukraine's parliament, from one of the patriotic-democratic factions. But what is he doing here? What in the world is he doing here? And then it comes to me. The young people's deputy has the same last name as Ivanna. This must be the older brother who traveled around with her to the US national parks. And their father, who also bears this familiar-sounding last name, is a former people's deputy who joined the executive body—a well-known statesman. Click.

I'm not sure how to end this story, but the following evening, the owner of the gallery calls me. He offers to organize some sort of PR campaign, immediately begins insisting on the indispensability of promoting our culture in any possible way, seamlessly transitions to Ukraine in general and its challenging fate, then starts talking about patriotism and inserts the words "price" and "payment" into the very same sentence.

Marmalade

"P is for Prospects," Markian proclaims, motioning at the swamp ahead with the sweeping gesture of a landowner.

With ominous, almost maniacal, laughter, he walks knee-deep into the first huge puddle in our path. For the next half an hour, I jump over and walk around pools of water, objecting and dickering over the depth of the proposed submersion. Then, I accept it, make my peace with it, and climb into the icy water past my thighs. Spring is very late this year. It's the second half of April, but the winter snows have just melted.

Markian is a young twenty-six-year-old with long, straight, fair hair, a sturdy and very tall build, and the first signs of a little belly from an excessive love of powdered beer. Right now, he's likely the most experienced "stalker" of the Chernobyl Exclusion Zone. He's made over fifty "treks" into the Zone as an "illegal" (his terminology). Six or seven times, Markian was detained. Two or three of them, he didn't actually want to be.

Today, Markian doesn't want us to be detained, so we enter the Zone via an inconvenient itinerary, namely, through swamps. There are more convenient and standard illegal entrances, but the cops know all of those, so there's a risk of being caught. Markian clarifies that he's never been "welcomed," so to speak, as he was entering the Zone.

Right past the standard entrances into the Zone—the ones we're not taking—the standard routes, accordingly, begin. They have established names among the illegals, like *Tsentral* (Central Prison), *Pivdenna Klasyka* (Southern Classics), and *Vilchanka* (The Vilcha Way).

The *Tsentral* route involves stupidly walking down the main road into the Zone at night. *Pivdenna Klasyka* involves entering the Zone from the south by following the power lines. Not wanting to be caught, neither of these routes work for us right now. The *Vilchanka* route leads you in from the west, through the village of Vilcha, over the abandoned railroad track. In many places, the track is overgrown with spruces and prickly bushes, making this route the most foolish, the most tedious, and the most ruthless. Markian describes it as fifty-five kilometers of hell and pain.

We're going to come out onto the Vilchanka route later, in the remote part of the Zone, but, for now, we're pushing even more foolishly, tediously, and ruthlessly through swampland. We use a beaver dam to cross a stream, then walk out onto dry land. But a kilometer later, we're once again knee-deep in a pool of water. Now that the snows have receded, the trees stand submerged in water. The trees are still leafless—even the buds haven't swollen yet—making it possible to see ahead through the forest. Like a young spring elk, Markian breaks right through the bushes, snapping and cracking as he goes.

That's how we craftily detour around the standard entrances to the Zone in order to avoid walking into a police hideout. The beginning of our trip turned out a little inane, however: Whispering quietly in his ear, we asked the driver of the Kyiv–Ovruch shared van to stop in the middle of the woods for us. Talking loudly across the whole cabin, he insisted on dropping us off in the village of Radcha instead. As a result, the entire van looked at us with a perfectly clear understanding of where we were heading—with backpacks to boot. According to Markian, the driver could have immediately called the security checkpoint, but that didn't concern him too much: "It's easy to get away from the cops because they're too lazy to walk through thicket," he explained. "It's harder with the border guards: they have thermographic cameras and a mandate. But you and I don't really interest the border guards."

For the first time in his five years of trekking through the Zone, Markian has brought a GPS he borrowed from someone and is feeling completely confident today as a result. We can go wherever we like and not get lost. That said, in the western part of the Zone, the radiation isn't high enough to affect the route we take.

"Calling stalkers a subculture would be too pronounced," Markian comments, half-turning to me as we wade knee-deep through the ice-cold water. "If you judge by our numbers, we're more of an interest-based group."

Few of the stalkers have read the Strugatsky brothers' 1971 Soviet science fiction novel *Roadside Picnic* because most of them don't read much at all—as is the case, incidentally, with the book's characters themselves. But every last one of them is, of course, fanatical about Andrei Tarkovsky's 1979 Soviet science fiction film *Stalker*. Yet the word "stalker" itself isn't popular in internal usage because it elicits excessive pathos. If you so much as utter the word "stalker," you get shot down by the stalkers right away. They mostly refer to themselves as "illegals"—in contrast to the "officials," as the official tourists are known. In Markian's estimation, there are at most fifty illegals who have gone into the Zone more than twenty or thirty times. One of these frequent stalkers is a legend. A Russian who has long since left the business, he used to go by the nickname of Flying Mouse and was, to put it mildly, odd. He was a "radio-phile," meaning that he brought things that "radiated" out of the Zone and kept them in his home. For instance, he once stole three kilograms of "radiating" sand from the famously most contaminated Red Forest.

"And that's in spite of the fact that he lived with his parents," Markian adds. "At the age of thirty-five. Yeah, and he had a day job as a schoolteacher. Go figure."

Flying Mouse did eventually get a suspended sentence, and for something that had nothing to do with the Zone. The majority of illegal tourists, however, don't bring anything out of the Zone. Therefore, they're looking at a maximum of an administrative offense, and that's in the worst-case scenario. Whether or not you fall into the hands of the police is thus more a matter of excitement than consequence.

We're following the GPS along a path cleared through the forest, which alternately appears and disappears beneath the surface of the watery mud. Markian pep-talks me as we go: "Another kilometer to the road . . . Another five hundred meters to the road . . ."

But when we finally reach this promised road, it turns out that we need to hop over it quickly and plunge even deeper into the swamps. By "road" Markian just meant the official boundary of the Zone. Life is pain.

A half-hour later, we arrive at the Vilchan Parallelogram. Illegals gave it this name by analogy to the Bermuda Triangle. The parallelogram is a destroyed train-car wash not far from the abandoned village of Vilcha.

"Train cars used to get washed down from radiation here. This area used to radiate a lot, but not anymore. Look!" Markian exclaims, pointing at the wooden railroad ties on the ground. "Even the rails have been stolen for scrap metal. Now that's what I call diligence!"

In addition to the illegals, who are drawn to the Zone by a purely platonic love, a fair number of more pragmatic people can also be found in these woods—fishermen and berry pickers, lumberjacks (we saw a newly felled square of forest in the center of the Zone, with freshly sawed logs still lying around and the smell of sawdust in the air), and looters, who steal metal first and foremost. Naturally, persistent rumors circulate that both the fishing and the looting—and, in particular, the noisy logging—take place under the warm and dry wing of the police. Or of the SBU, the Security Service of Ukraine.

The illegals separate the villages in the Zone into *sokhran* (literally, "preserve") and *destroi* (borrowed from the English "destroy"). Markian knows the names of all the abandoned villages and has visited most of them. Some of them he "uncorked" himself or with a few friends, that is, he was the first illegal to stay in them. Our end goal today is Lubianka, one of the best *sokhrans*. Squatters lived there for a long time, and a few people remain in the village to this day. But on the outskirts of the Zone, like in the previously mentioned Vilcha, the villages are complete *destrois* because they're too easy to get to. As Markian points out, abandoned villages are made into *destrois* not by Nature, but by Man.

"There's a legend about how an old female squatter from Vilcha died. The cops didn't want to go fetch the corpse, so they told a known local looter, 'If you bring out the corpse, you can plunder Vilcha for three days.' And not just rob," Markian clarifies, raising a finger, "but in a car . . . with a utility trailer attached!"

There are some well-known characters living in the surrounding villages. One of them is an alcoholic woman who carried fifty-five kilograms of metal in one go out of the Rozsokha "graveyard" for radioactive equipment and vehicles back when that Point of Temporary Localization of Radioactive Waste still existed. "Now that's a heroic woman! Just imagine: fifty-five kilos, through forests and swamps, on the hump of her own back."

There are other local celebrities, like the settler Beaver, who rules over the only clean-water well for a few dozen kilometers (because drinking water is a problem in the boggy Zone, which is why we're carrying all of ours with us right now). There used to be a villager named Noah, who got his nickname because he was forever building rafts. Apparently, he smuggled contraband on them to and from Belarus. And then there was Alik in the village of Potoka on the outskirts of the Zone. He was a respected personality, a businessman. Alik eliminated money as an unnecessary link in the trading process, instead "paying" alcoholics for stolen metal with denatured alcohol.

From the Vilchan Parallelogram, we're supposed to walk on a dirt road because we've already entered the remote part of the Zone. But we hear a dog bark to our left. A single time. Markian freezes.

"Dogs don't stray far from people around here—because they get shredded by wolves."

And so, we head back into the swamps. Life is pain.

"We need to make it to Kliviny by nightfall. It's this abandoned whistlestop where we hold the annual Kliviny Party. The theme of the party is always 'everything is rot.' We spend the night there, gorging ourselves on the cheapest of vodkas—deliberately to the point where we're dying the next morning—and then force ourselves to go on. After the suffering, we purposely see to it that the cops show up and write us up. Vilchanka really is a route for masochists."

Markian and I do make it to Kliviny before nightfall. In the twilight, we walk on along the overgrown train tracks. The young branches of prickly, wet spruces whip us in our faces. My feelings are intense, but not those of an enthusiast.

We're being "led" by two wolves. Behind us, between the spruces, their eyes flash fluorescent yellowish-green. Markian keeps reassuring me that wolves haven't attacked any of his acquaintances a single time: there are a lot of animals in the Zone, and a human is too difficult a prey for wolves to bother with. What's more, there are two of us. "Now, if there was a group of us, and a whole pack of them, and if it was winter and one of us was lagging a kilometer behind and was clearly weak . . ."

After twenty kilometers of walking on wet, chafed feet, I'm limping badly. But I'm trying as hard as I can to not to lag behind, doing my best to exude vigor and vitality. I keep looking around, searching for the flash of eyes in the darkness.

Markian had brought a half liter of cheap whiskey with him that he'd bought on a promotional sale. At first, I had said that I wouldn't drink it, but as we continue our trek, I start sipping it—for anesthesia. We reach the village of Lubianka at three o'clock in the morning after thirteen hours of walking.

"Let me show you the village first tomorrow, and when we're done with that, we'll go see those self-settlers of yours," Markian decides at the outset. "The cops have changed their tactics and don't bother the self-settlers anymore. Instead, they bring them food and do what they can to support them. And the self-settlers have walkie-talkies and can call the cops whenever they need. Therefore, the village first. It's worth having a look at it. After all, it's one of the best *sokhrans*."

The illegals avoid contact with the self-settlers. Despite having visited the Zone fifty times, Markian has interacted with the villagers only a single time. He isn't convinced they wouldn't give him up.

We spend the night in one of the few abandoned houses in Lubianka that has a working stove. We light it and heat the place up. The illegals have brought furniture from other houses to this one, so I even get to sleep on a mattress that's soft, even if it's of questionable cleanliness.

The entire following morning, we walk around the village. The copper wiring ripped out by looters has left long, jagged lacerations on the walls and ceilings of the houses. Light fixtures have been taken down and removed. In contrast to Vilcha or Poliske, the windowpanes are intact everywhere, so the houses are relatively dry. This has allowed for thirty years of *sokhran*. People hung on here for a long time after the nuclear disaster of 1986. In one house, a newspaper from 1993 advertises that any ordinary person can become an Alfa Romeo dealer, guaranteeing "an increase in self-confidence and creative development of the imagination." In another, a wall calendar from 1996 hangs alongside a portrait of some hero of the Soviet Union decked out with orders and medals. And in a third, there are copies of the newspaper *Kyiv Region Sports* all the way to 2005.

Finally, we go to the other end of the village, where the self-settlers live.

Before heading over there, we debate whether to hide the backpacks we're leaving in the house. After discussing it, we decide to make our peace with being detained should the police come in advance, so there's no need to hide our things. At the last moment, Markian convinces me to take my legal documents and anything valuable with me. The Zone looks to be empty, but there are looters roaming around. All sorts of things can happen.

"Well, we've seen the village, so we can head out. In twenty minutes, the cops will be here," Markiyan says with a chuckle.

We're deliberately making as much noise as we can as we walk up to an inhabited house. There's a cat on the little earthen embankment that runs the perimeter of the house, a cow in the yard, and roosters on the roof. We're holding packets of food in our hands.

"Knock-knock!" Markiyan calls out in a sweet voice. "Good day to you and your home!"

I chuckle and think to myself, if I were a self-settler, no way would I open the door. You're an old granny, living alone in the middle of the woods, and here two big dudes that are suspiciously friendly come to visit you.

We walk around the perimeter of the yard, then we knock again.

"OK, there's nothing we can do," Markiyan says, sighing. "Let's go to The Commendatore."

The Commendatore is a nickname that a particular old self-settler got for unclear reasons. He's the only one whose location Markiyan knows definitively. And he knows just as definitively that The Commendatore will turn us in. But the desired contact with a self-settler will take place; the mission will have been accomplished. And while we're at it, we can also "get registered" with the cops.

As we walk to the main street of the village, we talk loudly and boisterously on purpose. The weather has been unpredictable all day: one minute there's sunshine, the next there's hail. Then, out of nowhere, even though it's the middle of April, a dense fleecy snow starts to fall. We duck into the nearest abandoned house to wait it out. And when we come out, we see a brand-new white minivan twenty meters away from us, parked in front of the gate of the house where we'd just knocked on the door.

Our humility evaporates, and, without consulting each other, we silently walk in the opposite direction.

"It's pretty unlikely that a self-settler would have a brand-new van," Markian says softly once we've covered some distance. "It's probably cops from the Dibrova checkpoint. Just as I had said: they arrived in exactly twenty minutes. Nice job."

It's difficult to explain a person's motivation, even your own. Literary attempts to do so are always fantasized convention. Of course, having invented a character, you'll also, with arbitrary detailing, invent the motives for his actions. But that's not how it is in life. Markian and I, as I've already said, had agreed to surrender when the cops came. It would have been interesting even—additional literary material, so to speak. But both of us acted differently than we had agreed on. Why? I don't know. Maybe it's one thing to surrender with dignity and quite another to walk up to the policemen that you noticed first and just hand yourself over. But even this explanation is the result of rationalizing and fantasizing after the fact.

In short, walking through backyards and gardens, we reach the house where we had left our backpacks.

Outside the house, a villager of about fifty whom we don't know is standing with his back to us. Instinctively, we drop to the ground and slither on our stomachs along the hedge into the garden behind the house. OK, so, in addition to The Commendatore, there's at least one other man in the village. And here Markiyan had thought that it was all just old ladies.

When, after calming down our breathing, we peek out from around the corner a minute later, there's a policeman wearing a jacket with a warrant officer's epaulettes and a cap standing two meters away with his back to us. Our spit could have reached him. And again, we have the same story as with the van: we see the police, but the police don't see us.

Without saying a word, we slip through the garden and into the neighboring house, plastic grocery bags of food that we had brought as gifts for the self-settlers in our hands.

"Well, I never thought that I'd be running away from cops through gardens at the age of thirty-three," I whisper once we've entered the abandoned house.

Then we sit down to catch our breath

We assume that they're going to come for us right away. But the cops are either too lazy to come looking for us or never even noticed us as we sprinted through the open space between houses. All of this is starting to get boring, and we're starting to get hungry.

"You don't happen to have any candy left, do you?" Markiyan asks.

"No. Oh, wait, hang on! We should just eat what we brought for the self-settlers!"

We open up the plastic bags with everything that my wife had bought in Kyiv. There, among other things, we find some marmalade.

"We should nickname whoever gave us up Marmalade," Markian suggests as he eats.

And that's how, alongside Noah, Beaver, Alik, and the alcoholic known as Fifty-Five Kilos, the self-settler Marmalade enters the folklore of the illegals.

We're sitting on the wood floor under a window and warming ourselves in the sun, which has again come out and is shining at us through the intact windowpanes and melting the snow that accidentally saved us. We're eating marmalade. We're waiting for the police. And I start interviewing Markian.

"There's a fair amount of humor specific to the Zone regarding government registration and official documentation. They're mostly primitive jokes, made up on the fly. When illegals are making plans to go into the Zone again with someone, they say, 'OK, so, we're going to go and get ourselves registered then?' There are also couplets, similar to those in traditional Ukrainian folk songs, but the majority of them also play on that same topic of the police and getting officially registered and documented by them."

As we talk, the policemen keep not coming and not coming.

We eat so much of that marmalade that our stomachs start to hurt. An hour and a half passes.

"As a rule, if the cops find backpacks but can't find you, they'll sit next to them and wait. It's convenient for them: there's a stove and heat in the house. Maybe they're gorging themselves on our cans of stewed meat right now. Who knows?"

"To hell with them. Let's go get our backpacks," I say. "I'm sick of this. If they're there, let them write us up."

We agree to act very surprised—as if we were just out on a walk and running into cops hadn't even crossed our minds. And then we'll suggest that, before registering us, they should take us to the self-settlers so that we can give them the food we brought.

But we don't encounter any police in the house. We don't encounter our backpacks there either.

This once more changes our plans drastically. To, once more, try to rationalize our own motivation: It's one thing if the cops find you or catch you. At that point, fine—they've won fair and square. But it's quite another thing if they're playing dirty by taking hostages (namely, our backpacks) and waiting for us to voluntarily surrender. We're proud, after all.

Our two sleeping bags, our alcohol burner, and all our food and water have vanished also, as has the half bottle of whiskey that we had saved for purposes of anesthesia on our trip back. The wily cops have even kidnapped my dirty hiking boots that were drying on the windowsill in the sun. Now, I'm left in soft-soled sneakers.

Markian and I had been planning to exit the Zone through a hole in the barbed wire next to the Dibrova checkpoint. Now, we make what feels like an obvious decision: if we're going to go ahead and fall into the hands of cops, then, as a matter of principle, we aren't going to let ourselves get nabbed by the same ones that were too lazy to look for or even wait for us, but simply took all our belongings. There's a bridge over the Uzh River in front of the Dibrova checkpoint that can't be bypassed and where we'll likely be ambushed by those very cops. So, we head in the opposite direction. To the west. On Vilchanka, that most hellish of routes.

As we're exiting Lubianka, we're met by a herd of cows that have gone wild: a few adults, a few calves, and one bull. The road is overgrown on both sides with dense bushes. We cautiously inch forward, ready to run away from the bull at any moment. The herd is retreating along the road, its horns lowered at us. Whereas ordinary village cows would have advanced toward us without even noticing us, these wild ones are backing up, keeping us at least a hundred meters away. Finally, the bull shakes his head, moos a brief order, and leads the herd into the thicket amid much snapping and rustling.

The sun is setting.

"And we proudly walked off into the sunset," Markian quips.

I would've very much liked for everything to have ended on this proud note.

But a hailstorm starts, which then turns into sleet. And that's followed by thirty-five kilometers in wet sneakers through wet branches that slap you wherever they spot bare skin.

After drenching us just enough, the clouds disperse. The moon comes out, and frost sets in. Steam escapes from our lips, rising in thick swirls in the moonlight.

"You do understand what we did, don't you?" Markian starts, pep-talking me again. "We deliberately entered via the most hellish route so that we wouldn't get caught. And then we personally pushed the red activate-the-cops button. And then we evaded them twice. And in the end, we got away from the cops again via the most hellish route—all the way into Zhytomyr Oblast."

To ensure that we had acted as true adolescents, of course.

At the end of our route, eight kilometers in wet, frozen sneakers over the jagged rubble of an abandoned train track eagerly await us. There's nowhere else for us to walk because the railway embankment is bordered by swamps on both sides. Every step is pain. In sneakers, my feet, which have already been pounded to the point of open wounds, feel every little edge of every sharp rock.

And yet—as, through bushes, we circumvent a checkpoint where a light is shining and dogs are barking, I keep thinking about how comfortable and safe I felt in the Chernobyl Zone after spending time in a war zone. Everything that happens to us here is just fun and games. When you're circumventing a checkpoint, you know definitively that you won't stumble across a mine or a tripwire. When you're running away from a cop, you know that he probably won't throw a grenade at your back. And on the chance that he does catch you, you know that you probably aren't in danger of being either tortured or shot.

We hobble the final kilometers through the inhabited village of Radcha right before daybreak at a pace of two kilometers an hour. I calculate our speed by the electric poles to distract myself from the pain.

As I climb out of the shared van in Kyiv, I understand why the path under the columns at the Polissia bus station is known as Invalid Alley in the folklore of illegals. Markian admits that even in his five years of visiting the Zone, this has been one of his most hellish treks. With lips chapped from dehydration and the cold, I'm sitting in a warm apartment, sipping tea and pondering whether I should go back to Dibrova, to give myself up for kicks and let them write me up. In exchange, I might learn the official fate of those expensive backpacks, sleeping bags, hiking boots, canned beef stew, and, last but not least, the whiskey.

Freedom for Papua!

I've known Artem for a long time. We met on the car ferry between Russia's Sochi and Turkey's Trabzon not long before the Russo-Georgian War. Just like Oksana and I—namely, without doing too much advance research or planning—he and his girl-friend at the time had decided to hitchhike through Russia, Abkhazia, and Georgia to Turkey. It was April 2008. The war hadn't started yet but, as I understand it, Russia had started men-acing the country already. Artem and Yasia had learned from drivers while still en route to Georgia that you couldn't make it into the country from Russia. Oksana and I, meanwhile, had crossed out of Russia at the Psou border crossing point, but the Abkhazians hadn't let us through. "Because your Yushchenko supports Saakashvili." That's why they turned us back in Adler, after which the Russian border guards kept prodding us, "What were you doing in Abkhazia?"

It was evident that Artem and Yasia were traveling on a tiny budget. Unlike us, they didn't buy tea on the ferry, just filled their Mivina-brand soup cups with the free boiling water and cooked their instant noodles. I took an immediate liking to them.

The four of us spent the night in Trabzon on the seashore, our tents pitched on rocks near a construction site. In the morning, Oksana and I went off to see the city. Artem and Yasia were heading all the way to Syria—this was before the Syrian civil war too—so we parted ways, so that they could make some headway sooner rather than later.

Naturally, we exchanged phone numbers and email addresses. And naturally, I was confident that we'd never see each other again, as happens with practically everyone you befriend on the road.

But a few months later, Artem hollered us down at the outdoor Petrivka Market in Kyiv. Oksana and I were just getting ready to meet one another's parents before getting married and were looking for gifts for the occasion at the bazaar.

Artem told us about the rest of his and Yasia's travels, and we told him about ours. And once more, we thought that we'd never see each other again.

A year after that, my wife and I returned back to Kyiv from abroad, where she had been studying for her master's degree. The financial crisis was in full swing; there was no translation work or honoraria to be had for a writer like me. We were out of money and had to borrow cash from our parents for cigarettes.

So, I headed to Odesa to look for a job. I had seen an advertisement somewhere that stevedores were needed at the port there. It sounded romantic. It echoed of draymen, scows, and Isaac Babel's fictional mob leader Benya Krik.

Unsurprisingly I didn't find any work, but as I was walking around in the city center one day, I heard my name. I didn't turn around because I didn't know anyone in Odesa and just kept walking. But then Artem caught up with me. "Hey! What are you doing here?"

As it would turn out, Artem had quit his previous job at the advertising agency in Kyiv—or also lost it as a result of the crisis,

I don't remember anymore. He and Yasia had broken up because of "different life priorities": she had dreams of having a successful career, and he of traveling. Artem returned to his hometown of Teplodar, not far from Odesa, and was for now trying to work in "the field of advertising," as he put it, as he had before in the capital. In practice, this boiled down to him printing handbills and announcements on a personal printer and taping them to utility poles. Or he would hand out flyers in the city center. Sometimes he hired university students when he couldn't manage on his own, but typically, he distributed the advertising products himself. "What matters is that I work for myself and not for the man," Artem declared optimistically. But orders didn't always come in, so the income was unstable.

That day, we sat down in a square in the center of Odesa, the one where artists sell paintings.

As we talked, Artem described to me how he and Yasia were robbed in Syria and how the Syrian police operate. Without much money to spend, Artem and Yasia set up their tent on the bank of the Euphrates, not far from a small town. The water was dirty, the vegetation wilting. They tried to hide the tent as best they could in the bushes in case camping wasn't allowed there. But there was a boatman with a ferry working on the river nearby. First, he ferried a peasant with a donkey from their bank, and then, from the opposite bank, three local old men.

During the night, two men sprang on Artem and Yasia, and, menacing them with knives, drove them out of the tent with threats. Then, one of them climbed inside and began to rummage around. He found a wallet and took whatever money was in it.

In the morning, Artem and Yasia went to the police in the nearby town. An interpreter from a larger city was sent for. Yasia and Artem assumed that the robbers were most likely the men that had been ferried across the Euphrates. They must have noticed the tent upon their arrival. It couldn't have been the boatman: they remembered his appearance well. As for the assailants, Artem recalled only that one of them had a gold tooth.

One by one, the cops started bringing nearly all of the town's men for Artem and Yasia to inspect. The Ukrainians, who were afraid of identifying the wrong men, didn't point out anyone.

"Then they brought one more in. I take a look: Is this him? Is it not him? 'I don't know,' I say. It doesn't look like he has a gold tooth. And then the cop peers into the man's mouth. Suddenly, here you go, he lands a first in the man's face, then he starts swearing at him in Arabic, and then again with the fist. The interpreter explained to us later that the policeman had seen traces of gold in the man's mouth and a hole in his gum. The man, obviously, must have heard that they were looking for someone with a gold tooth. And so, he pulled out his own tooth. But damn— they beat him right in front of us, without any hesitation. Yasia said, 'Maybe bring him a lawyer?' The interpreter translates what she said, and all the policemen burst out laughing. Like, you must be joking! A lawyer? Ha-ha-ha! Well, in short, we were led out of the police station. Him they kept, and two hours later, we were given all our money back. After that, we were driven to the district center, together with the interpreter, and brought to the police chief's office. He was very apologetic that that's what their people were like. He drove us to his home and fed us. And now, I don't know: on the one hand, I, naturally, feel bad that it was because of me that that old man with the tooth was . . ."

After three chance meetings—each time in a new place, as well—it became clear that my friendship with Artem would continue. When I traveled to Teplodar to visit Artem a few years later, he was still living just as he had the last time we had seen each other: looking for clients, taping up handbills, and distributing flyers. In the preceding months, he had been working a lot: he was trying to set aside money in order to hitchhike to

Southeast Asia. That was his long-cherished dream. That's why, even though I had gotten very lost on my way and had arrived in Teplodar after 9 p.m. already, Artem had just returned home from working in Odesa.

Over the course of that trip, I stayed in an array of private residences, and none of them were lavish. But his apartment, which he had inherited from his parents—now that was something. Dilapidated walls—without wallpaper, just gray concrete. In lieu of beds, old Soviet mattresses on the floor. A dark-brown wall unit dating from the seventies.

Artem lived in a Soviet-era communal apartment building that had been converted into a building of separate apartments. The construction of a nuclear power plant had been originally planned in Teplodar in the 1980s: that's how the town was formed. But the power plant was never finished, so most of the former builders and intended workers of the plant now work in Odesa, forty kilometers away. The town, which consists of a few dozen high-rises, is a geometrically regular rectangle about eight hundred by three hundred meters in size. From any tall roof, you can see all four edges of the town, as well as the steppe beyond it.

I had bought a liter-sized box of the cheapest wine I could find and a large bar of chocolate, and Artem now set about making a salad and frying mushrooms. I sat in the kitchen next to him and told him stories about my travels around Ukraine.

"So, here I am, finally coming home, feeling all inspired and thinking to myself happily, Yes, Ukrainians are fucking awesome! Feeling like that, I walk into the elevator, and there's piss all over the place. Here you go again. I walk out, thinking, Fine, I'll take the stairs up to the ninth floor. And guess what? There's piss on the stairs too! In three different places. It must have been a planned diversion."

While I was sitting on the toilet at Artem's with indigestion from my bad diet and abuse of instant coffee while on the road, Roman Bilyk came over. He was a motorcyclist, well-known in his circles, who wanted to meet me. But I didn't come out of the bathroom for another forty minutes.

Roman turned out to be as chatty as Channel 1 on Ukraine's public radio. For the sake of etiquette, he had brought beer even though he didn't drink himself. He launched into a long, ten-minute explanation about how his body didn't handle alcohol well. More precisely, it's not that his body couldn't handle it at all, it's just that he tried alcohol but soon realized that it wasn't his thing. When Artem and I went out onto the balcony to smoke once again, Roman transitioned to the subject of how he—analogously to how he didn't drink—didn't smoke either. He didn't even need to be encouraged with questions: he could chatter nonstop and about anything you pleased. He told us about how a few years back he had driven through Iran and Pakistan on an old Czech Jawa motorcycle, all the way to India. According to his story, his motorcycle got so beat up over the trip that my Mamayota was brand new by comparison, as if fresh out of the factory. As was the case with me on my Mamayota, the principal problem he ran into was with the suspension: On bad roads, the entire chassis gets completely beat up. So, by the time Roman made it to India, there was no front shock absorber left. Every little pebble relayed right to the handlebars, and he had to absorb all the impacts with his hands. His muscles trembled, his joints ached. Roman told us about how the police in Pakistan wouldn't leave him alone: they were worried that the foreigner would get kidnapped for the sake of a ransom payment, and they'd get stuck dealing with it. He told us about how they drove through areas controlled by the Taliban under increased security. An escort was mandatory for foreigners, but because each patrol tried to ferry him into the neighboring district as fast as they could, to hand him over to the next patrol, he was constantly being hurried. He slept and ate only when he couldn't push any further. He would stop at some gas station and collapse right there, down on the nearest strip of grass, and an hour later he would be woken up and forced to drive on. The cops wanted to go home to their families, but before they could do that, they needed to get rid of the damned foreigner. They were carrying out an order, but that didn't make Roman feel any better. Without so much as a pause, Roman also told us about his relations with various motorcycle gatherings. At any one of these gatherings, there are at most a hundred people hanging out, but the forums seemed to serve as the foundation of life for Roman. He had always wanted to become famous as a biker. And that's why he traveled to India specifically. He wanted to end up on TV and tell all of India that it was imperative they read Napoleon Hill's book *Think and Grow Rich*. This master-piece, in his opinion, contained an unusually profound idea: in order to become rich, you needed to become famous. But when Roman actually ended up on a morning entertainment show on the channel M1, the hosts started asking him unexpected questions that made Roman flounder, and so he never managed to tell them about the best book in the world. He also told us about his views on the most well-known personality among Ukrainian motorcyclists, Roman Martyniuk—who, it seemed to me, was his chief competitor. This Martyniuk had made a round-the-world trip on his bike back in the day. Roman Bilyk, by contrast, was intending to carry out a different project on his motorcycle: he had decided to drive through all the district centers in his oblast, down to the very last one. He had already covered two-thirds of his itinerary. However, you can't execute such an ambitious project at your own expense. Sponsors were needed. And sponsors demanded advertising in every district center. He ended up having to talk to people about all kinds of products, projects, and opportunities at every destination, which made Roman feel awkward and like he was wasting the time he had allocated for the trip on advertising. For now, he had put all of this aside and resumed his old work again. He earned a living by shooting wedding videos and was trying to improve as a photographer. On top of everything else, riding a motorcycle had become difficult for him. A year earlier, he had broken his leg in a stupid accident. In a district center he wasn't familiar with, which he was visiting in the framework of the oblast-traveling project, he hadn't noticed a speed limit sign because it was obstructed by a commercial kiosk placed right on the side of the road. Roman had been convinced that he was on a main road, while, in reality, he was driving on a secondary road. Later, the court decided that the motorcyclist wasn't at fault in the traffic accident, despite his speed. Forensic experts even came and photographed both the kiosk and the sign.

And so, Roman talked, and talked, and talked, effortlessly moving from topic to topic effortlessly and imperceptibly and never stopping. Agh, he's talking about something else already? And how did we segue onto this? Well, OK.

We were sitting on two mattresses in an almost empty room. In the middle of the room, on a crate covered with newspapers, stood three-liter metal bowls with salad and fried mushrooms. We were eating right out of these big common bowls. We ended up not even eating half of it because Artem had prepared a lot of food. Roman and I leaned our backs against the dark-brown, Soviet furniture wall that Artem stored barely anything in. Roman had placed a camera on a tripod off to the side to record me should I suddenly start telling an interesting story. But he never got the chance to because he was the one talking ninety-nine and a half percent of the time.

He told me about how one time, together with Artem, he had made it into the Ukraine Book of Records for the longest distance ever traveled in a bathtub. Roman had welded four wheels onto a bathtub and outfitted it with a motor from a scooter. The two of them submitted the requisite paperwork to the necessary authorities and drove the so-called autobahn from Odesa to Kyiv, then headed back.

"My cheekbones hurt," Artem said, finally getting a word in. He grabbed his cheeks with his hands. "I was grinning the whole way! Everyone who saw us would immediately begin to laugh and waive at us."

"At one point, some cops stopped us," Roman continued the story. "We showed them our permit from the administration of the State Motor Vehicle Inspectorate. But they called the inspectorate anyway because they couldn't believe that they had let us out on the road in this form of 'transport.'"

Despite setting a record, Roman and Artem didn't finish the return trip. After all, the Ukrainian autobahn—as it was then, newly opened, hailed by the press—is a Ukrainian autobahn. A bathtub has zero shock absorption. On the way back, the rear wheels fell off. The bottom rasped against the asphalt. Sparks flew. Fortunately, bathtubs travel slowly. It didn't skid; they didn't roll over.

"And there was so little left to go! We were in Kryve Ozero already, almost two-thirds of the way there!"

I remembered Kryve Ozero. One time, I was hitchhiking from Odesa back to Kyiv without a penny in my pocket, and night caught me outside a village. Workers who were building the autobahn hollered over to me from their trailer as I was walking past. They fed me, gave me some moonshine to drink, and put me to bed on a bunk.

So, Artem and Roman left the broken bathtub at a car repair shop in Kryve Ozero and hitchhiked to Odesa. They were picked up by a ramshackle Soviet truck that was driving very slowly.

There was a small problem in that that was the day Roman was getting married.

"And here we are, crawling along in this truck. In the meantime, the bride in Odesa is already wearing a white dress, and the relatives from her side are cursing the groom, while the groom himself is in a rusted cabin of an army-green Soviet ZIL truck. Once we finally rolled in, never in my life have I ever changed clothing that quickly. They pulled my travel clothes off me, wiped me down with a wet towel, and put a formal suit on me. All of this together took maybe thirty seconds. Another thirty seconds went to my shaving. And I made it to my wedding."

Artem and I chuckled as we listened to all of this and, little by little, got drunk, first on the wine out of a cardboard box, and then on the powdered beer. Roman left at three in the morning.

Finally, Artem was able to tell me a story too. At that time, I was in the middle of riding around Ukraine and, as I traveled, was asking everyone I encountered what they dreamed about. And so, Artem told me about how he'd been dreaming of hitch-hiking to Southeast Asia for several years already. He was hoping to raise the needed funds by taping advertisements to poles and handing out flyers in the streets.

To be honest, I didn't think he would pull it off. But I was wrong.

A few more years later, I saw Artem again. This time it was in a news photograph because he himself was far away.

He had realized his dream. While still en route to Southeast Asia—in Russia or Mongolia, I think—he was robbed twice. The money he had earned on flyers was long gone. He did, nonetheless, achieve his goal, ultimately making it all the way to Indonesia. And from there, Artem was deported.

This is how it happened: Artem befriended some villagers in the Indonesian province of West Papua. Overstaying his visa, he lived among the ethnic Papuans for a long time. He taught them how to cook *borshch*, Ukrainian beet soup. Artem grew to love these kind, open, and sincere people very much. Papuans are discriminated against in Indonesia, and one time Artem went out to a protest with his friends. Foreigners are forbidden from taking any part in politics in Indonesia. Distinguishing a Ukrainian from a resident of Papua, even West Papua, proved uncomplicated for the police. When Artem was detained, he was engaged in active resistance and shouting loudly, "Freedom to Papua!"

The Ukraine

She and I converged on a sullen love for our country. A hate-love, some might say. A love with a dash of masochism, I used to say. A love in defiance of pain, she used to say. And that's how she and I loved each other too—through pain and a bit frantically.

Almost every weekend, she and I would get on a train or bus and head off somewhere. And, in Ukraine, you can get far in the course of a weekend. And make it back home too. Only once were we late for work on Monday—when we were hitchhiking back from Milove in the Luhansk region in January. It's the easternmost point of the country. We made it there on buses and headed back on foot along a snow-covered road, hand in hand. We had just fallen in love. Guys in Soviet-style Zhiguli four-doors were giving us rides, no problem, but each time they'd give us a lift for only a few kilometers, then drop us off at the side of the road and turn off toward their villages. We shivered in the blue twilight, but we were happy.

We felt a melancholy love for precisely everything in Ukraine that annoyed many of our acquaintances. The random thrashiest of thrash metal on intercity buses. The obligatory multi-hour sessions of awful comedy shows like *Evening Quarter*. The flat-screen TVs at the fancier bus stations, like Dnipro, where the thrash on the speakers was even harsher—like that little rap that goes, "The best feeling's when you're the coolest of 'em all"—and performed by Ukrainian performers who write their names in the Roman alphabet because they think that will be more familiar and appealing in the West. The sour smell of the alcohol that was poured in semidarkness on the lower bunks of the economy-class sleeper car while we were trying to fall asleep on the top ones. The instant coffee in plastic cups and the plasticky sausages in hot-dog buns. The cheap train-station food, like cabbage-filled patties or meat pies wrapped in paper; even back then I wondered why it was that she didn't care at all about her health.

Or the more tender things: the slightly squat, chubby mother and daughter speaking Surzhyk, that slangy combo of Russian and Ukrainian, so alike in appearance—dark, cropped hair, their faces wide, a deep beet-colored flush on their cheeks—who wouldn't have been all that pretty if it weren't for the huge, kind gray-green eyes that made them beautiful! They were the proprietors of a cheap café at the bus station of a nameless town, with tables covered with oilcloth carelessly slashed by the knives of previous guests, which the daughter rubbed with a gray rag before bringing out plates of food that her mother had prepared for us. We had a meal there—for less than a dollar, if you add it up—of mashed potatoes with a sun of butter melted in the center of the plate, pork chops fried to a crisp, and homemade sour-cherry juice in tumblers. Or the people with gray faces, smileless and weary after a long shift, on the buses of Donetsk. The wet autumn leaves stuck to the footpaths of the Storozhynets Arboretum in Chernivtsi, where we had gone just to take a stroll—likely the only people ever to make a day-long excursion to have a look at a city where, when push comes to shove, there's nothing much worth looking at.

She was quoting Serhiy Zhadan, her favorite poet: "*Ya liubliu tsiu krainu navit bez kokainu*"—"I love this country even without cocaine." I prosaically chimed in, "And without antidepressants either." It was then that she stopped taking antidepressants; she said they made her gain weight—the only vanity I noticed in her in all those years. And now she always resurfaces in my mind along with a line from my favorite poet, Tom Waits: *She was a middle-class girl*... She had spent a few years living in the US: her father had gone to earn some fast cash, then brought her over too. While there, she finished college, got married, and quickly divorced. It was a past I was jealous of, and that was why we rarely talked about it. One time, she told me that her friends in the US, and even her ex-husband, used to call her home country "the Ukraine." With the definite article. Even though they knew that in English it was correct just to say Ukraine, their tongues kept reflexively pronouncing "the" first. Why? she would ask her ex-husband. One time, after some thought, he said, "I think it's the 'U' sound." The USA, the UK, the Ukraine. She and I laughed about this, but from then on we began to notice and point out to each other situations and instances when it was actually correct to say "*the* Ukraine"—because there's Ukraine as such, but there is, in fact, also a *the* Ukraine—a "*voila*-Ukraine." A Ukrainian Dasein.

For example, it's the middle-aged men in peaked caps, with long mustaches and leather jackets over their warm sweaters. It's the middle-aged women in chunky knit hats. The college girls who, on their way back to the dorm after a weekend at home, step over puddles of oozy mud in their fancy white boots, clutching the handles of checkered plastic tote bags with fingers red from the cold, trying not to chip their long painted nails. It's the old lady in the ankle-length brown overcoat and cheap white sneakers who's carting apples on a hand truck. The coiffed, aging blonde behind the wheel in a traffic jam in Donetsk who's calmly smoking out the car window, watching life pass by.

Once in a blue moon, during the worst frosts or protracted rains, she would plant me in the red Škoda Fabia her father had given her—because, of the two of us, only she had a license—and then we would look out at the country, separated from our fellow Ukrainians by glass and music: usually, Tom Waits, who, for some reason, perfectly suited the Ukraine. But, in the end, the trip would sour her mood because, separated in that way by music and glass, we could only watch and not experience, not identify. The following weekend, we would once again buy tickets for a train or a bus and be among people.

The Ukraine, for us, was a gigantic and empty new bus station, dusted with snow, at the edge of, I think, Cherkasy. I didn't understand why it was so gigantic or so empty. She and I stood in the bitter cold in the middle of a snow-covered, concrete field beneath an open canopy, alone. Opposite us was a single minibus, a white Mercedes Sprinter—ours. I opened the door, but the driver barked, "Shut the door! Don't let the cold in! This isn't the stop."

So we stood and blew on each other's fingers until, fifteen minutes later, he pulled up fifteen meters. Her face flushed in the frozen air. In the van too, our breath turned to vapor. We paid the driver, who grumbled, "This is the stop." She giggled softly and whispered in my ear, "This here is the Ukraine."

She was generally quick to laugh, though sometimes with a dark sense of humor. For instance, one time in Khotyn we were taking a selfie at her prompting in front of a store called Funeral Supplies and Accessories. She let out a ringing laugh and said that this too was the Ukraine.

When the bus stopped on the highway north of Rivne and in climbed an old woman whose sheepskin coat smelled of hay and cows, the people turned up their noses, not appreciating that this old woman was, in fact, the Ukraine. The official folk kitsch—that stereotypical woman with ribbons flowing from her hair, holding bread and salt on a traditionally embroidered towel—is a fake, but that dilapidated mosaic at the entrance to the village, depicting a Ukrainian woman with ribbons in her hair—only she's missing an eye—now, that's the Ukraine. The Ukraine is also the romance of decline. The unfinished concrete building on the outskirts of Kamianets-Podilskyi. The bottomless, purple-green lake in a submerged quarry in Kryvyi Rih, which you're looking at from a tall pile of bedrock, fearfully watching as a single minute swimmer slowly does the breaststroke, holding himself up above the lake's impossible depth on the treacherous film of the water's surface. It's the slow destruction of the Dominican Cathedral in Lviv, grayed by rains, and the faded-white plaster Soviet Pioneers with lowered bugles in Kremenets, in a gorge between the creases of mountains, unanticipated among all the fields overgrown with withered grass. The abandoned Pioneer camp outside Mariupol, where we sat on rusted swings, thermoses in our hands, with a view of the Sea of Azov, which swished with ice, pushing its surf, layer by layer, onto the shore. And even in Kyiv—the gray, multilevel concrete interchange at the Vydubychi transport hub, framed by the smokestacks of the TETs energy plant, which belch a thick, dense smoke into the deep-blue sky.

We were wanderers: we glided on the surface and often saw the Ukraine through misted windows. In the final years, she'd have her treatments in the summer, and we couldn't travel then. That's why the trips I typically remember were in late autumn or very early spring, when the country is in a palette of gray, rust, faded yellow, and pale green. It is unimaginably beautiful. Side roads along alleys of poplar or birch trees, winding through hills, lead you to places where you haven't been and aren't visiting, and you feel the urge to stop, to climb out of the bus, and go—actually go—to those places where you haven't been and aren't visiting.

One time I dozed off, my head resting on my hat against the steamy pane, and, when I awoke, through the window I saw, right next to the road, large and seemingly metallic waves frozen in time.

"Is this a reservoir?" I asked her. "Where are we?"

She laughed softly and stroked my temple.

"Rub your eyes."

Those waves frozen in time turned out to be large hunks of plowed black soil.

Once, at night, behind a belt of forest, bare in November, a tractor was running with four blinding headlights, two on the bumper and two above the cabin, and this detail struck me as particularly romantic, for some reason, yet somewhat mysterious. Another time, the minibus driver stopped at a café in the middle of the woods—near Chudniv, I think. The café was encircled by a wall of logs, sharpened on top like pencils, with frightening, elongated, crested faces of Cossacks wearing large earrings carved on them. It was trash and kitsch, but it was the Ukraine. The night was frosty, and star-pierced deep space loomed, black above the forest road.

I think that fatigue, too, affected our perception on these trips. We were under-rested, and everything struck us as a little unreal and simultaneously über-real. Blurred objects and people emerged through the fog, becoming distinct as they approached. In silence, with a shared pain and delight, the two of us could spend whole minutes watching a droplet trickle down the other side of the pane. Even then, she was succumbing to mood swings, which were rubbing off on me too. One time, I recall, the other people in the bus were mouthing, "Starkon, Starkon. We're heading to Starkon." There was something cosmic, futuristic, and damply mysterious in this word. When an hour later it turned out to be Starokostiantyniv, for some reason she grew disenchanted, pouted, and withdrew into herself. For the next hour, everything seemed horrible. In Starkon, two young men sat down behind us, reeking of alcohol. All the passengers were gray in the partial darkness of the cabin and swayed like sacks on the rugged road; no one was smiling. Then, suddenly, one of the drunks behind us began to tell the other one about his little son.

"I look over, and he's got a snotty nose and he's crying. I tell him, 'Open up your mouth, I'll take a look.' He shows me his mouth, and he's got a little side tooth that, you know, had pushed through in two places. I felt so sorry for him. 'Poor little kid!' I say. And I start kissing him, and I grab him in my arms . . ."

The bus was suddenly bathed in love and beauty. All the people who had been sitting silently, swaying with the bus's motion, lost in their own thoughts and their own problems, ceased to be gray mannequins: inside each of them, behind the mask of weariness, was an entire universe, a gigantic cosmos brimming with internal stars, and she leaned over and whispered in my ear, "People are beautiful, even if they don't realize it."

Sometimes she and I would set out on our weekend journeys on foot. In the early years, when it was still possible. Outside Yuzhnoukrainsk, on a Polovtsian grave field in the steppe, we ate a stolen watermelon. Outside Konotop, we got lost in the meanders of the Seim River; emerging from waist-high mud, we walked onto a farmstead, and a young woman, whose husband had gone off fishing in his boat, fed us boiled perch and polenta flecked with scales. And, when we paid her, the woman tried to refuse, but her hands began to tremble because it was an enormous sum of money for her. While it was still possible, we climbed a mountain overlooking Yalta, and from a kilometer up we saw clearly that the earth was round: the deep-blue sea segregated itself from the pale sphere of sky in a distinct arc.

I had anticipated that during our early trips she and I would be making love constantly, particularly in the fields or in secluded and beautiful spots like that mountain over Yalta. Yet she almost always said, "Ew, we're dirty." Once or twice, during a mood swing of hers, she initiated lovemaking on her own—like in the transit hotel on the highway in the bogs of Polissia, where we startled the long-haul truckers—but I quickly understood that, for her, our trips weren't at all about that. She was catching time, which was trickling through her fingers. Particularly in the final years, when she needed more and more treatments and we traveled less and less.

I was jealous of her past in the US, of her learning, which came from I don't know where. Or, rather, of her chaotic erudition. For example, she had this category: "random fact." We could be traveling in a black vehicle through a snow-dusted field in the boondocks, which, between the two of us, we referred to as "Kamianka-Znamianka," and we'd be marveling at the greenish hue of the asphalt when, out of nowhere, in response to some mental association, she'd burst out, "Random fact: When Voltaire died, his relatives sat him up in a carriage as if he were alive. And just like that, seemingly alive, the corpse was driven to a remote eastern region. You know why? To beat the mail. So that the Church wouldn't have time to give the bishop there an order prohibiting Voltaire's burial in consecrated ground."

I was jealous of her past in the US, the past from which these paroxysms flared, while she, it seems, envied me those years which she had missed in Ukraine. I would tell her stories. I told her about how in the nineties, as a schoolboy, I was forever digging in our gardens with my parents because, at the time, we had amassed as many government-issued plots as we could till from elderly relatives and relatives who had gone abroad for work—so that there could somehow be enough food for all the children through the winter. I told her how the electricity would be shut off in winter, and my entire family—clad in thick sweaters, because even the gas heat wasn't all that warm—would gather in the kitchen, first around candles and eventually around the car battery Dad had bought, which enabled a light bulb to emit a pale glow; and how, on those kitchen evenings, Mom would bake flat biscuits with a dollop of jam in the gas oven or fry crêpes on the stovetop, which we ate with preserves; and how at the time, of course, I didn't understand that these would be the happiest memories of my childhood.

I told her how my brother and I traveled to my grandfather's funeral from Kyiv. I was living at the Polytechnic Institute then, not far from the train station, while my brother lived in a hostel in the Vydubychi neighborhood. We bought tickets for the no-frills train that was leaving for Radyvyliv in the middle of the night, when the metro wasn't running, so my brother came to my place, in order to be walking distance from the station. We sat and sat, talked, smoked, but, when we headed out, it turned out that we were running late, and so we sprinted the last kilometer, as fast as we could, panting and sweating, and jumped onto the moving train, teetering on our bellies on the already raised steps. The conductor saw all this and scolded us: "Dumbasses, you could have had your legs chopped off!" I wanted to laugh in relief but thought that laughing wasn't appropriate. We ended up late for the funeral all the same, and, when we arrived in the village of Boratyn, our dad and the neighbors had just returned from the cemetery and were sitting at a table beneath the old pear tree in the yard set with cheap booze, cheap smoked sausage, and homemade pickles. They tried to force me and my brother to have a drink. A minute later, the neighbors were recounting how good each of them had been to the deceased old man and what he had promised to bequeath to whom. Our dad, his son, sat at the table in silence, and later, as he led me and my brother to the grave, he complained, "The body isn't even cold yet, and they're already divvying up the inheritance. I don't need anything, but at least don't start in front of me."

After I told her this, I recall, she and I took to saying that thoughts of the Ukraine always, sooner or later, led to memories of funerals. Why?

"Maybe love is more acute when it's mixed with the feeling of inevitable loss," she surmised.

I think I finally understand what she meant.

One time, in her last year, I told her about how my best friend's mother was dying of cancer in the hospital. And about how he had to take a syringe to the head nurse and give her a twenty-hryvnia bribe each time he wanted her to fill it with morphine for his mom.

She laughed. "That is most certainly a contender for *the* the Ukraine."

And then she began to cry.

For the two of us, the booming talk of "official" patriots about their "love for Ukraine" that you hear everywhere—that talk was pompous and stilted, hackneyed, and, above all, it was what the Russians called *poshlo*: passé, tacky. Or, if you prefer English, it was lewd. Paraphrasing an American saying, she used to argue that patriotism was like a penis: irrespective of its size, it's not a great idea to go waving it around in public. Choral singing and walking in formation. *Sharovary*—the bright-colored ballooning pants of the Cossacks—and everyone on the same day sporting traditional embroidery, on shirts and even plastered on cars. Waving flags on sticks or, better yet, flying the biggest flags possible! Ukrainian tridents on chests. It was all a pretentious demonstration, a showy show. It was an aesthetic on the same level as putting up a billboard beside the road with a picture of your beloved holding a Photoshopped bouquet and the caption, "Natalka! I love you! Your Tolia!" Only in this case it was done collectively: "Natalka, lookie here at how you arouse our patriotism!" It was group exhibitionism.

Sincere feelings don't need megaphones. Love is quiet, barely audible. It's in the comma and in the reiteration: "I love her so, I so love my poor Ukraine." Today, I almost let out a sob when I came upon this line. Taras Hryhorovych Shevchenko. In defiance of pain, a bit frantically. Tenderly. Acutely. With a fear of loss. In love, the imperative is acceptance.

During one of our final trips, in the heart of winter, the rural bus we were on broke down, mid-ascent, outside Dunaivtsi. Little by little, the cabin of the bus began to freeze. Outside, a cold damp wind blew, piercing through our flesh all the way to the marrow. The driver was poking around in the engine. The bus was old: that was why it had broken down. Someone began to grumble, "And here we have the perpetual 'Are we part of Europe or are we not?'" I, too, was growing irritated. But she was warming her hands in her armpits and smiling. She said, "I've never heard that someone up and froze to death in Ukraine from a bus breaking down. OK, it isn't pleasant. But it happens."

I was learning acceptance from her. When her mother called and invited me to the funeral, it was bitterly sad, but I wasn't surprised. She hadn't said anything to me directly, but now, looking back, I saw that all along she had been living a life short on time. Just as she had gleaned satisfaction from depression and from a sullen love in defiance of pain, I was confident that she had even gained a certain pleasure from her suicide. I only hoped that the physical pain of it had been less than the pain she had had to live with.

> But now she's dead
> She's so dead forever
> Dead and lovely now

I didn't notice when I stepped on the edge of the freshly shoveled, soft mound of earth. Her mother looked at me judgmentally. Lips compressed into a thread, painted with dark-red lipstick. A thin, properly contoured, made-up face. Her mother had a wonderful figure for her age; she would have had a similar one had she lived as long. Her mother wore a light-colored business suit, a white overcoat, and black high-heeled shoes: that was why she stayed on the concrete path and didn't approach the mound. She had a scarf on her head because, after all, it was a cemetery. Her mother probably thought I wasn't displaying enough grief. All those years her mother had thought that I was a bad influence on her daughter. That it was me dragging her "who knows where or what for." That it was me refusing to formally start a family, or at least live together full time. I'm curious, did her mother understand the pain her daughter lived with? Someday I'll tell her about it. Or maybe not. Her mother was very orthodox and concealed the truth so that her daughter's body—her body—could be buried in accordance with the rules. In consecrated ground.

I was learning acceptance from her. Clay from her grave stuck to my shoes, and I recalled how she and I had walked around the cemetery in Krasnoilsk the previous spring. Fake flowers adorned almost all the crosses. We read the inscriptions, written in a mix of Romanian, Russian, and Ukrainian, and yellowish clay stuck to our feet in just the same way then.

Her mother and I heard muffled cursing behind us. Apparently, the two cemetery workers who had filled the grave were squabbling over the tip that her mother had given to one of them. If I recall, they were a little drunk. Her mother glanced at the workers, her painted lips clenched, then turned away and snugly tightened her scarf, which she would take off upon leaving the cemetery.

"What horrible people," her mother murmured.

The gravediggers asked my forgiveness with a gesture. They quieted down and walked past me and her mother, their shovels over their shoulders. When they thought I could no longer see them, one punched the other's shoulder, then gesticulated: idiot. Yes, they had had a bit to drink. They smelled. They were filthy. Gray, in tattered jackets. They probably consume that TV trash, I thought. They weren't European, they weren't civilized. What else was there to say? Inside everyone there's a universe, a gigantic cosmos brimming with stars. And so be it that an uninviting exterior, humdrum labor, thoughtless amusements, and squabbles over money often keep it from being seen. Sometimes people forget that it exists inside them. Sometimes we do too.

I turned to her mother: "You know what she used to say? People are beautiful, even if they don't realize it."

ARTEM CHAPEYE has published widely in his native Ukraine, including two novels, four works of nonfiction, and a book of war reportage co-authored with Kateryna Sergatskova. The Ukrainian edition of *The Ukraine* was one of three finalists in the 2018 BBC Book of the Year Awards Nonfiction category. The title story appeared in the *New Yorker* in late March 2022, making him one of the first Ukrainian writers since the start of the war to find a wide readership in the English-speaking world. *The Ukraine* is Chapeye's first book to appear in English.

ZENIA TOMPKINS is an American literary translator and founder of The Tompkins Agency for Ukrainian Literature in Translation (TAULT, tault.org). She has devoted 2023 and 2024 to working exclusively with Ukrainian authors who have enlisted in Ukraine's armed forces since the Russian invasion.

About Seven Stories Press

SEVEN STORIES PRESS is an independent book publisher based in New York City. We publish works of the imagination by such writers as Nelson Algren, Russell Banks, Octavia E. Butler, Ani DiFranco, Assia Djebar, Ariel Dorfman, Coco Fusco, Barry Gifford, Martha Long, Luis Negrón, Hwang Sok-yong, Lee Stringer, and Kurt Vonnegut, to name a few, together with political titles by voices of conscience, including Subhankar Banerjee, the Boston Women's Health Collective, Noam Chomsky, Angela Y. Davis, Human Rights Watch, Derrick Jensen, Ralph Nader, Loretta Napoleoni, Gary Null, Greg Palast, Project Censored, Barbara Seaman, Alice Walker, Gary Webb, and Howard Zinn, among many others. Seven Stories Press believes publishers have a special responsibility to defend free speech and human rights, and to celebrate the gifts of the human imagination, wherever we can. In 2012 we launched Triangle Square books for young readers with strong social justice and narrative components, telling personal stories of courage and commitment. For additional information, visit www.sevenstories.com.